the ROADMAP of LOSS

For all who believed in this and in me, those who didn't make it to the end, the ones who joined somewhere in the middle, and the few who were there the whole way through.

the ROADMAP of LOSS

LIAM MURPHY

echo
PUBLISHING

echo
PUBLISHING

An imprint of Bonnier Books UK
Level 45, World Square,
680 George Street
Sydney NSW 2000
www.echopublishing.com.au

Bonnier Books UK
4th Floor, Victoria House,
Bloomsbury Square
London WC1B 4DA
www.bonnierbooks.co.uk

Copyright © Liam Murphy 2024

All rights reserved. Echo thanks you for buying an authorised edition of this book. In doing so, you are supporting writers and enabling Echo to publish more books and foster new talent. Thank you for complying with copyright laws by not reproducing or transmitting any part of this book by any means, electronic or mechanical – including storing in a retrieval system, photocopying, recording, scanning or distributing – without our prior written permission.

Echo Publishing acknowledges the traditional custodians of Country throughout Australia. We recognise their continuing connection to land, sea and waters. We pay our respects to Elders past and present.

This is a work of fiction. Names, characters, businesses, places, events, locales and incidents are either the products of the author's imagination or used in a fictitious manner. Any resemblance to actual persons, living or dead, or actual events is purely coincidental.

First published 2024

Printed and bound in Australia by Griffin Press

The paper this book is printed on is certified against the Forest Stewardship Council® Standards. Griffin Press holds FSC® chain of custody certification SGS-COC-001185. FSC® promotes environmentally responsible, socially beneficial and economically viable management of the world's forests.

Page design and typesetting: Shaun Jury
Editor: Jessica Friedmann
Cover design: Lisa White
Cover image: A guy in a dark shirt sits in a car, tilting his head to the side, by Karyna Bartashevich/Stocksy

Lyrics from *ME AND MRS. JONES*, pp. 199–200:
Words and Music by KENNETH GAMBLE, LEON HUFF and CARY GILBERT
© 1972 (Renewed) WARNER-TAMERLANE PUBLISHING CORP.
All Rights Reserved. Used by Permission of ALFRED MUSIC

NATIONAL LIBRARY OF AUSTRALIA

A catalogue entry for this book is available from the National Library of Australia

ISBN: 9781760688295 (paperback)
ISBN: 9781760688301 (ebook)

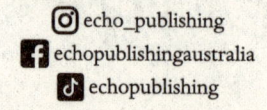

echo_publishing
echopublishingaustralia
echopublishing

Praise for *The Roadmap of Loss*

'Liam Murphy has taken a great and familiar form, the American road novel, and infused it everywhere with his own lyrical and melancholic exploration of a young man's pitfalls as he traces his father's footsteps. Fuelled by bitter grievances and restless sorrow, Mark Ward faces numerous challenges, but none are as confronting as when he is forced to drag forgiveness from within himself. Beautifully structured, imaginatively conceived, *The Roadmap of Loss* is a compelling story about loss, failure and self-destruction – but also about human resilience, and how grace can appear from the most unexpected places.'

Debra Adelaide
Author of *The Household Guide to Dying*,
The Women's Pages and *Zebra*

About the author

Liam Murphy is a professional writer, based in Sydney. After graduating from the University of Technology Sydney with a Master of Fine Arts in Creative Writing, he went on to work for various News Corp and Nine–Fairfax mastheads. Liam is now working with the NRMA, and his writing features in *Open Road* magazine. *The Roadmap of Loss* is his first novel.

1.

I remember the call. The way the woman took just too long between her words and how the phone felt unbearably heavy by the end. My rushed apology as I stole the taxi from a couple in front of the cinema. Disinterest from its driver as he alternated grunts between two phones. Raindrops on the window that gained momentum as they found another; ones that wandered alone until they reached the sill. How the staff seemed to know who I was as I arrived.

'Neighbours found her and called for an ambulance,' the doctor informed me. 'It appears she suffered a myocardial infarction ... a heart attack.'

I nodded as my jaw fell away and hung in the air – the automatic response of someone who should have something to say. He paused. I had nothing to fill the space, though I tried anyway.

'I guess it was always going to be one or the other.'

'Pardon?'

'Her heart or her liver, I mean. They seemed to be in a race towards the finish line.'

'Hmm, I see. Is there anyone else I can call? Any relatives or close friends?'

'No,' I said. 'There's no one else.'

We took the lift and glided down a corridor in silence, moving past rooms of the new, the expiring, and everything in between. I wasn't sure what marked the shift from growth to decay in those hallways, but was sure I'd passed it.

We neared the only closed door. He approached and gestured towards it with a slow, upturned palm, like a robot mimicking compassion. 'Take as long as you need,' he said. I pulled down on the handle. 'I'm sorry for your loss,' he added. I pushed the door open.

The room was bright with artificial light. In the corner, a bed with a drawn curtain. Through caustic odours of hospital-grade cleaners, her perfume. I closed the door behind me and flicked off the lights.

The curtain swayed as I approached and bunched its edge in my hand, wondering if a good time to draw it back would ever arrive. Its hooks let out a screech as they slid along the rail, jolting me backwards. I knocked a pan from a cart and stood frozen while it bounced and shook against the floor, ringing out with a chime. I squeezed myself between the curtain and the wall.

Sliding a seat up to the bed, I took her cold hand in mine, somehow expecting a squeeze back. I brushed hair from her face and tucked it behind her ear. Deep wrinkles rested in her brow; bite marks of a life spent bottling things up.

'Hi there,' I said, my voice like dried leaves underfoot. 'I don't know what to say. I wish I could have given you more. I wish this life had given you more. You never took from those who take and it killed you ... it killed you so long before you died. Oh, god, that can't be all there was for you.'

I buried my head into her shoulder as the city fell to night. The air conditioner hummed as rain tapped on the window, like static from an LP after the final track.

No warm sunset pierced the blinds to rest across her face in gentle strips of gold. I never got the chance to say goodbyes. There was no rainbow for my mother.

2.

The day was shaping up like any other in a Melbourne autumn. The weather's ambivalence mirrored my own as I stumbled out of bed at 10 a.m., washed my face and leant forward, staring at myself in the bathroom mirror as if the whole scene was some disappointing news I'd just received. Two years out of university and I was still working in the recording studio of a small performing arts school in the city. What began as a Bachelor of Music and a make-do, part-time job had concluded in a degree in sound engineering and my entire foreseeable future. 'Dreams are important,' my mother insisted, 'but nothing's more important than security.'

Night shifts had become my bread and butter. Session fees were much lower in off-peak hours, and there was a near-endless supply of amateur, aspiring artists who couldn't afford larger studios at busier times. Given their limited understanding of good mixing, it meant the job was easy and, most importantly, 'secure'. The days bled into one another.

The previous night's shift had run a typical 5 p.m. to 1 a.m. slot – its only notable event being when I forgot to start a recording as the hand of a wall-mounted clock ticked over to midnight. 'Seriously? The whole fuckin' thing?' the drummer asked from the other side of the glass, leaning into his snare's mic.

'Yes, sorry, I was watching the clock. I just turned twenty-five,' I replied into my own.

He shrugged at his colleagues and leant back in. 'Yeah, alright. Happy birthday, mate. Can we go again now?'

I sat on my apartment floor later that day, flicking pages of a photo album as the midday news interrupted music on the radio. Stalling on the same page I always tended to, I ran fingertips back and forth along the foreground of a particular photo.

Me, sporting a dumb hat and grin with blank space where teeth should have been, holding a balloon displaying a large '5'; my mother standing behind me; a man with his arm around her; a fluorescent orange '12 3 77' in the corner dating the scene. I'd studied this photo before, always focusing on one detail more than the rest, unsure if it was the ink of the print or my own memory that seemed to fade each year. The man's eyes seemed empty – as if the film had failed to render them, or had maybe done it perfectly. I stared at the print for some time before turning to the next page. There were far fewer after it.

That evening, I walked up steps and flicked my knuckles into a Richmond home's front door three times. Rustling came from inside, then the creak of floorboards interrupting the vague resonance of a television.

'Who is it?' a woman asked through the door.

'Ma'am, please, I just escaped from the prison. I need a place to lay low for a while.'

The door opened as a hand thrust out, fingers bent into the shape of a gun.

'Bang,' she said, feigning recoil.

'Argh!' I keeled over with a hand on my gut.

'You know,' she said, blowing imaginary smoke from her fingertips, 'they'd give me a reward for that.'

'Ha. And you'd deserve every cent.'

'Happy birthday, Mark,' she said, wrapping arms around me.

'Thank you, Mum.'

The house wasn't large, but was too much for one person to maintain. She'd long since resorted to closing off rooms when they became too much work. I'd tried to convince her to live with me or find a smaller place after I'd moved out. 'There's been too much suffering in here,' I'd reason.

'A life doesn't fold up inside cardboard boxes,' she'd retort.

She poured herself a gin. I caught a whiff and felt ill, still unable to smell the stench of alcohol without hearing arguments, glasses smashing, doors slamming, and her cries. As a child, I'd believed that stench to be a ghost far exceeding any horror I'd seen on television, one that knew only anger and sadness.

It would sometimes blow in through the front door at night, forcing its way between the floorboards or through the keyholes, filling the house. When it entered my room, it would consume the air and make it cold. No position in my bed could stop it from reaching me and exhaling rancid breath into my nostrils.

One night I ran downstairs to confront it and was met with a shout so loud it shook my bones. I stayed in my room after that. Then, all of a sudden, the arguments went away, although the stench and my mother's cries did not.

3.

Children ran unrestrained, young lovers swam in each other's eyes, almost every person bumped into my chair as they passed. The restaurant had the ambience of a cafeteria ... or a zoo.

I twirled spaghetti around a fork and watched it slide back into the bowl over and over. My mother finished another glass of wine and told me I didn't eat enough. I said I'd try harder.

'Are you okay?' she asked, already seeing the answer on my face.

'I'm fine.'

'I'm glad you took tonight off. So, anything noteworthy today? Besides the obvious.'

'Was like any given Wednesday, really. A sleep-in had, coffee drunk ... McCartney knighted.'

'How good, and each well-deserved!'

'I was confident one of them was, then they played "Silly Love Songs" and suddenly wasn't so sure.'

Her mouth shaped into a familiar, guilty sort of smile. I'd watched the creases that formed around it grow a little deeper over the years – the attempts only ever made to rouse me from whatever downhearted bullshit was going on in my head in those moments. The response I was able to muster seldom varied.

'Sorry. You, just, you know I don't like birthdays. Especially not when they're my own.'

'I understand, but today's is a milestone, Mark; your quarter of a century. It mightn't seem like it now, but you're doing well.'

'Oh yeah, it's a milestone alright ... You know, I was thinking earlier,' I said, shifting in my seat. 'You know it's been almost twenty years?'

'Since what? Your last thought?'

'Ha, very good.'

'Then what? Twenty years since I was proud of you on your fifth birthday?'

'Twenty years since he left.'

Chanting waiters brought out a birthday cake for a nearby table, filling the little remaining space with noise and sparks.

'Oh, Mark, I don't want to talk about that. Tonight is about the future, not the past,' she said, turning her head with a thin smile, pretending to be distracted by the apathetic performance.

'But I want to talk about it.'

'You know all there is to know. I've told you everything.'

She wouldn't look at me. The ensemble's vigour dipped as it reached the recipient's name. I wasn't getting any answers. The kid blew out his candles and everyone applauded him for it.

'You haven't. You know you haven't,' I said. A child clipped my chair as she ran past and began crying. 'Can we please get out of here?'

We headed to the nearest pub. I placed a drink in front of my mother, dropped my weight into the bench seat across from her and waited.

'For fuck's sake. Why now?' she asked, lighting a cigarette with jittery hands. 'Years without mentioning him, letting me believe you'd moved on, then you go and bring this up – and tonight of all nights.'

'I'm sorry. I guess today being some sort of twisted anniversary brought it out. I spent most of this morning looking through that photo album – the one I took when I moved.'

'Nothing worth keeping is already behind you.'

'This will be the last time I ask, I promise.'

She drew on the cigarette and stared at the exit. 'You've obsessed over this and broken that promise before.'

'I just need to know what ...' my voice trailed off, diluting in the hum of after-work-drinkers.

Looking into my eyes, her resolve broke. She exhaled and ushered me on with a swift nod.

'I need to know what was so wrong with me that he had to leave.'

'There isn't, and never was, anything wrong with you; it was always ... I'm sure he had his reasons for leaving, but don't you ever think it was because of you,' she said with a calm anger.

Another of her rehearsed platitudes – the same I'd heard scattered throughout my entire life whenever I'd asked these questions. Though, still, her eyes became glossy, which made my chest hurt. I readied myself yet again for the defeat of accepting that not upsetting her meant more to me than the answers did.

'I don't know what you want me to say. I was much, much older than him ... He was still a boy in many ways,' she continued after a moment, unprompted, much to my surprise. 'And he went searching for something that wasn't there – as boys tend to.'

My belt let out a long, awkward squeal against the bench seat as I leant forward in awe, the only sound in our silent corner of the loud pub. I'd never heard this reflection before. Glancing at her drink, I tried to count backwards the number she'd had, but found no real deviation from any other dinner. Something in her seemed different.

'Okay,' I said, snapping myself back into the present, desperate to maintain whatever momentum I'd stumbled onto in this unknown territory of the conversation. 'And what was he looking for?'

'Oh, god, who knows? Adventure? Enlightenment? Some great frontier that existed only in his mind? The bloody American Dream?

'I never believed he was ready to be a husband or a father. There was always this restlessness, right up until the last time I saw him – the type I'm not sure a man ever truly outgrows. I think even he'd realised he would never be the man he'd simply assumed he would become.'

'So, what?' I asked with an unexplainable anger building in me. 'You want me to believe that that meant more to him than the wife and son he left?'

'We were never technically married.'

'Then why did I get his surname?'

'Because he was your father.'

'Fathers don't run away.'

'I don't know if he ran away, just like I don't know if he was ever truly here. He lived with one foot always out the door. The grass in both fields was perfectly, equally green to him and he'd have rather torn down fences than be forced to live in one. He was frustrating, but the good in him was so tightly bound and woven with the bad that you couldn't separate one without risking damage to the other. It made him the easiest and hardest person to love that I ever have,' she said, sincerity in her voice, a smile forming on her face.

I sucked on my gums and tried to calm myself.

'Why do you still defend him …? He abandoned us without a trace and never came back. He only ever took from us – he only ever took from you, and you let him. And still, now, you defend him like he was some kind of martyr.'

'He would've come back if he'd had the choice.'

'Had the choice!? You mean if he hadn't rolled a car off some Californian freeway and killed himself a few months after my fifth birthday? You've got to be kidding me. Had the choice!? He had the fucking choice, and it was made the second he closed our front door with you and me on the other side.'

She fixated on what remained of an ice cube melting in her glass. I took notice of some pub patrons watching on with concern.

'I'm sorry, I just –'

'I'd like to go home now.'

'He never even said goodbye, Mum.'

'I'd like to go home now.'

We sat in silence in the taxi. She climbed her front steps without poise, as if she'd aged ten years since walking down them earlier that evening.

Pouring herself a nightcap, she stood before me in appeal. 'Please don't obsess over this. You've already spent enough of your life wondering.'

'Maybe, but ... I still think you should be angrier. He left, and you never allowed yourself to fall in love again or anything; you just switched it all off. Now look at you. You can't get through a day without poisoning yourself with that piss just to feel something.'

'You've got it all wrong, Mark. It was no fairy tale, but your father gave more to me than he took. I have you. Also,' she said, taking a sip, 'I've come to find people drink for one of two reasons – and for some, yes, it's because they can no longer stand feeling nothing.'

'And the others?'

'The others? Well, the others do because they feel absolutely everything all the time, and that can be a kind of agony as well.'

'So, which are you?'

'I'm the one that's just about ready for bed,' she smiled, brushing hair behind my ear. 'Please take care of yourself.'

'Goodnight.'

'Goodnight. I love you.'

I got halfway down her street before turning back. As I pushed the gate open, the light glowing through the closed curtain of her bedroom window vanished. I closed the gate and stepped backwards onto the footpath. 'Love you too,' I whispered.

Work kept me busy for the following weeks. Our daytime engineer left for a holiday, so I took his shifts. Keeping on with the night slots as well meant fourteen-hour days weren't uncommon. I became friendly with Claire, a new-hire receptionist tasked with organising studio bookings. I hadn't spoken to my mother since my birthday.

Arriving at the studio on a Friday afternoon following three long days in a row, I was ready to sleep until Sunday. I kept checking my watch to see if the clock on the wall was slow. It wasn't. Pushing a taped cable back against the wall, I switched on the recording light and a band began another take.

A minute in, the studio phone rang. I lifted the handset and hung up before anyone noticed. Within a few seconds, more ringing. I raised and slammed it down again. The vocalist saw me and hesitated. A moment later, Claire burst in. The band ground to a halt.

'What are you doing?' I demanded, standing and ushering her into the hallway, closing the door behind us. I pointed to the red, illuminated sign above.

'You know what that means, yeah?'

'I do –'

'No calls, no second attempts at calls, definitely no barging into the studio.'

'I know, but –'

'Claire, there are no buts. It's never that important.'

'Mark,' she said, drawing her shoulders back and looking at me with sad, slick eyes. 'There's a call for you and you really need to take it.'

4.

The funeral was painful in every sense. Painful in how little money I had to spend for a woman who deserved everything. Painful for those who had to listen to me stumble through my excuse for a eulogy. Painful for me to hear all the people say how sorry they were for my loss and how great a woman she was. How come I never saw you around then? I thought. 'Thank you,' I replied.

I walked behind the coffin as she was carried on the shoulders of husbands of friends and acquaintances. I thought it just our luck that when she was finally walked down the aisle, it was in the wrong direction. She'd have laughed at that, which made me smile for the first time in days. By my request, the church played 'Throw Your Arms Around Me' by Hunters & Collectors. When I was sixteen, I'd returned from school one day to find it filling the house, my mother dancing in the living room after what must've been an especially deep dive into a gin bottle. 'Isn't this song wonderful? I want this to play at my funeral,' she said, spinning her dressing gown, making me sick at the thought. Libraries could've been filled with those throwaway utterances she thought I never heard, not knowing the size of the mountains and valleys they carved in me.

I took leave from work. They said, 'Take all the time you need,' which I interpreted to mean a week or two. Friends I'd left drift out of my life sent their regards, but our reunions were short-lived and superficial in ways that didn't surprise me. What did surprise me, however, was Claire and her daily check-ins. How much of her fondness was legitimate and how much was an innate need to nurture broken things, I wasn't sure, but I took what I could get, deciding along the way that men did not deserve women.

I revoked the lease on my apartment and moved back into my mother's empty house, visiting the bank to see what kind of outstanding mortgage I'd inherited along with the place.

'We received a notice of discharge for this loan back in ... August ninety-four,' the branch manager said, sliding glasses down his nose and leaning into his screen.

'I'm sorry, I don't follow.'

'We were removed from the property's title almost three years ago. The mortgage was paid in full.'

'How is that possible? She never kept a job for more than a few months.'

'Well, I'd say she must have been very good with a budget. I mean, there wasn't a single late payment for the entire duration of the loan.'

5.

The world seemed colder. Framed photographs of me and my mother dotted around the house haunted me. I turned them down then faced them back up because she'd put them there. The whole situation was numbing and unbelievable. I expected a call from someone to say there'd been some mistake, but the phone sat unmoving like a piece of furniture.

One night, when the house felt especially full of emptiness, I put her records on and opened one of her bottles. I closed my eyes and tried for a moment to imagine she was in the room with me. The smell did not waft like I'd hoped, so I poured and swirled the gin in a glass, studying the stuff as it diffused light. There had to be something in it – something more than chemical. I'd watched it transform people: turn lovers into fighters and fighters into lovers; give confidence or take it away. There was power in it.

I took a gulp and immediately retched over the bench. Ice, she always had it with ice. I added some cubes and watched the gin cascade over them in little waterfalls to collect at the bottom. Again, I sipped – this time keeping it down. After a few minutes, my body was lighter and heavier at the same time. I felt better, so had another.

LIAM MURPHY

I kept going, expecting the cycle to be finite, but never finding a plateau. It was brilliant. Thumbing through her mammoth stack of records, past The Doors and Anita Baker, I landed on James Taylor and laid the needle down. The music seemed richer with each sip and I laughed at my hindered motor skills, leaning against the couch after dropping a glass onto the carpet. I found a pack of cigarettes in a cupboard, smoked one and felt even better. I kept drinking. The ceiling light blurred, the records turned, and I slipped away.

I woke with my first ever hangover. After a coffee and shower, I felt okay, wondering how much of the hangover's reputation was because it often followed the best that people had felt in a long time. I reclined on the floor, the vague thud of my pulse in my arm tapping against the back of my rested head. Above, the ceiling fan rotated a lazy cadence; a tick with each revolution. For a moment, the two were in sync, and I felt as though I'd become the room. A few more beats and I could sink into the floor and be dispersed through the walls and the furniture. I could be inanimate, with the impossibility of thinking or feeling the wrong thing. I could be timeless as long as the timing was right.

I felt the calmest I had in days, but also the furthest from her. It was a selfish feeling to have. Rhythm was for the living, I decided. It was the only thing they shared. The earth flies around the sun; the moon spins around the earth; grass sways in the breeze; children rock on swings; the cursors of computers blink; and hearts beat in chests.

Death has no rhythm. It doesn't start and end on a day or in a week; it cannot be marked on a calendar. It arrives inside the ticks of clocks, during the nothingness of a blink. What was living becomes dead – the space between immeasurable. Infinity created in an instant. A moment between moments, one which tears us down the middle and forever leaves us in two: before and after.

The days passed too slowly. I hoped they would start later and end sooner, like a prisoner serving a sentence, carving lines through a calendar hung in the kitchen. But the hurting didn't ease with each dawn, and I began to wonder what my crime had been, and if redemption was ever coming. Before long, I found myself reaching for a bottle each time I sensed sadness seeping in through the walls.

Claire and I slept together one night.

'I love you,' I said, leaning in as I buttoned my shirt. She pulled back, turning wine-stained lips away.

'God, don't.'

'What?'

'Just... come on.'

'I do,' I said, trying and failing to kiss her again. I moved to the kitchen, poured a drink, lit a cigarette, and watched her wriggle into a skirt.

'You're all sorts of fucked up right now, I get it, but don't grab onto anything you can just because it's within reach. I'm glad to see you're remembering how to enjoy yourself, but there are healthier ways to do it,' she said, taking and butting out my cigarette. 'I'll see you soon, Mark.'

She kissed me and was gone. I stood for a moment, emptied the remainder of the bottle into my glass and lit another smoke. 'Remembering? I'm just learning how.'

6.

Going back to work felt premature, but to say I was making progress on the couch felt dishonest. The night shift was returned to me as being the least stressful option by Martin, the head of the audio-visual department. My days felt bereft. I yearned to be wherever I wasn't: at work when home, home when at work; on the tram while waiting at a stop, waiting at the stop when on the tram; with Claire when I wasn't, and alone when I was.

I became an aficionado of the late-morning bottle-shop run, soon cosying up to whiskey – especially the American types. The stuff could make a man feel like a scholar or a sailor, make him muse or sit in desolate silence, want to mend the world or tear it to pieces. I began having a few during the day to accelerate the time until work, and soon found myself having a few during work to accelerate the time until I could return home. If my sentence was to be life itself, I was going to make it as quick and painless as possible.

I put my feet up on the desk at work one night and took a sip from my flask-enhanced coffee. The client was running late, which meant they would undoubtedly expect missed time to be tacked onto the end of the booking, pushing back the others. I'd be the arsehole whichever way it played out. I'd expected a buzz from the front door's bell, but instead there was a knock on the studio's door. I sat, wondering how they'd gotten in before the door opened, and Martin stepped through. The head of the department had no reason to come in after hours, though I feared he'd found a compelling one.

'Martin, hey,' I said, moving my feet off the desk and standing.

'Hello, Mister Ward, how are you?' he asked without looking at me, perusing the studio as if he'd left something behind – his usual demeanour of being just too preoccupied for sincerity was more pronounced.

'Fine. Waiting for my eight o'clock.'

'That would be me.'

'You? Ah, you want a session ...?'

'No, no. Just needed you to come in,' he said, stepping closer to my desk.

'You could've called; I would've come in early.'

'I wanted to see how you work. There's been some ... concerns.' He wrapped a finger around the handle of my mug. 'May I?'

I envisioned appeasing the situation by knocking the mug out of his hand. How we might laugh about how clumsy I was and forget about the whole thing. In the time I'd daydreamt, he'd sniffed and sipped – his taste buds confirming suspicions with a scrunched face. He nodded.

'You had a group last week, Mark,' he said. 'They called the next day claiming their engineer was drunk. You know what I told them?'

I shrugged.

'I told them to piss off and have their work done elsewhere. But then, today, we get another call from one of your clients. You know what they said?'

'What?'

'Well, more or less the same thing. Peppered with expletives, though.'

He paused as if expecting a defence, but I had nothing to offer.

'We have a serious problem here. Do you understand?' he asked, shaking the mug at me.

'I do.'

'You do? Really?'

'Yes, I need to finish my drinks before the bookings start.'

'You think this is a joke?' he demanded, bringing it back down on the desk so hard it almost broke. 'I've shown you nothing but compassion and fairness and you're snubbing your nose at it? This is a small industry, Mark, which makes this a big deal. People talk.'

'Let them talk,' I said, with mounting irritation.

'Look, I'm willing to give you a chance here. Take another month off, get the help you so clearly need. Come back to the night shifts.'

'You can keep them.'

'You're going through a rough patch, I understand. I'm sorry about your mother,' he said, raising his voice and posture over mine, 'but this attitude's not the solution.'

'Martin, my entire life has been a rough patch. I just get thrown leftovers and told I don't say "thank you" loudly enough. This job is shit, this place is shit,' I said, ripping back the tape holding loose cabling to the wall that'd bothered me for months, taking a large flake of paint with it. 'Everything is shit and nothing ever gets better. We just sit around talking about how shit it all is, but nobody ever does anything about it.'

'Alright, Mark,' he sighed, 'if that's how you feel, consider this your notice of termination. Effective immediately.'

I dropped my keys into Martin's upturned palm as he stood blocking the doorway of the school's entrance. He seemed a lot more hurt by the whole situation than I was. But I had to hate him; in those seconds he was everything I'd ever hated.

'All the best, Mark. I hope you get better,' he said.

LIAM MURPHY

'Fuck yourself,' was all I could muster.

The door slammed in my face and I heard the lock turn. I lurched backwards into the cold wind. Lighting a cigarette, I looked up and let out a plume of smoke. The buildings seemed somehow taller and I smaller. With a strong sense this world was slowly rejecting me like some kind of bacteria, I turned, crossed the street and walked into the first pub I saw.

7.

I came to find hangovers are like love or loss, and your next always feels like your first. I watched bad television and didn't leave the house. Claire didn't come knocking. A realtor valued the house.

'Thus concludes our tour. Pretty great, huh?'

'Could do with a tidy-up,' she said, navigating empty bottles in heels while I led in my dressing gown, a beer in hand.

'But it's worth *something*, yeah?'

'Of course. I don't see why we couldn't get a buyer up past one-twenty-five or so.'

'Thousand? Dollars?'

'What? Yes. After some time bringing it up to a saleable condition, I think that's a perfectly reasonable expectation.'

'Interesting ...' I said, finishing the beer and dropping the bottle onto the carpet as we continued back into the living room. 'Let's say we skip the tidying part and put it up for eighty?'

'Excuse me?'

'I'd like a quick sale.'

'You and I both, but that is a massive, unnecessary loss.'

'Hmm, of course, you're right. Let's say eighty-five.'

'With all due respect, Mark, taking a forty-grand loss over what could be a few weeks of your time is absurd. I don't exactly see Melbourne house prices tanking at the turn of the twenty-first century.'

'Lady ... Linda?' I said, lifting my arms and gesturing around the room. 'With all due respect, do I look like a guy who's concerned with the twenty-first century?'

'I suppose not. Okay, if you're insistent. I'll draw up the paperwork and bring it around same time tomorrow.'

'I'll clear my schedule.'

'You do that.'

She headed to the door. I watched her body move inside her skirt; the tide of her hips pulling and pushing. Those gentle currents capable of steering a leaf down a stream or tearing a ship apart. The bottomless ocean of a woman.

'Hey, Linda.'

'Yes?'

'Are you, ah, are you seeing anyone?'

'I'm seeing you tomorrow, Mark,' she said, closing the door from the wrong side. I stood alone in front of my audience of empty bottles while the fan slow-clapped.

There wasn't much of a plan. I woke the following morning unsure if having the house valued was something I'd dreamt, until a contract was thrust at me between painted fingernails a few hours later. I hesitated to sign it; she did not hesitate to leave right after. I gratified myself in the shower to the idea of her having stayed. The first day of the rest of my life.

Cleaners came and mess disappeared. Linda rearranged furniture and threw down rugs I didn't own to create a façade of larger rooms for the photographer. I yelled at a cleaner for being rough with one of my mother's photos as they were taken down. An obnoxious sign with an auction date and inspection days was hammered into the grass by the footpath.

'What do I do during the inspections?' I asked.

'I don't know. Find a bar that allows dressing gowns or something,' Linda replied.

Claire came knocking.

'Jesus Christ...' she said as I stood in the doorway.

'What do you want?' I asked, scratching stubble. If she'd been around a few hours and drinks earlier, I might've been able to muster actual anger towards her.

'To be invited in would be nice.'

'I recall you having something to do with a door being slammed in my face,' I said, walking back inside.

'You think I knew that was going to happen?' she asked, following me, closing the door behind.

'Your handwriting on the booking. You knew Martin wanted to see me and he didn't want me to know. As far as I'm concerned, it was a goddamn ambush,' I said, pouring a drink and struggling to take myself seriously.

'This is somehow my fault...?'

'Your words.'

'Did you or did you not turn up to work drunk and tell the guy to fuck himself?'

'Well, yes, but, you know what?' I replied with a pointed finger and dignified pause. Claire and I both waited for me to resume. 'Maybe he does need to fuck himself. Why's nobody considering that?'

'You're a child.'

'Sure, but you didn't call or come by for weeks – that says something to me. You felt guilty.'

'Yeah, I did, and why shouldn't I? Look what you've managed without me. What the hell is that sign out there?'

'Pretty snazzy, huh?'

'No, Mark, it's ridiculous and obnoxious.'

'That's what I said! But my realtor, Linda, massive hard-arse, she –'

'Shut up, for the love of god! Go on a holiday or something, whatever, but don't just sell your mother's house. That is a ridiculous and obnoxious way to deal with your problems.'

'Maybe it is, but you have no idea what it's like to live here and be constantly reminded of the things I grew up without,' I snapped. 'Of the childhood I had taken away from me; of a 'good' day being one where my mother didn't feel compelled to drink herself into a stupor; of how ugly this world and the people in it can be. This life is a losing game, Claire.'

'The world is only against you if you're against it. It doesn't have to be. That's your choice.'

'I was never given the choice.'

'What are you afraid of . . . ? You avoid anything real – it's like you'll do anything but face it. Right now it's selling the house on a whim, but what next?'

I had no words.

'I want to help you, Mark, but you don't want to be helped. Your pride isn't some trophy; it's an anchor, but you're too fucking stubborn to let go, even when you're beginning to drown and . . . I should go, this was a mistake.'

She turned away, tears traced the lines of her face, shimmering as they caught light. I wrapped my hand around her arm, held on and kissed her. We tumbled onto the hideous rug, attempted to make something beautiful, and I felt better – if only for a little while. A drink and a woman was all I needed. The world had nothing else to offer me.

8.

The auctioneer's hammer banged down at one-twenty-seven, Claire squeezing my hand as if it were an executioner's gunshot. I breathed out smoke and watched the small crowd in front of the house from the other side of the street. A woman jumped into a man's arms with a scream.

'You okay?' Claire asked, looking up at me.

'I think so.'

'What now?'

'Maybe I'll have a drink or two then move to Sydney.'

She went home after that.

Documents were signed, hands shaken and a deposit paid while I prepared to farewell another thing on the increasingly short list of what had made up my life. Linda spread a 'SOLD' sticker across the sign – a lone air bubble irking me.

'Well, you made this unnecessarily excruciating, but it was good doing business,' she said, shaking my hand.

'It's what I do. Thank you for everything. Don't worry, I won't suggest a drink.'

'I've got time for a celebratory one, but just one.' She heaved a cheap bottle of champagne from her expensive handbag 'It's tradition.'

We clinked glasses together in the living room. Already I felt like a guest there.

'You know, you never mentioned why you were selling this place,' she said, relaxing into one of the beige couches dumped in there for the open houses.

'You never asked.'

'You didn't seem like the telling type.'

'Fair point. I grew up here with my mum. It was hers, but she passed a little while ago.'

'Oh, I'm sorry. No father in the picture?'

'He ran off to America when I was a kid and neither of us heard from him again. He died over there later that year – a car crash. Left in March of seventy-seven, dead by September.'

'I don't know what to say.'

'There's nothing to say. He got what he deserved; it was me and my mum who didn't.'

'How so?'

'He might've stuck around if I hadn't shown up.' I exhaled. 'But I did, so, there goes that. I deserved two happy parents; she deserved someone by her side in those final moments.'

'You really believe he left because of you?'

'Eh, maybe,' I said, finishing my glass and pouring myself another.

'Hmm, so, America? He was from there?'

'No.'

'Why then?' she asked. 'I'm sorry, this is really none of my business.'

I stared into space.

'You know, I've spent most of my life asking that same thing. Now I realise I'll never have the answer. Only two people might've known why he did what he did and now they're both gone. I'm just left behind, sort of ... stranded with the questions.'

'Maybe accepting there isn't an answer is kind of an answer?'

'Maybe you're right.'

Linda left me with a kiss on the cheek and a 'good luck' more sincere than I'd imagined her capable of. I closed the front door and leant back against it, looking around the room of the home which was no longer mine. No shower of relief or happiness rained over me like I had expected, nor even the sadness I'd felt before. There was nothing, and it was more agonising than anything else could've been.

9.

Removalists heaved my belongings into their truck. You don't realise how little of the stuff you have until it's packed up into cardboard boxes. The curtain fall of the roller door came down with a crash, and everything I owned went off to a storage shed in Footscray.

My mother's bedroom door creaked open. I reached for the light switch and flicked it back and forth; the globe was blown. I opened the blinds. It was one of those days where the morning air and light turn into a sunset and you wonder if there was anything in between. Maybe most lives go the same way.

Her perfumes and jewellery went into boxes for donation. I figured it's what she'd have wanted, and there wasn't anyone to disagree with me. The living speaking for the dead is a dangerous thing. I slid the door of her built-in wardrobe open, and took down and folded clothes. When there was just her antique shoe rack in its corner remaining, I heaved and dragged it to the centre of the room and got to work. All her shoes were laid out in perfect order – tidy and precise like everything she did. Touching them made me feel ill. Each pair I moved became one less thing in the world that would remain exactly as left by her.

I wiped down the last pair and placed them in the garbage bag.

Sitting against the wall across the room, I lit a cigarette and noticed a lone shoebox in the wardrobe that I'd somehow missed, resting between indentations left in the carpet by the rack. 'For fuck's sake,' I mumbled, climbing to my feet. Lifting the box to fling it at a pile of rubbish in the corner, the sound of contents moving within made me pause.

I looked from the box to where it had been in the wardrobe – too big to have fallen through gaps in the rack to rest beneath. I pried its lid, seized by dust and humidity that'd crept into the cardboard. It came free with a pop and I peered inside.

A pile of photographs, a beat-up flip lighter and an envelope. The lighter's lid croaked open. I pressed down on the wheel with my thumb, harder and harder, until it twisted free, coughing sparks over a blackened wick. I spun it a few more times, each becoming easier than the last and the sparks more abundant, yet still no flame. I slid it into my jeans' pocket.

The photographs seemed well preserved. Some familiar, but many I had never seen. All contained my mother and father, though, and most appeared to have been taken before I was born. I flipped through. They were not the type of photos framed and displayed around a house; they seemed more candid. Drinks toasted in bars, cigarettes smoked on park benches, lips pressed together. There was a shot of him reading with his head on her lap while she painted her nails. I'd never imagined the guy as being able to read, let alone picking up a book at will. One photo captured them on a bench at a beach I didn't recognise. The light looked different there. They both looked happy.

I placed the photographs down and fished out the envelope, drawing back its seal. Inside rested a wad of yellowed papers, thinned at their folds like worn hinges; flowing indentations of a pen tip showing through their other side. I opened them with care, as if unearthing some delicate, ancient tomb.

The first page began, 'My dear'; 'March 30th, 1977' dating its top left corner. I ran fingertips across the words resting on the page, feeling how they'd been engraved so long ago. A collection of ramblings, signed with a name I'd grown to resent. A letter, written to my mother by the man who was supposed to have left without a trace, sent from the other side of the world twenty years earlier.

A few lines into the second of the letters, I broke from my trance. Slamming the pages down on the dresser, I stepped away, holding back the feeling I was going to be sick. I didn't drink that day. The removalists took the remaining furniture and I sat on the floor of the empty living room with my back against the wall, staring at nothing in particular.

I'd been lied to, about her having no idea where he'd gone, about him never making contact. Answers I'd gone my whole life believing I needed had only resulted in more questions, and suddenly, my mother, the only real measure of goodness I'd ever known, had shown another side.

10.

'You're telling me honestly, truthfully, in absolute earnest, you had no idea these existed?' Claire asked with misty eyes as she returned the final page of the letters to the pile on my motel room's benchtop.

'No, I mean yes, fuck,' I replied, trying to manage my nerves and a lighter. 'I told you, Mum always said the first she heard of him after he vanished was during the coroner's first international call.'

'And you didn't read them all?'

'I couldn't. I got to the second one and it was like my body started rejecting them.'

'I think you should.'

I ignored her, staring at the downward-facing pile.

'He mentions buying a car to travel across the country ...' I mumbled, my curiosity punctuated by a half-baked attempt at upward inflection.

Claire didn't want to play this game, trying to outlast the silence but soon losing. Pursing her lips, she nodded with tight, concise movements.

'And did he really die in September that year like she told me ...?'

Her tongue crept out, wetting a dry bottom lip before it was pinched between teeth. Her eyes went pink again as she turned her head left then right – only a few degrees, but enough.

'Fuck me,' I said, blowing smoke and feeling another twang of nausea as I ran my hands through my hair and squeezed the back of my neck as if it were the only thing keeping me upright.

'You need to read them, Mark. All of them.'

'I don't want to.'

'Why not?'

'Because that man's already taken enough from me. I'm not letting him take the only good memories I have of my mother as well. I mean, Jesus Christ, what kind of monster lies to her kid about his father being dead?'

'Come on, don't speak like that. She was a kind woman and I think she had her reasons. It sounds to me like he – like your dad – might have had his own as well.'

'You're defending him now too, are you serious? I don't care if he can string a sentence together; I don't believe a word of this hollow, pseudo-sincere wank. Putting a bow on ugly things doesn't make them any less ugly.'

'I'm not defending him, Mark, I'm just saying –'

'You know, the only thing you two share is neither of you were around to see the damage caused. The nights I had to listen to my mother cry herself to sleep, watching her stay alone because no man could undo what my father did. Being branded a "fatherless bastard" and told he left because of me by the kids at school. I've never even left Melbourne because I couldn't stand the idea of not being here if she needed me. And her – you never even met her, what the hell would you know?'

'I didn't have to. I heard the way you spoke about her. There was love in your words, Mark, pure love. The kind I'm beginning to think you don't believe you're capable of anymore.'

'Get out.'

'Excuse me?'

'Just ... get the fuck out of here.'

And that she did. Too many of my conversations were beginning to end with a slammed door. Maybe I truly was my parents' son. I glanced between the letters and a rubbish bin in the corner, thinking they might be a good match for each other.

Sitting outside a café, I browsed a newspaper. A full-page ad caught my attention: an aerial shot of an expanse of buildings disappearing into the horizon, headed by: 'Wake up in The City That Never Sleeps!' I couldn't figure out why on earth anyone would want that, but found myself scanning the fine print anyway.

My stay in the motel hit the two-week mark after what was supposed to be a few days. Anxiety crept in; I couldn't bear to stay in my mother's house, but I couldn't bring myself to leave Melbourne either. Something had to give. I read the first letter again and got annoyed at myself for feeling a throb of excitement and curiosity about what came next, as if I were betraying my mother with the thought. It was a shame, though: if the man who'd penned it hadn't been such a loser, it might've made for a good read.

An apology to Claire seemed to stick, which I knew I didn't deserve, but I had nothing else anymore. She came around and I told her I was taking a holiday after all.

'Why New York City?' she asked.

I produced the full-page advertisement I'd botched tearing from the paper.

'Because of half an ad for it?'

'Ah, never mind that. Look at it – doesn't it look great?'

'You can't even stand the crowds in Melbourne. How would you cope in New York?'

'It could be exciting. You said it yourself; I should go on a holiday.'

'I did, but ...'

'What?'

'If I answer and you tell me to leave again after I've come all this way, I'm going to stab you.'

'Deal.'

She drew in a calming breath.

'Are you sure this has nothing to do with those letters?'

'What? I can't visit an entire continent because of a few pieces of paper?'

'It just seems less than coincidental considering the first of them was sent from New York, is all.'

'Your point being?'

'My point is I'm worried you think these letters are the beginning of something, instead of accepting they're the end,' she sighed. 'You're like this little race car full of pent-up energy, waiting for a green flag. You wanted your mum's okay to dream bigger than Melbourne; some absent dad's approval to feel like you're worth more than dirt. I don't think you'll like what you find if you pursue this, Mark, and I don't want you to be all alone if that happens.'

'But if going to New York might help me put this to rest?'

'Then, I guess ...' she looked to the ground and sucked a pout into one side of her mouth, then raised a hand and dragged an invisible flag back and forth through the air above us with sarcastic exaggeration.

I smiled and felt a wave of relief as I pulled her into me. She managed to force a 'dickhead' out between our lips as they met.

March 30th, 1977

My dear,

I'm not sure when this will reach you, but by the time it does, you will probably be aware my absence over the last week hasn't been just another bender. You always told me to take some time away, though I always thought it was a bit like expecting a dog not to be loyal.

My thoughts had become so self-destructive in the last few months I decided some time without me, and our seemingly inevitable infernos of arguments, might be better for you and Mark.

I'm sorry I didn't make it to Christmas, but I'm glad I was there for Mark's birthday. He looked like he had a good time, though I couldn't ignore that look in his eye. The distrust and disappointment in his baby blues when he looked at me, the one that turned back to a gleam when his mother came into sight. Maybe he knew I was leaving before you or I did. Maybe he never believed I was really there to begin with. He's intuitive, our kid. He takes after you – a trend I can only hope continues.

I am writing because I don't think I could bear to hear your voice right now – not with all the things you hide behind your words. You said to leave for a while but I never know if you mean more than the things you say. The way your pain and resentment towards me take indifference and make it poison. The way I fulfil your lowest expectations, time and time again. I am writing to you because of this, but also because I don't want these words to be lost in time. I hope this letter might serve as your memory instead of your recollection of a conversation on the telephone, or an argument had in doorways. I hope the words on this page will not be skewed or corrupted by time like we will surely be. I write because if this is your memory, then you can keep it folded in your jacket pocket or throw it onto the fire as you please, and when it's gone, it is gone, and that is all.

I have arrived in America. New York City, to be more specific, just like I always spoke about. This city is everything they say it is and more. I'm staying in Chelsea – right in the heart of it all. The wind is freezing, the streets are filthy, and the people are hard, yet the city has a warmth to it. Nobody ends up here by chance; it's a city that takes you in – swallows you whole. It takes your body, your mind and your soul but it gives back something that's so much more. If you have a dream, it will be tested. Nobody rides for free in New York City. I hope to really, truly feel this place before I have to leave, because anything less would be a tragic waste.

A man offered to sell me his car yesterday, and with it, a cascade of thoughts about driving across this country began flooding my mind. The idea of moving across this country in such an unhindered and unabridged way is too exciting to ignore.

Regardless, I need you to know this is not forever. You and Mark are my world and I will return home someday; I just needed to go into orbit for a while. I will continue to write until I can speak words to you again.

Always yours,

Dylan Ward

PS: *Keep his fingers on that keyboard. I know he wasn't too excited when he opened it, but I think he's got an ear for it.*

1.

I felt a shot of nerves as the plane descended towards early morning Los Angeles. The pink glow emanating into the cabin faded to drab grey as we fell through the clouds. We skidded along the drenched runway and taxied to the terminal. I watched rain trickle down the window and decided 'California Dreaming' must have been penned by its tourism department. Struggling to decide if either of the options presented by the customs officer really suited me, I dribbled out an unconvincing, 'Pleasure,' and with that, I had entered the United States.

I was delirious by the time I reached JFK. I'd departed Melbourne on Friday morning, spent what felt like days in the air, and touched down in New York on that same Friday's evening. I trudged through the airport with my backpack over my shoulder and stood at the baggage collection. The gentle hum of the carousel's conveyor belt almost put me to sleep where I stood. A familiar shape and hue moved towards me. I heaved my bag off the belt and staggered along as I tried to counterbalance its weight with my own.

Catching a bus to Jamaica, I transferred onto the E line. Eyes fixed onto me and quickly darted away when my stare met theirs. I wondered how dark the rings around my eyes were. The sun was setting behind houses extending to the horizon as we moved through Queens – the train tracks elevated from the streets. I was surprised; my idea of Manhattan had, until that point, been a markedly empty skyline multiplying in height and complexity by a few thousand all of a sudden. Queens looked like a jungle of its own, but I had no idea what was waiting right down the line.

I tried to fend off exhaustion. Despite whatever 'good work' smiling news anchors proclaimed Giuliani to be doing, a lifetime of television and filmic impressions of the city had me convinced one was only ever a few seconds away from being mugged. Unable to fight it any longer, I drifted off, repurposing my backpack into a pillow as I keeled over.

Departing Lexington station, I was snapped awake by three thunderous bangs. I scanned the faces of the other passengers for any kind of reciprocation of my panic, but saw only indifference. Again, three bangs travelled through the car. Only the sounds of quiet conversation and the subway groaning along its tracks, filled the silence between the storms. I leant forward to look down the car.

A man in ragged clothes stood in the centre beside an old, rickety cart covered in bizarre fabrics and patterns. In his right hand was a small pot; in his left, its accompanying lid. I teetered between sadness at how invisible he must've felt to need to draw attention to himself on a busy subway car, and anger at how obnoxious his chosen method was. He raised his instruments up high, turning the empty pot for all to see, and again married them with force. Once, twice. This time on the third strike he held them together, smothering their clang back to silence. With a concentrated look and peculiar finesse, he brought the sealed pot down from above his head, revolving its rim to horizontal during the steady descent. Holding it in front of him for a moment, he scanned the car to make sure he'd retained the attention of his audience, of which I comprised roughly a third. I inched forward and cocked my head to get a better look.

With a confident smirk, he lifted the lid. Following it, a small white figure reared its head. Twisting and turning, its beady eyes scanned the car, locking onto me for a moment before shooting off to its next focus. The man showed the pot around as the thing stood tall, rising from the metallic confines and shaking itself off. A single, perfect, white dove, illuminated by the fluorescent lights of a grimy New York City subway car.

In my disorientated state, I was certain this was the most incredible thing to ever happen – some sort of cosmic metaphor for myself, perhaps. A woman noticed the awe in my expression and smiled.

The car began decelerating as we approached the next stop and, like clockwork, the magician had his cart packed and was moving down the carriage, taking tips along the way. Most ignored him, but I eagerly retrieved a crisp one-dollar note from my wallet and pushed it into his upturned hat. He nodded and stepped off at the next station, ready to board another train and do it all over again. With a grin, I eased back into the seat inside my own metal container and waited for it to open inside the heart of New York City.

A crescendo built inside me as I moved up the stairs towards the loudness of the city, growing with each step of my weary legs. It burst as I stepped out onto Seventh Avenue from 23rd Street station and was hit by a wall of sound. A sea of car lights disappeared into the distance in all directions; sirens and horns wailed; revellers laughed and cried. Illuminated buildings reached for the sky while the subway roared underneath, millions of people bustling somewhere in between. A man winked and waved at me as another barked 'Excuse me,' and moved through the door of a convenience store. I bee-lined down the busy footpaths against the flow of traffic, my bag colliding with a few. I turned to apologise but saw only their backs as they disappeared into the night, unaffected.

I reached the hostel I'd booked on 20th Street and signed in. The receptionist led me to my room, past a group of French girls who fell silent as we moved by – displeased looks on their faces as they blew out cigarette smoke. My shoulders and neck ached as I dropped my bags onto the floor and slid them under my bed. It was a shared room with three other guys already checked in: two young Brazilians, I guessed, and another Australian. The Australian instantly assumed a level of camaraderie when I spoke, shooting up to his feet and thrusting a hand towards me.

'Nice to meet you, mate, but to be honest, I was hoping you'd be a girl,' he said, chuckling as he shook my hand a little too hard.

'Why's that?' I asked.

'I've been here five days and still no pussy! What's the go with that? I thought American girls loved the accent.'

'Ah well, maybe it's a numbers game.'

'What?'

'Never mind.'

'Hey, we should go out for a drink.'

'Maybe another night. I just got in.'

'All good, brother.'

The others had gone out by the time I'd shaved, showered, and crawled under the covers. I'd lain in many beds, staring through darkness at many ceilings, but I'd never been this far from home. I could hear the chaotic hum of the city; its heartbeat so frantic it seemed to vibrate the room, the bed, the very cells in my skin. New York City. A billion little processes all taking place at once – each seeming microscopic compared to the larger being of the thing, yet all integral to its survival. And I was in the middle of it.

My fatigue vanished at the thought. I got up and dressed, not content with wasting another second. Walking back into the chilly night, I found a bar packed with people on the corner of a block. It was swanky – not the type of place I'd have gone to back home. An orange glow shone through the wall of spirits behind the servers, while the underside of the bar counter splashed neon blue over crossed legs on stools and flowed down to the tips of high heels.

I moved through the crowd to the bar and ordered the only beer I recognised, then took a free stool on the end of a long table with a loud group at the other. The girl nearest looked over, and I smiled and saluted with my bottle. She stood and moved closer. The table was reserved, she told me. I offered her my stool, hoping hospitality might afford me an invitation to join, but she returned to the group, her friends seeming uncomfortable as I watched her saunter away.

I moved to another area but found myself always in someone's way. The speakers repeated the same few bars of monotonous, uninspiring beat over and over. I finished my drink and left. Walking the long way back to the hostel, I found a deli on a corner, ordered two slices of pizza and sat at the window. A man had been knocked off his push-bike by a cab in the middle of the intersection outside moments before I'd arrived. I chewed and watched as the gathered crowd argued about how to best help him. Then he was loaded into an ambulance, everyone left, and it looked like nothing had happened there at all.

The Brazilians were in bed when I returned. One slept and snored; the other looked up and smiled at me before returning to his book. I don't think he knew English, but he knew how to smile. I got into bed and tried to drift off. The other Australian returned a while later – liquored up.

'This fucking guy! He's snoring again. I told him to cut it out last night,' he grunted.

'I don't think he's doing it to upset you,' I said.

His eyes narrowed. I turned over, not wanting to antagonise the Neanderthal.

I moved in and out of sleep with the volume of the snoring, sensing mounting frustration across the room each time it climaxed. Suddenly the Australian was at the snoring Brazilian's bed. 'Shut up! Shut the fuck up, cunt!' he screamed, grabbing him by the collar and shaking him ferociously. The other Brazilian rushed over and grabbed the Australian's arm to stop him. I watched as the three silhouetted figures wrestled in the darkness, their shapes outlined by moonlight creeping through the window.

The centre figure drew back an arm like a slingshot and launched it into the one holding his arm, knocking him back onto his bed before turning to the other. 'I hear another fuckin' peep out of you and you're getting the same, alright?' he screamed, giving him one last shake. The Australian went back to his bed and threw the covers over himself. I was frozen, my pulse throbbing in my ears. As it slowed, I stared into the darkness and fell asleep to the quiet sobbing of one of the Brazilians.

2.

I woke alone the next morning. The Brazilians' bags were gone, the Australian's were not. On my way to the bathroom, I noticed blood on the pillow of the one who'd tried to help his friend. I got dressed, went to reception and requested a room change.

Gruesome clouds filled the sky. I took a folder from my bag, placed it on the bed of my new room and sat by the window overlooking the courtyard. I lit a cigarette and yet again read the letter my father had penned here. Nothing new was going to jump out from between its lines. The words weren't going to change; only I was. I was in the exact neighbourhood where he'd pushed pen onto pad, declared his self-righteousness, and signed off on my mother's and my fate twenty years earlier. It had all begun in these streets, in these buildings, in these rooms. This was the closest I'd ever been. I threw on my jumper and butted out my cigarette.

I moved east along 20th Street. Rubbish was piled high; murky water filling crevices between roads and footpaths. Pools of the stuff collected at crossings, forcing crowds to move around them like a trail of ants encountering a pebble. I passed a homeless man, then another. Horns blared almost incessantly while opportunistic motorists tried to gain a foot's advantage in miles of gridlock. I came to a construction site narrowing the street and a driverless cement truck blocking the way. A bus tried to navigate the tight gap to no avail, its driver getting out and approaching the truck as its driver returned.

'Man, move this damn truck. You blocking the whole street with that bullshit!' he yelled at the small, Eastern European-looking man. I felt a rush of nerves, expecting violence to ensue.

The small man looked up and down the street for a better place he could've stopped, before shrugging and replying, 'What you gonna do? It's New York City.'

'I know, motherfucker, I'm born and raised!' he exclaimed, drumming his thumb into his sternum as he walked backwards to his bus. 'Get that shit outta here!' he added, throwing his hands in the air. The truck driver shooed him off with stiff joints as he climbed back into the truck. Noticing me watching, he shrugged the same 'What you gonna do?' expression before driving off. I buried my hands into my pockets and continued on my way, unsure if I'd just witnessed my first taste of New Yorkers' particular brand of pride.

I continued to weave through Chelsea and its immediate neighbourhoods, refusing to acknowledge the rest of the massive city. People walked their own paths from A to B, unwilling to stray from the straightest line between the two, with a stubborn indifference to those around them. I became more adept to these patterns and had fewer collisions with each block I traversed. After a few hours, I began to wonder what I was expecting to find. With every turn moving me further away from an answer, I called it a day and did the most unoriginal thing I could think of: I walked to the Empire State Building, bought a ticket, got in line and took the lift to the top.

Winter was holding on, or so I overheard in the queue. The wind at the top was icy and my jumper couldn't stop me from shivering. I paced the packed lookout. The sun was setting through the clouds, casting streams of light in patches onto the mammoth expanse below. From a distance, New York City seemed a singular whole; as if a forest. But only when inside could you see each tree, string of bark and leaf comprising it, and the impossibility of being aware of them all at once descends on you like a dark cloud.

Sunlight and shadows fought for control of the city as I made my way back to the hostel. A small bar nearby appeared closed from the outside, despite its big, illuminated 'OPEN' sign. The bartender saw me as I peered through the gap between the door and blocked-up window, lazily gesturing me in with a raised hand. There was very little seating except for stools around the bar, most of them filled by hunched-over men. An Eagles song played through worn speakers. I approached the bar.

'What you having?' the bartender asked me.

'A beer, please,' I said, looking at the unrecognisable can gripped in the hand of a man sitting next to me. I pointed to it. 'One of those.'

'That's a PBR. You want a beer or a PBR?'

'Is PBR not a beer?'

'Kinda,' the man interjected. 'I mean, they put "beer" on the label, but it's really fermented horse piss, is what it is.'

He threw the rest of the can down his throat and tapped the bar twice with his finger, not once looking at me. The bartender cracked open another for him and one for me. I didn't speak another word to anybody in there for the rest of the night, or them to me. The seven or so seats around the bar were on a constant rotation of silent men who pushed the door in, ordered their poison, drummed on the bar at intervals, unfurled their notes and left – never saying a word or sitting beside each other if they could help it. The place had the feeling of a medical centre – the barflies like patients who had self-diagnosed their illness and written prescriptions only a bartender could fill. I sat, listening to the music, not realising how drunk I'd become without the distraction of conversation. I stumbled back to the hostel and went to bed.

The next morning I awoke to a guy fumbling through his bag. The other two in the four-person room were gone. Sun streamed through the window and my watch said 1 p.m.

'Oh, man, I'm so sorry. I didn't mean to wake you,' he said.

'No, no, that's okay. Something had to. Fuck...'

I turned my head and the hangover began straight away.

'Danny,' he said, extending a hand in front of big, white teeth.

'Mark,' I said, taking it.

'You sound like you've got a bit of an accent there. Where ya from?'

'Australia.'

'Australia, beautiful! I've always wanted to go, it looks so great.'

'It's something.'

'You look like you had a big night on the sauce.'

'Yeah? I feel like it too.'

'It's all good, enjoying a vacation in New York City! You've gotta make the most of it. I'm up here for a buddy's buck's party tonight. You want to get a drink tomorrow maybe?'

'I never want to get a drink again.'

'Alright,' he said, laughing. 'Well if you change your mind, let me know. I'm heading off the day after.'

His enthusiasm worsened my headache, though I couldn't help but like the guy. He seemed to take energy in from the world, amplify it somehow then send it back out. I lay in bed listening to the city through the walls, feeling somehow excluded from it. There was a knock on the door. I wandered over, underpants-clad, and reached for the handle as it turned from the other side. A short, Hispanic housekeeper stood there, armed with a bucket of brushes and sprays.

'Hi,' I said.

'Hello, sir.'

'Hmm, you looked different in the picture.'

She raised an unimpressed brow.

'I come back later. You no be here.'

'Okay.'

Even with the afternoon sun out, the wind was icier than it had been the day before. A bell chimed as I pulled open the door of a thrift shop. I flicked through clothes on a rail and stopped at one. A jacket, leather – a fabric I'd always loathed. It was brown, with cuffs and an upright collar in wool. A small belt ran through loops around the collar, meaning it could seal snug against the neck. It was ridiculous, like something a 1950s fighter pilot might've worn, yet I was drawn to it. I placed it on the front counter.

'Ooh, I was wondering when someone was going to snatch this up,' said the round woman behind the counter.

'Really?'

'Oh yes, it's very nice. If you want, I got some boots that'd go real nice with it.'

'No, just the jacket, thanks.'

I walked back out onto the footpath and began moving north. A girl looked me up and down. Waiting at the next intersection, I glanced down at my worn Chuck Taylors, splits forming at the bends of my toes. I turned back, pushing through the crowd gathered behind me, and chimed the bell. 'Show me these boots.'

I tapped and clicked my way through Central Park. I'd never owned a pair of wooden-soled shoes before and the sound made me more conscious of my walking than I'd ever been. I sat on a bench in the sun and watched a group play baseball. Joggers jogged, children laughed, dogs barked; I smoked a cigarette and took it all in.

A winding path wrapped around a lake with rowboats drifting along its surface, lovers intertwined in each.

    A group of drunken French girls on their backs in the middle of a path gazed up at the trees. They threw sour looks as I stepped over them and continued. 'Hey, fuck you, man!' one yelled to me. I walked without turning back. 'Hey!' she yelled again. 'I don't like you; I only like your arse!' The others erupted in laughter. I continued along the track and headed south towards Chelsea.

3.

Danny's flight back to Orlando was at 4 p.m. the following day. We went to a bar to pass the time. He loved to talk, and I didn't mind listening. His spirits were high considering how big a night he said he'd had. I tried to make eyes with a big-nosed girl further down the bar, much to her eventual annoyance.

'What's with this fucking guy?' she said to her friend, loud enough for me to hear. 'He a fucking bird-watcher or something? Hey, yo! Do I look like a fucking bird to you?' she yelled down the bar.

'Yeah, a toucan!' Danny countered before the embarrassment could even hit me. We doubled over in laughter.

'Fucking assholes,' she muttered, shaking her head and going back to her drink.

'Damn, that was mean,' I said to Danny.

'Hey, man, she was mean first. Gotta live and let live, ya know.'

'I don't think you're using that correctly ...'

'Aren't I? Eh, whatever.' We both cracked up again and ordered another round.

Laughing and swaying, we walked east along 34th. We didn't know each other, but it felt good to have something close to a friend. I carried Danny's bag for him until we got to the subway station.

'Was awesome meeting you, my man,' Danny said as he went in for a handshake and I missed.

'You too. I'm glad you talked me into that drink.'

'Enjoy the rest of your trip. New York is great, but if you've got the time you should check out some other cities. There are great ones all over this country.'

'I don't doubt that, but my flight home is in a few days. I think I'll just stay around here.'

'All good, man. Take care,' he said, throwing his bag over his shoulder and heading down the stairs.

I stood for a moment and felt a familiar wave of loneliness wash over me. I turned and began walking. A hand tapped me on the shoulder.

'Actually, take this,' Danny said, dropping his bag to the ground, pulling out a pad and pen.

He handed me a small, torn-off piece of paper reading 'Danny' and a phone number.

'Hit me up if you ever find yourself in Orlando.'

'I don't know why I would be ...'

'Well, take it anyway,' he said. 'You never know when it might come in handy.'

And like that, he was gone again.

The following days in New York City were more of the same. An abundance of wealth and poverty, footpath collisions, honking horns, bright lights and dark corners, big personalities getting caught up in little issues and me somewhere in the middle of it all. I wandered more and more of the city, coming to grips with its enormity and the futility of trying to find anything particular there. The place was a circus where every worldly extreme collided at every moment. If some god had ever been reincarnated, only to be pushed into

THE ROADMAP OF LOSS

obscurity as he waited on the ears of passers-by while shaking an empty can, it would surely have happened in New York City.

I read the letter again, wondering what I'd expected to find and what my father had hoped to. Maybe he had a clearer vision in mind. Maybe he didn't have one at all. To think he'd found something here worth staying for was insane, but to think some fire in him burnt so strongly that he'd pursued this elusive meaning from city to city across America trying to find it, was something else. He may have been a loser, but he was ballsy, I'd give him that much.

The doors of the bus wheezed open outside the departure terminal of JFK. I wrestled my bags over my shoulders and walked in. Large screens listed flight numbers, destinations and delays. My flight home popped up. I imagined touching down in Australia, Claire greeting me, and the sad, perpetual nothing of my days starting all over again. Another screen refreshed to another list of places – most within the United States – all with their own history, people and stories; their own beauty and ugliness. I waited with my back against the wall as the minutes fell away. Screens updated as flights arrived, boarded and departed – others taking their place in an endless, indifferent cycle. I watched mine update to pre-boarding, but I didn't move. The clock hand continued moving and my flight began boarding, but still I didn't budge. I heard my name called over the PA system three separate times then watched as my flight updated to: 'CLOSED'.

I walked back outside and boarded a bus to Manhattan.

4.

The hostel in Chelsea was booked out for weeks. The receptionist suggested a place in Brooklyn doing cheap short-stay. I caught the subway there and checked in. Something inside me was running the show now. A concoction of fear, sadness, excitement and anger, all mixed in the perfect ratios to fuel me with nervous energy. I felt as though I was doing something I shouldn't be, and if I slowed down, then I'd be caught by some invisible enforcer and the game would be up.

I called my bank and asked if the total amount for the house sale had been transferred yet. It hadn't. I was comfortable for money from the house deposit, at least for a little while, though the cost of the empty seat I was paying for to fly across the Pacific at that very moment didn't help.

I grabbed a newspaper and searched for the classifieds with such ferocity I ripped some pages. A payphone on the corner of the block swallowed my coins with a metallic gulp. Wiping the handset with my jacket cuff, I scanned the page I'd torn out. Three circles, drawn so quickly the paper had punctured, encompassed three used-car listings. Two had accompanying photos, one was just words, but they all fitted a particular theme: they were in my budget, and ridiculous, but no more ridiculous than what I had planned.

The first's contact was simply: 'KING'. I punched in the number and waited. 'What?' barked back through the phone. I asked to see the car as soon as possible and within half an hour I was on my way to the Bronx. Walking downstairs from the station, I rounded a corner and there it was – a champagne Ford Mustang convertible. I extended a hand more upwards than outwards to its huge Black owner as he stepped out. He seemed taken aback by the formality, but shook it.

'Mark.'

'King,' he snarled, showing teeth of diamonds and gold.

'What's your real name?' I asked, following him to the car. 'It's, just, I don't think the DMV would accept "King" on the forms.'

He stopped and turned back with low brows. My smile disappeared.

'Call me King.'

I drove around the block, deciding halfway through my first lap that peak hour in the Bronx was not the best place to pilot a left-hand-drive car for the first time. The Mustang pulled to the right when coasting and to the left when braking, but it was mean. The engine and the sound it produced were burly – any pressure applied to the throttle translating back into my gut tenfold as the car surged forward. The car was made to live on a highway carving through some desert, but the body was badly rusted and the brakes made an awful noise when used too much. I knew nothing about cars, but even I was seeing red flags.

'How much do you want?' I asked King.

'Five-K-five, my man.'

'That's a little steep. How low could you go?'

'Hmm. Five-K-five.'

I took the subway back to Brooklyn and used a bar's phone to check the other listings. One had been sold; the other could be viewed the following afternoon. I called Claire and told her I'd pushed my flight back to spend more time in New York. She said she was glad I was enjoying the city so much.

The next day I caught the subway to lower Manhattan and boarded the Staten Island Ferry. I walked quiet blocks of white picket fences and manicured lawns, beautiful houses and perfectly waxed cars in driveways, pretty birds chirping in pretty trees. This was an America I'd always imagined, but never thought could exist so close to Manhattan's chaos. Approaching the address I was given, I saw the car out front. 'Oh, god,' I said to myself, almost turning back right then.

Its owner stepped out through the front door with a swinging wave. A young Hispanic guy. His name was Carlos, but he told me I could call him Carl. He showed me around the car, which he seemed to take more pride in than its appearance suggested.

'It's a 1989 Mazda Miata,' he told me. The diminutive convertible wore its eight-year age worse than I thought possible. A skewed, chipped bumper wrapped around pop-up headlights at the front, with a cracked panel and black soot around the exhaust pipe garnishing the rear. Its red paint had faded from a glossy finish to more of a chalky one. The wheels had been spray-painted black – I assumed to cover damage – and the antenna was stuck at full-mast, bent almost ninety degrees. Rust festered beneath the doors and patches of paint were missing.

'Let's go for a spin,' Carlos said, throwing me the keys. I pulled on the driver's door handle and nothing gave. 'Oh, yeah, that only opens from inside,' he added, reaching over the passenger seat, unlocking and pushing it open for me.

'Cool,' I said, lowering myself into the seat and pausing.

'What's up?' Carl asked.

'This is manual.'

'Sure is. Five-speed manual transmission, and smooth as a waxed pussy.'

'I don't know how to drive manual. Your ad didn't mention it.'

'Come on, man, it's a sports car. Of course it's gonna be stick. Just give it a try.'

I started the engine and found my feet, and Carl's, swimming in an ocean of red, blue and green light.

'What is that ...?' I asked.

'Oh, yeah! I put these lights down there and wired them into the speakers. They pump to the bass of whatever song you're listening to. It's awesome.'

He fiddled with a controller fitted to the side of the transmission tunnel, pushing buttons that cycled through various modes of the light show.

'Cool, huh?'

'Can they be turned off?'

'Yeah sure, I mean, if you wanted to. They'll just turn back on next time you start her though.'

'For fuck's sake ...'

After a two-minute explanation of how to drive a manual car, I bucked my way out of Carlos's driveway and we were off. The engine was smooth but loud, due to a rusted-out section of exhaust. The Miata didn't have the same grunt as the Mustang, but it would rotate with enthusiasm wherever the wheel was turned. We settled on $1300 and filled out the bill of sale.

'Whoa, what state is this from?' he asked, studying my licence.

'Victoria, in Australia.'

'No shit ... you live here now or what?'

'No, just travelling.'

'Why not rent a car then?'

'Don't know how long I'll need it.'

THE ROADMAP OF LOSS

Carlos's mother arrived home during the sale. In a matter of minutes she'd decided my story sounded suspicious and was on the phone to her husband. In a matter of a few more minutes, she'd decided I looked like I needed to eat. She warmed up a chicken cutlet and put it down before me at the table. It was the first meal I'd had in America that wasn't eaten at a bar or a deli or a fast-food outlet. It was nice to sit in a home where people lived, to eat with the company of framed photographs of families, not baseball stars or musicians.

Carlos's father decided my story checked out. Carlos cleared his belongings from the Miata, one of which was a crowbar. 'Never know when you might need one. There's a lot of looneys out there,' he said when he saw me staring. He drove his family's car back to Brooklyn while I followed in the Miata and stalled or bucked away from each stop along the way. Carlos uninstalled the hardware holding the plates on – which consisted of one bolt and three zip ties – shook my hand and was on his way. I leant over the passenger seat and locked the driver's side door. Taking a step back onto the footpath, I placed my hands on my hips and took in the magnificence of my purchase. 'What a pile of shit,' I muttered.

Registering the car was painful. After three days of back-and-forth subway rides, photocopiers, waiting rooms and being turned away for inadequate documentation, a clerk finally disappeared into a backroom of the Manhattan DMV and returned with two fresh New York state plates. I ran my fingers over them as he spoke.

'Secure these to the front and rear of the vehicle in a visible location. You have ten days to have the vehicle inspected. Next!'

'So it's done?'

'Is what done? The vehicle is registered, sir. Next!'

'Like ... it can be driven? I can get in it and drive wherever I want?'

'Yes, that is typically what a registered vehicle is used for. Next!'

An old woman sitting next to me on the subway back to Brooklyn looked at the plates in my lap.

'I just registered my car. I'm gonna drive it,' I said.

'Good for you.'

I justified staying the following days in Brooklyn on the basis I'd already paid for a week's accommodation, but there was something else hindering me. I loathed admitting it, but my father's eloquence rang true, even two decades later. New York City was brutal in so many ways, but I felt safe. I couldn't tell if the city was made hard by the people, or the people made hard by the city. Nevertheless, it belonged to them, and they to it – like a parasite and its host, the order of which eluded me. Its geography, with the Atlantic just over its shoulder, gave me a sense of being at the edge of the earth. People tend to feel their safest or most vulnerable when cornered.

My room key disappeared into the letterbox at the unmanned reception. I stepped through the front door and into the morning sun. The air was cool and still, the sun unobscured yet forgiving. My favourite type of weather. The boot lid fought back as my bag was squeezed against the floor. I hadn't thought to check if my luggage was larger than the available space. It was. I transferred clothes into my backpack and threw it onto the passenger seat and placed my weight onto the boot lid for a second attempt. The latch clicked shut and I moved back in small steps with raised hands, expecting the rear of the car to pop like a shaken champagne bottle at any moment, then walked into a deli around the corner to fuel myself.

'Morning, do you do coffee?' I asked.

'Yeah.'

'Great, I'll have a flat white then.'

The shopkeeper scrunched his brow and opened the display between us. He removed a white bagel, laid it on the chopping board, and began sawing it in half.

'No, no, a coffee.'

'You want a coffee or a bagel?' he said, slamming his fists down on the board.

'Sorry, a coffee. A flat white coffee.'

'I don't know what that is.'

'Okay, what type of coffee do you do?'

'Caw-fee,' he spat, pointing to a dispenser in the corner with a large, red tap handle protruding through a photo of a white-toothed woman smiling over a mug of brew she obviously hadn't bought there. I looked at the machine and back to him. He continued pointing at it with his left hand, his right against the board, white knuckles wrapped around the knife handle. The machine gurgled as I pulled the tap, a molten black mess spewing into my cup a moment later. It was immediately too hot to hold, and I sleeved the first cup into another.

'Hey, you can't take two cups,' he said, still watching me.

'Fuck yourself. I'll pay for two,' I retorted, to both of our surprise. He shrugged and went back to preparing sandwich ingredients. I walked to the counter and threw two ones down as the clerk opened the register.

'For that, you can throw in the hacked-up bagel as well,' I said to him, not breaking my stare. He looked at me for a second, then bagged the bagel and handed it over.

'You have a good day, sir,' he said.

'And you too.'

As I sat in the car, sipping coffee and chewing a bagel, I laughed to myself. In my final moments in New York, the city had given something back. A forgettable breakfast to most, but a trophy to me. I had seen something I wanted, and I had taken it.

Taking a breath, I tested my newfound self-assuredness right away. I removed the letters from my pocket and turned pages until I reached the second. Nausea swelled as I consumed the words, but not stemming from fear like it had in Melbourne. This was different: it was an overwhelming sense of anticipation.

I started the engine, turned off the footwell disco lights, and clunked my way from the kerb out into the street, following signs into Manhattan. I dropped the soft top at a set of lights and put on my sunglasses. Two women covered their mouths, laughing and pointing as they crossed the road. After a few more turns, I was in a tunnel under the Hudson River, emerging from its other side into sunshine. A long, sweeping left-hander guided me higher and higher before opening out at the top of a large crest. Roads and buildings and greenery stretched in all directions under the blue sky.

I removed a cigarette from the pack resting in the cup holder, and the beat-up flip lighter from my shirt pocket. Turbulent wind pummelled me. I leant forward under the windshield to escape it. The flint spat sparks, and the fresh, white wick I'd replaced while hunched over a bar the night before was engulfed in flame. I sat back and drew a deep breath through the cigarette. A large, imposing sign ahead arrowed towards each lane: 'Pennsylvania' marked the furthest right.

It glided over me like some great gatekeeper deciding if I was worthy to pass. 'Sorry, Mum,' I said aloud. I moved to the right lanes, getting the Miata into fifth gear as I worked it up to seventy. With another deep breath, I headed for the horizon.

April 28th, 1977

My love,

I apologise for not writing again sooner, but I've struggled to find the words. A letter doesn't deserve to be written, nor your time wasted, unless I've something worthy to say. I've been embarrassed by my behaviour, so I hide, then teeter constantly between running away and tackling my fear head-on. Much the same could be said about how I've handled everything in my life thus far, I suppose. I've wired you some more money, which should have arrived by now. If it hasn't, then I fear for the teller who has to take your complaint. The women in New York are strong, but they're Coney Island cotton candy compared to you.

I've left New York City, for now. There was too much lingering beyond that horizon to stay. It would take a million lives to see it all, and we're only gifted the one. I was not falling out of love with her, but the city is too fantastical for its own good. I never thought I'd find myself saying that about anything, but maybe even the shine of a brilliant sunset can wear away when every day is punctuated by one. Perhaps it's the shine within me that's wearing. It's getting harder and harder to tell.

I did something impulsive, though I think you would say entirely predictable: I bought that car. I couldn't help myself. It was a good buy though. I think it'll end up paying for itself in saved bus or train fares, and I can sell it on before I come home. I started driving in the vague direction of Chicago, and have found myself in a small town in Pennsylvania named Kane.

It's so quiet here, and green. There is one bar and no traffic lights. I like it. I met a man who builds houses, called Rodney. He said he has some work for me if I'm fit and willing, and I figure I have at least a week or two before he realises I don't know anything about building houses. Of what I earn, I will keep only what I need and send the rest to you. I'm sure you're enjoying some time off from me, despite the circumstances. I hope you and Mark are well. Has he asked about me? If he has, tell him I'm just fine. If he hasn't, then this absence is necessary to become the type of man he would ask about.

1.

Pennsylvania rewarded me as I moved off the interstates. Winding country roads shaded by thick, ancient trees squeezed themselves between hillsides with small farms resting at their feet. Sometimes they passed through townships that had dodged the merciless hands of time. I stopped in one and had a sandwich, bought a book of road maps as thick as an encyclopaedia and filled the tank. The further west I moved, the more eyebrows were raised and questions posed about an accent I'd never considered myself to possess. A few hours from New York City and I'd already entered an America where most people had never met an Australian.

After plotting a vague route on my map, I continued north-west into the Susquehannock State Park. The forest was the most dense I'd ever seen. Every piece of land seemed to vie for control over the space around it; they pushed forward and against each other like troops marching to a frontline. Not a single spot was left vacant by a tree or bush, a pebble or a stream. The roads were at the will of the hills, creeks and rivers. Every twist or turn, elevation shift and contour that they produced, the road would passively mimic as if not to intrude, only taking a stubborn stand of defiance with the occasional rickety bridge passing over water. There was a gentle feeling to those roads, like you were floating down the river while driving beside it.

Every once in a while, the road would steer away from the bank – the land flattening out and opening up. Small townships made up of trailers and shacks nestled themselves between the bitumen and the water. Streets and intersections forming blocks ran throughout, created from grass ground into dirt by truck and bike tyres, not by bitumen and city planners. I slowed when I passed each community to look in. These people lived wherever they wanted to, or perhaps wherever they could. Maybe they were just like the trees.

Reaching a somewhat larger town, I stopped in the gravel car park of a gas station. There was a shack-bar next door sharing the same car park, with some of its outdoor patrons taking note of my arrival. I used the station's bathroom and pulled a gallon of drinking water out from a fridge.

While standing in line at the counter, I noticed two men standing by the Miata. One placed his boot against a wheel and leant in with all his weight, as if trying to roll it over. The Miata's tiny mass wobbled back and forth on the tyres' sidewalls as the man pushed himself off. I paid for the water and watched the men through the glass storefront, pretending to browse the aisles until they'd walked away. When I got back to the Miata, I opened the passenger door, put the bottle on the seat and reached through to open the driver's door. I stood and turned to see the two men standing a few yards from me. One of them sucked on his gums and spat on the earth between us.

'What's with the tin can Jap crap?' he asked me, his friend remaining silent.

'Nothing. It's, ah, it's just a car.'

'Yeah? And you *just* some New York City faggot too?'

I looked over his shoulder to the bar's patrons watching on in glee.

'No. No, I'm just some guy who stopped in the wrong town and was about to leave.'

'Mm, that's smart.'

Releasing the clutch on gravel was difficult with a quivering leg. I drove out of the car park with the two men walking beside me, and every eye at the bar following me. I watched as they all shrank to nothing in the rear-vision mirror. The sun was starting to sit low, casting sandy light into the valley and drawing long outlines of the forest. I followed the river west.

2.

I pulled over on what seemed like the main strip in Kane, though I was the only soul around. Another car passed every few minutes, but otherwise, nothing. A fog loitered over the streets and footpaths, finding its way into alleys and driveways and locked doorways. It had a luminance from the yellow street lights and rolled over itself like something alive and breathing.

When another car drove by, the fog would recede; a pocket of still, clear air left behind for a moment before the fog would fill it, chasing and reaching for the back of the car like an outstretched hand. I already didn't want to be here.

It was 7.40 p.m. and Kane was asleep; I was a far shot from New York City. Doubling back, I passed a motel I'd missed when driving in. It was a white, two-storey house on a lawn, with a more typical-looking motel building behind. The air around my face and arms was cold, but the fog had turned my legs to ice. The screen door creaked as I heaved my bags through and walked into the reception, which looked like a converted living room.

Lowering them to the floor, I let out a deep breath of relief. A small doorbell rested on the counter, 'Press ONCE for assistance' printed on a laminated card taped down beside. I pressed the button, once, and a tired chime sounded in another room. A minute passed as I fought the urge to press the button a second time, distracting myself with photos hung on the walls. An old woman opened the door behind the counter.

'You after a room?' she asked, her words trickling out like a leaking faucet.

'Yes, please.'

'How many nights?'

'Just the one for now.'

'Can't promise there'll be any tomorrow night.'

'That's fine.'

'Thirty dollars,' she said, leaning over the counter, sliding her glasses back up her nose and looking at my bags on the floor. 'You haven't done much of this, have you?'

'Much of what?' I asked, handing her two twenties.

'Travelling, or whatever it is you're doing.'

'No, I haven't.'

'Mm-hmm,' she said, opening a small money box in slow motion. She fished out a tenner and handed it to me. 'None of my business,' she added, 'but there's no point lugging those bags all this way just to ask if there's a vacancy. Eventually, you're gonna get all worn out, only to find there was never a place for you.'

I walked down to the one open shop on the strip, a pizzeria, and made it in before closing time to wash down two slices with five beers. 'These numbers are usually the other way around on the bill,' the clerk joked. I swayed back to the motel, pulling against the embrace of the ghosts hiding in the fog along the way, and stripped down for a shower. With my shirt off, I saw the aftermath of the day. Dark red painted my arms, the sunburn stopping in an abrupt line at my shoulders before beginning again in a crest along my collarbones and consuming my face. If you're going to chase the sun, prepare to get burnt.

I ran cold water over my body and drank up as much as I could from cupped hands, then collapsed onto the linen bedcovers, naked and fatigued, and began to sink into sleep. The fan whirred and cast a soft breeze over my damage. I was too young to be this worn.

3.

The room flickered with light for a moment before returning to dark, the cycle repeating over and over. I fell out of bed, opened the blinds and stood at the window, looking up at the patchy, overcast sky and down at the town. The only two cars within sight almost collided at the intersection, a hand gesture of mutual apology following from both drivers. Rush hour in Kane.

A woman walking on the footpath below happened to look up at me. She did a double take then picked up her pace. 'Strange town,' I thought, before putting my underpants on and getting dressed. My sunburn had gone down, already turning brown. I'd been told the sun was gentler here than back home, but now I was convinced.

I walked down to the reception, pressed the buzzer, once, and played the same waiting game as the night before. The door opened and an old man emerged.

'You after a room?' he asked, words dripping from him.

'Yes, I already have the one upstairs; I was hoping to stay another night. Your ... colleague said it might not be available.'

'That would be my wife.'

'Alright,' I said, waiting. 'Okay, well, your wife said it might not be available.'

'Let me check,' he said, licking his finger and turning the pages of the registry. 'That room is vacant, thirty dollars,' he added after a few more finger licks and pages turned backwards and forwards.

I handed him a fifty and lapped up the déjà vu while waiting for him to source change from the metal container. Some people just find their soulmate, I suppose.

I wandered the town. Only a few streets had traffic and businesses. A shopkeeper selling electronics seemed fascinated to meet an Australian.

'What the heck are you doing in the icebox of Pennsylvania?' he asked me.

'I'm asking myself the same question.'

'It's not much, but here, take this,' he said, handing me a hat proudly proclaiming the town's name on the front.

I put it on and asked if anywhere did a decent breakfast. He said I could get a good, hot meal down on Field. There I ordered and inhaled pancakes, syrup and bacon and downed two cups of coffee. A sign on the wall read: 'Serving Kane for four generations – and counting!' I queried one of the waitresses about how long the place had been there. 'Real long,' she replied, topping off my coffee. A man approached when I asked if I could speak to one of the owners.

'Well, there are a few home builders in town. Not sure I recall a Rodney though,' he said, rubbing his moustache.

'It was a while ago. Quite a while ago.'

'Hey, Joey!' the man yelled to another who was halfway through serving a table. 'You remember a guy who used to build houses 'round here a while back? Name's Rodney or something.'

'Hmm, yeah, actually. Yeah, I do. Was a friend of Pops'. Rodney Barlow, I think,' Joey supplied. 'Yo, Pops!'

A leather-faced man came out from the kitchen to join the other two.

THE ROADMAP OF LOSS

'Rodney Barlow, he was a buddy of yours, right? A builder in town?'

'Yeah, he was. Jeez, I haven't heard that name in a while,' Pops replied, flustered.

'Would you happen to know if he still lives in the area?' I asked.

'No, Rod's ... unfortunately, Rodney's no longer with us.'

'Ah, I'm sorry to hear that. That's a real shame.'

'Yeah, was a real shame for him – caught his wife with some hired help that rocked into town one day. Some fuckin' kangaroo that was lucky to make it out of here alive if you ask me. The whole town knew. Rod and the missus split the sheets not long after; he sold up and headed for Buffalo. I hear from him sometimes, but, eh.'

I took a sip of my coffee and missed my mouth.

'Oh, jeez, here, let me get that for you,' said Pops, as he and his sons jerked napkins from the dispenser and cleaned me up. I smiled, toasted the coffee to them and finished it. Pops looked out the window of the diner, his smile fading as he looked back to me. I quickly stood and thanked them for their hospitality, tipping excessively.

'Hey, son, I didn't catch your name,' he added.

'Oh, it's Mark,' I said, forcing neutrality in my pronunciation.

'I haven't seen you here before, Mark. You new in town?'

'No, just passing through and heard this was the best hot breakfast around.'

'Right, right. Just seems strange, is all, that you'd be passing through here and bringing up a name I haven't heard said in this town in almost twenty years,' he said, his comment rousing suspicion in his sons, who also took a sudden, keen interest in me.

'A, ah, friend of my uncle's, came through here yonks ago. Told me if I ever found myself in Pennsylvania, I should get a beer with his mate Rodney in Kane.'

'I see,' Pops paused. 'Well that's nice. Rodney did love to make new friends.' He seemed placated, which meant the sons did too.

'He sure did,' I said, getting up and moving towards the door. 'Well, thanks for breakfast.'

'Yeah, you're welcome.'

I pushed the door open but before I was through it, Pops addressed me again.

'Hey, Mark, I didn't catch it. Where'd you say you were visiting from again?'

'I didn't,' I said, walking out into the brisk air and back to the motel.

I collected my things, placed the room key on the counter, pressed the bell and left. If there were answers out there, I was beginning to wonder if I even wanted to find them. The fog was gone now. I eased out of the town.

May 17th, 1977

My everything,

It turns out home building is not my forte, and I've found myself back on the road sooner than expected. I made it as far west as Cleveland before tiring of the northern cities and terrains. They are all spectacular and forgettable in their own ways. I stood at the edge of Erie, one of the great lakes. It seemed an ocean in itself – a blue, million miles meeting the sky in such a way that makes it impossible to tell where one ends and the other begins. I squeezed the air swimming between my fingers, for a moment expecting to feel your grip, and my hand had never felt so empty.

I've begun my travels south. The damage done to the American psyche can still be felt in these small towns scattered along the highways of my descent, even years after the soldiers left Vietnam. The people are confused. Their America can be, and has become, the loser – something they'd never fathomed. I suppose I'm the opposite. I've always considered the US to be the home of losers as much as it is of winners. Without this equilibrium, the nation would not have produced the brilliant minds it has. People who only know how it feels to win are among the most boring I've ever met.

Columbus welcomed me, followed by Cincinnati, then Louisville. The plan (if it can be called one) is to move through Nashville and on to Memphis to meet the Mississippi and follow it south. My stays in each have been brief, but when a new destination enters my mind, it becomes all I want to see. Right now, it is New Orleans, Louisiana, but who knows what it might be tomorrow. If I knew anything of the future, then you wouldn't be reading these letters, I suppose.

I am trying not to rush this journey or myself, to not forget about 'the places between places'. Do you remember that expression? You used to use it a lot when you were pregnant with Mark and when he was very little. I used to nod back, though I never really understood what you meant by it. Now, though, I think I'm beginning to. We are made of these places between places, these moments between moments. And I'm realising, yes slowly, that there is no surer way to waste a life than to place the soon above the now, or a there over a here. If these are the parts that make us, then I have already lost enough of them. And I wonder if a jigsaw can ever be complete with any of the pieces missing.

I'll write again soon.

1.

Back roads won out over highways wherever they could. The Miata parked by a field or creek with a street directory spread over its boot, myself leaning over with a cigarette hanging between lips and eyes darting like a mad scientist cracking some code of the land, became a familiar situation.

I moved north through the Allegheny National Forest, a small expanse of land stretching into a body of water compelled me, testing the Miata's grit as I moved down the bumpy trail. I stood by an abandoned campsite – the only remnants of which were a burned-out campfire inside a ring of stones and a litter of empty beer cans. Geese drifted across the lake and occasionally a fish leapt from the water and crashed back in. I watched them until a bush near me moved faster than the breeze, accompanied by a baritone grumble. I stepped on my cigarette, got back in the car and moved on.

The more I drove, the less of a chore it became. I didn't hesitate to plot routes taking me three, even four times as long to reach my destination, knowing what I lost in efficiency, I more than made up for with what I saw and felt. Growing up, I'd often admired how a patch of land or a street looked from afar, but never ventured to it for risk of it not being so alluring up close. I'd lived all my days like that, but now something within me yearned to push forward with massive amounts of enthusiasm. For maybe the first time in my life, I was acting like someone I wanted to be without having to try.

By just the third letter, they'd already begun to feel like a challenge. I may not have been dictating my travels in any way other than steering the Miata down whichever winding road I chose to take to wherever the next letter led me, but the decisions were my own and I took pride in them. 'Look, Dad, I can be a wayward dickhead too. Are ya proud?' I asked myself aloud as I turned from one back road to the next, beginning another long, scenic detour.

Visiting the town of Erie felt like ticking a box on a checklist more than anything. I entered the Presque Isle State Park, what was effectively a large head of land protruding into Lake Erie, wrapping around on itself like a fishing hook to almost seal off the Presque Isle Bay inside.

The park had a single, narrow road cutting through, looping back on itself as if laid by a man who'd forgotten where he built his house. Small lakes dotted the park, some of which contained floating homes – not houseboats, but well-maintained shacks atop raft-like foundations, with footpaths of jetties extending to their doors. I wondered what kind of person would want to live like that and then remembered all the times I'd looked up at towers and thought the same thing.

The rain fell slower that day than anything seemed like it ought to, but had coated everything by the time I reached the lighthouse at the end of the park. It sat tall and proud on the farthest part of a long, thick pier with men fishing off the side and waves crashing below them. I decided that's where somebody like me belonged: not quite welcome on land, but not yet banished to the sea.

I walked down the pier and stood next to the lighthouse with hands pressed into my pockets and chin into the collar of my jacket

THE ROADMAP OF LOSS

to escape the wind. The sky was grey and still full of rain, Lake Erie extending to a place I couldn't see, to meet with it in a distinct line. How different the same thing can look on another day. Of course it had been sunny when he stood and looked out over the same view. It was always sunny for my father.

I drove the two hours to Cleveland. The place was New York City with a decent night's sleep. The temperature doubled in the days I was there and I sweated for the first time in weeks. I wandered around the city because it was something new, the same reason for visiting in most of the places I was finding myself. There was more and less pressure in a city like Cleveland: it was one my father had mentioned, but to no specific or meaningful extent. I could walk its streets freely without the sensation I had to be dusting for clues, but not without guilt I was wasting time being there.

The Rock and Roll Hall of Fame was the only thing that interested me. I strolled through its exhibitions for an entire day, feeling good. Flicking through CDs on a stand, I noticed a plaque on the wall. The museum had been erected in 1983. The place wasn't even around when my father had been in this city, and there I was messing around in its gift shop. As uncertain as I was about my purpose in America, I was sure this wasn't it.

I stood outside the museum, at the edge of Lake Erie as it reflected the blood orange of the setting sun. I rested my arms atop the railing and started to, again, wonder what I was doing. Was this place the world, or was it some place I'd come to hide from the world? How often our minds make oceans out of lakes.

2.

Forgetting the time difference, I phoned and woke Claire. I needed to hear a familiar voice, and figured she'd be the only person who'd care where I was. Even in her befuddled state, she seemed unconvinced when I told her I was staying a bit longer to see Boston and Philadelphia. I hung up knowing I had no number I could be called back on, and that soon I'd be in another town and it would be the same story there. I'd just be some figure who'd roll in and vanish as quickly as he'd arrived. Nobody would know my name unless I wanted them to. Something about it excited me, though I felt like it shouldn't.

I zigzagged south-west, taking convoluted routes passing through as many towns and green-shaded areas of my map as possible. It could take an entire day of winding roads and old bridges over creeks twisting through valleys and towns to move a straight two-hundred miles towards the next city on the map. On the road, I didn't have many people to speak to. My days' most meaningful connections were made with the bartenders, motel receptionists or gas station clerks of towns I found myself in. I would dawdle and prolong conversation to try to feel some form of companionship with these people. I found I was talking to myself a lot.

I called ahead and booked a room at a hotel in Louisville North, Kentucky. Its foyer was connected to a Mexican restaurant with a bar. At least I wouldn't have to walk far that night. I picked up my room key and drove towards the rear of the hotel. The sun was setting behind the wing my room was in, casting a shadow across the adjacent pool. A group of shirtless men stood on a balcony, drinking cans of beer and smoking cigarettes on the second floor. I parked in the late afternoon sun behind the building, knowing it would be shaded come the morning I was to leave.

I put the roof up and my shirt back on. A few days earlier, I'd discovered the Miata's air conditioning did zilch and had resorted to driving with the top down for as long as I could each day to manage the heat. My shoulders and chest had burned raw a few times already and were beginning to darken, along with my face and arms. The strap of my bag cut into my pink skin as I hiked up the staircase at the end of my wing.

The group was still there, five of them, loud, most no older than me. I took note of the room numbers as I walked along the balcony and counted ahead to mine. It was one door past where they were: perfect. They quietened as I approached, turning sideways to fit through the little space the group made for me.

'Recede, motherfuckers. Let the man through,' said a guy with blond tips, as he leant his back against the railing, elbows on top, a knee bent to rest his bare, dirty foot flat against a rail. They did. He brought his head down to the cigarette between his fingers and not the other way around. 'Cut him some slack. Can't ya see the man's been deep-fried, flipped and fucked?'

The group laughed. Blondie was the man.

'Cheers,' I said, dropping my large bag to the ground outside my door and pushing my key into the lock.

'You look like shit, brother. Where'd you come in from?' he asked.

'Cincinnati.'

'Oh, no wonder then.' The group laughed again and even I found myself smirking. 'Tell you what, drop your stuff off inside, wash up if you want, and get back out here. We'll have a beer waiting for you. Ice cold.'

'Yeah?'

'Yeah,' he said, smiling. He slid off the railing, hiked his jeans up over his exposed pubis, and walked over to me with a proffered hand. 'Chris.'

'Mark.'

'Alright, you motherfuckers hear that?' he asked, addressing his followers. 'This here is Mark, and he's gonna be helping us drink all that beer we got. You remember the name so you know who to thank when you wake up tomorrow able to remember which city you're in for a change.'

The group roared as I closed the door behind me. The sounds of cans being crushed and new ones cracked open made its way through the wall. A night on the drink would be nice. A night off it might be nicer. I took a long shower, towelled off and got into bed. I listened to the laughter and hollering outside. None of them sounded lonely. None of them were lying in empty beds in empty rooms either. I got up, put on only my jeans and stepped outside barefoot.

Chris was a man of his word, thrusting an unopened beer at me before my door had even closed behind me. The group was different now. Three of the guys had gone, and another two and a girl had taken their place. The girl sat with her back against the wall, facing out towards the pool, listening to someone speak. She looked up at and through me. I smiled and lifted my can; her expression remained unimpressed and unchanged. She turned back towards her friend.

I drank a beer and then another. I'd been drunk more times than I cared to remember in the past few months, but that evening was the closest I'd come to the first time's euphoric sensation. The dread of tomorrow and the pain of today melted away. All I needed was a few drinks, or maybe a few friends. I mingled, being introduced to someone and forgetting their name right away. They seemed to be on a constant rotation, one or two disappearing at a time into a room along the wing and another one or two emerging from another, about nine in total, the group on the balcony seldom in the same arrangement twice. Chris explained they were roadies working a gig in town and had every room on the floor except mine. 'We were wondering which poor bastard was gonna end up with yours,' he added.

We polished off a case of beer and opened another as the sun set. The sky was tinted pastel, seeming somehow both impossibly far away, yet close enough to be grasped and scrunched up into your pocket. I found myself sitting next to Chris with my back against the railing, across from the girl who hadn't moved. Monica was her name, but I hadn't found out because she'd introduced herself.

The group quizzed me about Australia in the same one-dimensional way I was getting used to. My answers had become streamlined after being asked the same things so many times. 'Did you ride your own kangaroo to school?'

'Yes, but only when the family one was in for repairs.'

'So what are you doing here?' Monica asked all of a sudden.

'I'm kinda ... driving around aimlessly.'

'Why?'

'Just trying to see as much of this country as I can.'

'Now why the fuck would you want to do a thing like that?'

She spoke softly but there was an edge to her words.

'Don't mind her,' Chris intervened, 'we get carted all over this damn country for work. Easy to forget sometimes people do it for fun.'

Monica looked at me for a moment before turning away, lighting a cigarette and sipping her beer. She'd had more than any of us, at least in the time I'd been there, and I was drunk. She looked South American, maybe, with crimson lips and dark eyebrows which framed her face in a way that made her seem angry. She seemed dissatisfied with everything, but especially with me for whatever reason.

I wondered what this world had done to her. I couldn't help but notice her legs. Brown skin charted her ankle, past her knee and up her thigh, disappearing into the darkness inside her skirt. She might've been Chris's girl so I looked at something else.

The roadies started trading stories, each more ridiculous than the last. Whoever held the floor would stand in the same place on the dark balcony – an exposed globe above like a spotlight over the bard. I was seated at the back of the group, leaning forward and looking on with a turned head. One of them stood and began the story of the cursed harness. 'Oh, this is a good one. Listen to Dave, listen to Dave,' Chris said, flicking my shoulder with the back of his hand without turning back to me, already enthralled by the story.

'So me and the regulars on this gig, we all got our own equipment, of course,' Dave said, 'but we were getting a few kids as extra help in each town. These kids are just, whatever, replying to ads in the classifieds, they don't do this kind of thing; they don't own their own gear. Anyway, we had these harnesses, helmets, etcetera, left behind from other gigs that had become "property of stage management". These kids used that equipment. I mean this shit was worn out, but the kids helping in each town didn't know that.'

The people who'd heard the story before started to squirm.

'We do this one town. It's all going pretty standard, right. Dave – Other Dave – any of you ever met Other Dave? Well, anyway, Other Dave calls in with a sick stomach. Probably shitting pure bourbon from the night before. He's meant to be on high rope with me. I try to get it all done by myself, but we're behind schedule. Stage manager and my boss put this kid – he'd done, like, two shows – on the goddamn high rope with me instead.'

The group all exhaled and shook their heads. High rope was bad, I guessed.

'I tell 'em not to do it, they don't listen to me. They put us up, and this was a thirty-five, maybe forty-foot rig. I tell the kid to keep an eye on his slack. He's trying to, but he's nervous and the buckle is worn to shit.'

I felt something press against my ankle. I looked across to see Monica's leg spanning the balcony towards mine, the dirt on the sole of her foot rubbing off against my denim. She was looking at me with the same bare, empty expression as before. I hadn't noticed her eyes before. They were deep; the kind of deep a man could fall into and never be seen again. I shifted my foot away from her.

'So we're making good time, the kid is a good worker, but suddenly he slips. Now, he was doing a good job pulling slack out, but that buckle would serve you a good six feet of it if you even looked at it the wrong way. The kid drops and almost goes ass-up out the harness when the rope takes. I get over there fast as I can.

'Now, here's the thing, it wasn't a big drop, but the kid is screaming. I'm talking the kind of scream that still sends a chill up my spine thinking about. I figure he's just afraid he's gonna fall the whole way out the harness and he's screaming for the Lord, but not long after I get to him, I see this blood, right? This little stream of blood, running from the inside of his shirt and down his neck onto his face. I look up. One of the leg straps, bitch had come so loose it's got the buckle of the other one caught up inside it.'

Again, I felt a rubbing on my leg. Monica's leg had straightened out further to reach my ankle. Her other leg bent at the knee, thigh pressed against her chest, hands clasped around her ankle. She placed her chin on her knee, looking at me with the same blank stare. 'What are you doing?' I mouthed to her without a sound. Nobody else had noticed. If I moved my leg any further I would've kicked Chris. I sat in checkmate.

'His pants are soaked through with blood already. What happened was the loose strap had caught on and brought the other buckle across like a goddamn guillotine on this poor kid's dick when the rope caught. So there I am, stuck thirty-five feet up, with this kid bleedin' out through his dick, upside down, screaming. Anyway, we got him down and into an ambulance. He was fine, a few stitches I think. So, then, the next day ...'

She wasn't tiring of it at all. She was a sadist. Maybe she couldn't get her kicks by embarrassing me so she'd settle for watching her friends kick the shit out of me. She rubbed against my leg through my jeans, and then, with a dextrous toe, slid the cuff up a few inches and rubbed my bare ankle with her foot. I felt myself start to rise. She withdrew the leg, tucking it up like the other. I looked into her eyes. They seemed like they held in a lot more than they let out. The tired dams of her life.

'I wake up, hung over as a motherfucker. I'm talking top-ten here. I manage to get myself in the car and start driving. Pull over to throw up a few times on the way, whatever. Venue is about forty-five away and I'm already late. I get to the parking lot, turn to the back seat, and ... I've forgotten my gear.'

I listened to the story, but watched her. She rested her head against the wall behind, mouth ajar. I don't think she'd blinked. I don't think I had either. Without even a glance to see if anyone was watching, she began to move the leg furthest from the roadies, its shadow on the inside of her other thigh descending as her knees came apart.

'Now, I know I'm not getting paid for a full day already, so I can either drive home to get my shit and lose another two hours, or take my chances. Then I remember the kid from the day before. I just ... I hear that scream in my head and it makes me cold. So you know what I do? I go the fuck home, call my boss and tell him I'm feeling unwell. He starts yelling, all tough, that if I don't come in today not to bother coming in at all, whatever.'

The shadow reached the valley as her knee reached the floor, and I could see it all. Taut and serious like the rest of her, adorned by a solitary tuft of hair worn high and proud like a crown. It stretched and sighed, the balcony's fluorescent light clambering onto and falling from its intricacies as they glistened and moved with her slow, deep breath.

'I go in the following day. Everybody's real serious – don't really want to look at me. I think I'm either getting my ass kicked or fired or both, for sure. Boss says he wants to see me. I go into his office; he asks me if I've been told what happened the day before. I play dumb, ya know, but, shit, turns out I didn't know anyway. Those dumb fuckers. They put another kid in that same harness and the same damn thing happened. Only this one's in intensive care and the parents are suing the asses off anyone involved.'

There was pain in her eyes, I was sure of it. She was probably thinking the same of mine. I stared into them and then back into her. She rocked her hips up and down on the tiny piece of skirt separating her arse from the ground, pulling herself tight and then relaxing. I took a drag of my cigarette and blew it out, watching her deep breath steal the smoke from the air between us, pull it in through flared nostrils and push it out through her hanging mouth. We didn't need words; this was maybe the best conversation I'd ever had.

'Cops, they seize the harness; my boss and the stage manager, they end up getting charged and doing time for it. I mean, that alone is messed up, but, man ... I could've been that fuckin' kid. I could've been the one hanging upside down, approaching those pearly gates with my dick in two. Shit, I got real lucky – someone was looking out for me that day. That harness is probably out there somewhere, too, you know, locked away in some evidence room ... Probably still has all that dried dick-blood over it as well. Fuck.'

Chris began clapping as the rest of the group erupted in cheers and whistles. He turned to me. Monica pushed her skirt down over herself just in time. She was swift but not frantic. She was a mystery. He gripped and shook me by the shoulders. I clenched up for a moment.

'Have you ever heard anything so fucked up? Ha!' he asked, wide-eyed, his words slurred as he tried to keep a cigarette between his lips.

'He got very lucky,' I said to him, projecting the words towards her. 'Could've ended real badly for him.'

Monica looked at me for a moment with her same expression. I waited until my swelling went down, then stood and headed into my room's bathroom. When I came back out, she had vanished.

'Where'd she go?' I asked.

'Mon'?'

'Bed,' another responded.

'Pretty sudden. She alright?'

'Eh, she gets like that. Bit loopy,' he said, running a circle around his temple with his finger.

The last case ran dry. Chris and I threw wrinkled, dirty T-shirts on and ambled into the foyer's restaurant-bar with dirty, bare feet. We took stools at the bar and ordered last-minute feeds and nightcaps. The staff looked unimpressed, but they didn't say a word. I assumed they didn't want trouble, and I assumed they didn't want it from Chris.

The following night was the last of the shows in Louisville before they'd pack up and head to St Louis. Chris told me to swing by his room before 11 a.m. the next morning and someone would have a spare ticket for me. 'It's fuckin' country music, but you've never seen so much ass squeezed into such little shorts in your entire life,' he said. His life sounded exciting – a lot more than mine. I daydreamt what it would be like to travel across the country with them. A tour convoy tailed by a Miata. Hard, dangerous work by day, Monica by night. I could manage both as long as they'd replaced the harnesses.

'How long have you been doing this?' I asked.

'The shows?'

'Yeah.'

'Too long, brother.'

'Why do you do it then? I mean, how can you spend so much time on the road?'

'The money is good – real good, and it's easy when you don't really have a home. You don't belong anywhere, so you can just keep ... leaving things behind.'

'Where was home before you started doing this?'

'I've, ah, I've got a little girl. So it's wherever she is. That's where my home is. Right now that's Kansas, but, I'm not welcome there no more.'

'Why's that?'

'I did some bad things. I did some bad things and I did some time and now her mother doesn't want anything to do with me. But ... she'll come around.'

Chris seemed different from there – less chatty; the charisma had been stripped away. What did I expect? I'd held a man by his ankle just long enough for whatever he was running from to catch up. I'd done what I resented other people doing to me. He stared across the restaurant in silence and then his head crashed down onto folded arms on the bar. He convulsed in what I thought was laughter, but then I heard a cry.

'My little girl, man. My little fuckin' girl. She's out there without a daddy,' he whimpered into the bar. Other patrons watched on.

THE ROADMAP OF LOSS

The bartender motioned to me that Chris was cut off and I nodded understanding. 'Come on, let's get you back to your room,' I said.

I walked with Chris past the pool with his arm over my shoulders. He could barely support his own weight and I wasn't in much better shape. I looked up to the empty balcony. His colleagues had all gone to bed. A good thing, I decided; I didn't know how they'd take seeing him like this.

'Hey, Mark,' he said as we reached the top of the stairs.

'Yeah?'

'Don't tell my boys about this.'

'Of course.'

'Man, please. I'm serious. If you tell any of my boys about this, I'm ... I'm gonna hurt you. I'm gonna hurt you real bad,' he said, pressing a finger into my chest.

'Alright, relax.'

'I'm not playing around. I'll put your nose through your fucking brain.'

He pushed me. He was strong, or at least a lot stronger than me. It launched me into the wall behind, my back slamming into it, my head following suit. I keeled over, bracing myself from my knees. Suddenly all I wanted to do was sleep. Chris walked over to me.

'Goddamn it, you see? This is what I do,' he said, labouring words out of his limp, drunk jaw.

He caught hold of me, lifting me by the collar of my slack T-shirt as if he was going to hit me. I clinched in preparation, but didn't try to stop him.

'You okay? You're being so nice to me, like a brother, and I hurt you. I fucking hurt you.'

'It's okay, I probably deserve it in some way,' I said, coughing.

I found my arm over Chris's shoulders as we staggered back down the balcony, bouncing off the wall and the rail.

'Hey, those arses in the shorts tomorrow though, eh?' I said.

'Oh, buddy, they're ... they're majestic. You're gonna love 'em. Hey, say ass again.'

'Arse.'

'Are-ess?'

'Arse.'

'Heh, that's funny.'

He left me at my door.

'You're a good man, Mark.'

'You too.'

I fell into my room, collapsed onto the bed and passed out.

3.

I was up at 9 a.m. the next morning to make sure I didn't miss them. I walked to Chris's room and knocked. No answer. I tried another then another. They were all gone.

I smoked a cigarette on the balcony and rubbed the lump on my head. My time as a roadie had been short. Onto the next town and gig they went without me. Another direction my life could've veered off in. Maybe those other directions always seemed more appealing because they weren't where I'd ended up. Maybe Monica showed it to a different guy in each city. Maybe she'd seen all fifty states and now wanted it seen in all fifty. I floated on my back in the pool and contemplated these things.

The next day I got back on the road. On the outskirts of Bowling Green, Kentucky, I hunched over a bar and scribbled numbers onto a napkin. Money had become an abrupt and real concern. I was spending too much of it, and not getting far enough. Although they'd seemed innumerable to me, the miles I'd covered were only a small dent in the hugeness of America. Where the letters would send me next remained a mystery, too. For a brief moment, I considered reading them to their end right then at that bar, but something inside prevented me.

I decided if I covered more ground in a day, I could spend less on accommodation. More time on highways meant I could save on gas. I decided luxuries like star ratings on accommodation or having more than one meal a day could go. I called my bank; the remaining amount for the house still hadn't been received. I just needed to watch my money until that came through, then I'd be set.

Going back to Melbourne and its routine, only to attempt mustering what had gotten me to America in the first place again wasn't an option. I was living in some part of my mind devoid of order and reason, and I wasn't sure I'd be able to find my way back to it a second time.

I tracked south-west along country roads into the evening under a southern sky. I passed a cornfield, a dirt road disappearing into it. A few miles further, the fuel light came on. I found a small gas station and filled the tank to the brim, bought a chicken sandwich and a forty-ounce bottle of beer, and headed back the way I'd come.

After a few wrong turns, I found that same dirt road and turned onto it. The road ran deeper and deeper into the fields before rising into a crest to clear an irrigation pipe. I stopped there, moved my bag into the driver's seat and myself into the passenger's. There wasn't much room to recline, but I took it as far as it'd go. The roof's latches clicked open and I dropped the top to feel the breeze wash over my warm, dirty skin as I looked up. The player swallowed one of the CDs I'd bought in Cleveland, rolling onto track one as I ate my sandwich and sipped. My head sat just above the crops and I felt as though I was suspended in them as they swayed, shimmering like a deep green ocean in all directions.

There was something about the air that night. Warm and cool all at once, oppressively thick and impossibly thin, an energy coursing throughout. For a moment, I felt as though it might have floated me from my seat, cradling me in its arms like a mother with her child, and taken me into the night. I breathed in, letting it rest in my lungs – full and proud. Drawn into my blood and pumped to every dark corner of my body. Then I released, letting it take with it another scrap of my hurting each time.

Something brutal and unforgiving in me melted away, and for the first time since her passing, I cried for my mother, unapologetically and unabashed. The tears came in surges, running down my face and past the edges of my mouth. The sun slipped behind the horizon, as it had so many times before. Stars showed themselves, dotting and filling the night. They weren't always seen, but they were always there. The sky changed above me as I changed below it.

4.

Sunlight woke me early. It was already hot. A farmer glared as he drove past on a tractor. I waved and opened the door – the empty forty-ounce rolling out of my lap and onto the road. I walked to the driver's door, leant over and opened it from the inside. There were no vacancies at any of the motels when I arrived in Nashville. 'It's Friday afternoon and it's a party town. What did you expect?' asked a very sage receptionist.

I found a hotel closer to the river and choked at the price. Maybe I could find another cornfield for the night. My aching neck disagreed. I booked the room and found a parking spot on the other side of the river. There were going to be some long driving stints to make up for this indiscretion. Sweat drenched me by the time I'd crossed the bridge over the river and got back to the hotel. I went to shave but decided against it.

A group of three girls and a guy entered their room down the hall as I left mine. They each had bottles of spirits in hand. 'Reckon you've got enough?' I asked in passing.

'I think we'll make do,' one girl replied with an Australian accent. I stopped and turned back as we shared a moment of mutual recognition through the gap of their closing door.

LIAM MURPHY

I had no interest in Broadway. It felt touristy, and I wasn't supposed to be a tourist. In a way becoming all too natural for me, I found myself gravitating towards uglier places with uglier people but with prettier hearts. This was good for me, because the man I was on the trail of was as ugly as they came. Instead, I found a bar around the corner from the hotel, half-sunken below the sidewalk. A thick haze of smoke filled the place as people with cigarettes sagging from their lips leant over pool tables and tried not to get smoke in their eyes for the brief moment it took to calculate a trajectory. I played a few games against the locals – poorly. Nobody looked at me twice unless I spoke, so I took to using a silent nod or a solemn 'hmm' of concurrence when I could.

When I caught my reflection in a mirror as I stood with arms resting on an upright cue, I thought it was another man in the bar. My skin had darkened, my stubble had graduated to a weak beard, and I'd lost weight. The only things I recognised were my eyes staring back at me through the mess of it all. Afternoon sunlight and the lower halves of bodies walking by showed through windows at the side of the room. They formed a triangle, thinning off to nothing as their lower frame traced the gradient of the street outside.

Occasionally, games would come to a complete halt when heels adorning exposed legs passed by; players and spectators alike all swaying in unison towards the windows like trees caught in a silent gale, trying to catch an up-skirt. The wind would pass as the legs did and the games would resume. I managed to sink a few shots by accident and quickly learned the only way a crowd could discern between a successful, calculated move and a complete fluke was by how surprised the person who'd played it seemed. The game spoke volumes to life itself.

Day turned to night, and I headed back. My hotel's lobby bar was too much to resist as I passed. Taking a seat, I ordered a nightcap.

'I'm afraid the bar is for hotel guests only,' the bartender informed me. I spun my room key around my finger. 'So sorry, sir.' He placed a bottle down as I removed the letter from my pocket, unfolded and read it again. A loud group took seats across the bar. I looked up and recognised the Australian girl among them, and she me. I raised my bottle and went back to reading.

'What's that?' she asked, suddenly beside me.

'Shit,' I said, jolting. I sunk it back into my jeans. 'It's a ... review.'

'Of this hotel?'

'Of this city.'

'Can I read it?'

'No, it's not finished yet.'

'What did you think of Broadway?'

'Haven't been.'

'You're reviewing Nashville and you haven't seen Broadway? What kind of writer are you?'

'Not a very good one.'

'Well, we must educate you. Come.'

'No, it's alright. Gonna hit the hay.'

'You'll do no such thing,' she said, taking me by the wrist. 'My friends have decided you're coming out with us.'

The Broadway strip was all gaudy neon. Music and crowds flooded out onto the street. Cops yelled at drunks as they ran across the street, squeezing between gaps in the traffic. It was chaos and I was falling asleep where I stood. The group consisted of two Brits, the guy and one of the girls, and the other two, a Canadian and the Australian.

We bounced from honky-tonk to honky-tonk. The Australian came over to me with a bottle of beer for each of us. We toasted and I took a sip. As I placed the bottle back down on the table, she raised hers and banged its base onto the lip of mine. Foam worked up the neck and began cascading out the top like a volcano.

'Now why would you do a thing like that?' I asked as froth covered my resting hand and the table.

'You're wasting it! Drink!'

'I shouldn't have said yes to you tonight.'

Returning from the bathroom soon after, I was greeted by an empty table. I scanned the dance floor and saw the group near a door leading back out to Broadway. Angry gestures were exchanged, before the group left. The Australian yelled something and chased after them.

The lift opened onto my floor. I swayed down the corridor and fumbled keys. As I neared my door, I looked up to see the Australian leaning on the wall beside it. Brown hair fell across her face, obscuring it, but I recognised her knee-high boots. She turned towards me as I approached. She'd done a decent job of wiping away the makeup running underneath her eyes, but I'd been raised by a pro.

'Mate, you look like shit,' she said to me.

'Yes, to be expected. I narrowly survived a kidnapping tonight, y'know?' I said, pushing my key into the lock.

'Oh, that sounds terrifying. Are you going to call the police?'

'I'm undecided. They might want me to describe the assailant to a sketch artist, and I wouldn't know where to begin.'

'Really? No idea at all what you might tell them?'

'Well,' I said, opening the door and leaning against its frame to face her, pressing my boot down as a doorstop. She linked her hands behind her back against the wall and looked up at me.

'I might say she's confident – perhaps a little too much for her own good.'

'Oh, there's such a thing?'

'Yes, though not because she shouldn't be. Because it makes her fearless.'

'And there's something wrong about a woman without fear?'

'A fearless anything can be dangerous.'

'I see. So it's not for her own good; it's for those she might intimidate in the process?'

'Yeah, I guess so. Goodnight.'

She clutched my arm as I stepped into my room.

'Wait, there's nothing else you'd tell this sketch artist? You're making their job very difficult.'

'I'd say she's beautiful. Stunningly beautiful. And I'd say there's not a fuckin' chance she's without fear, because she's cried enough in her life to know how to be even more beautiful with puffy eyes and mascara running down her cheeks than without, and that's the most fearless thing about her.'

She squeezed my arm tighter for a moment, waiting for some other part of her to make a decision.

'I'm ... I'm not really sure how they're meant to draw that, but –' I added.

She thrust me into the room and followed behind.

'Steph,' she said, pushing me onto the bed and lifting her top. 'My name is Steph. You didn't bother to ask.'

5.

I reclined in the bed and lit a cigarette. Steph wore only a shirt of mine draped over her body and it lifted high enough to see the folds of her arse against the back of her thighs as she opened the curtains. The light came in and was too bright for me. I asked if she could close them a bit and she did. I watched the shirt lift again.

She had been abandoned by her friends. It didn't bother her, though, to find her belongings in the hall outside their room the next morning, as if it were routine. They had met the day before, and I'd pieced together through the haze of my hangover that her waiting outside my room was somewhat of a backup plan. I hadn't been making friends to lose, but I knew too well the feeling of people wanting to get away from me, and felt a sense of camaraderie with her.

We had coffee and she told me of her travels and how you can do it on the cheap if you're willing to make friends. 'So you're somewhat of a parasite then?' I asked. 'I prefer nomad,' she quipped.

She was from Brisbane, Australia, but lived on Canada's west coast. When the weather was cold, her days were spent working at the ski fields she lived near; when it was hot, they were spent moving across America, seeing as much of it as possible on the least amount of money. She'd 'done' New Orleans, a few times, but what she hadn't done, she told me, was camp in and hike the Great Smoky Mountains.

'Sorry, not on my itinerary,' I told her.

'Then put it on your itinerary.'

'I don't have the time.'

'Why not?'

'Because I don't have the money.'

'People trade one for the other all the time. Which matters more to you?'

I wanted to say, 'Getting to New Orleans,' but I hesitated.

'You're pretty good at this, aren't you?' I asked.

'The best,' she replied, kissing me on the cheek and then pissing with the bathroom door open.

After some rearranging, the Miata's boot clicked shut. We squeezed into the cabin and headed east. Steph remarked how cute she thought the car was, but after an hour of bucked launches, cramped heat and the drone of highway speeds with the section of exhaust pipe missing, her feelings began to mirror my own. We passed through Knoxville and followed directions to a Walmart.

We entered the massive store and lost each other right away. She found me with fingers hooked through a caged door, studying a collection of hunting rifles. I'd never fired a gun – the only ones I'd ever seen had been hanging from the hips of police officers.

'Browsing the freedom and liberty aisle?' Steph asked.

'There's just something about them. They fascinate me.'

'Well, you're a dude, so that's probably why.'

'Probably.'

'Got a favourite?'

'That one,' I said, straightening a finger towards one with a rubber butt, which looked especially powerful.

'Ah, the one resembling a bulging cock, of course. Let's go.'

We found the outdoors section and Steph selected a two-person tent. I looked at the price tag.

'This is too much,' I said, scanning the cart. 'All of this is too much, even if we go halves.'

'We're not buying; we're hiring.'

'I don't think you can hire this stuff.'

'Mark, anything and everything is for hire with a return policy, a complaint and a bit of bravado.'

The land changed as we approached the Smokies and reached Cherokee. The roads became winding and mountainous, the Miata's small engine struggling to pull us up. The temperature shifted in huge increments, almost between breaths, as we drove into clouds lingering on the road and through the other side into perfect sunshine. The place was beautiful and surreal, so lush that everything seemed as though a pinprick might cause it to pop and water come gushing out, even the air itself. We stopped at a gas station with a hill of grass becoming dense forest behind. A few creatures lingered, attracting a small crowd. Steph and I joined to look on. Three of them stood with large, sandy bodies, downright massive with the span of their antlers added, perusing the grass at their feet.

'Wow ... what are they?' I whispered, lighting a cigarette and closing the lighter as quietly as possible.

'I think they're elk,' Steph told me, leaning away from the smoke.

The elk were aware of their audience, but didn't mind. They wandered and occasionally looked into the distance, moving with an agile grace which seemed almost impossible for their size. My ears waited for sounds that never came when their hooves made contact with the earth after they'd jumped and soared. In unison, as if speaking a telepathic language, the two smaller elk looked to the larger one, who began moving into the forest. They rushed to him, covering the ground with rapid ease, and the three disappeared into the wall of flora together.

Steph directed me from an opened map too big for the Miata's cabin. We left a main road sunken deep into a narrow valley and crossed a bridge over a creek. The tight road on the other side trailed the water for a few minutes, before coming to a small cabin with an office sign above its door.

'Perfect timing,' she said, looking at her watch.

'What is?'

'It's just past six. The rangers clock off at six.'

'Why does that matter?'

'If you take a site before they clock off, you have to pay upfront, but get in after six and you pay in the morning.'

'How does that help us?'

'We'll be gone in the morning.'

We drove through and passed families at other sites, their laughing faces lit by the glow of dusk campfires. We found a free spot near the back of the campsite, away from the creek and backed up against a hill of trees so steep it seemed like a wall with a forest painted onto it. Steph set up the tent and I tried to help. The light was disappearing fast, so we had to move faster. I tried to clear away large rocks and sticks on the ground where the tent would go; Steph questioned my priorities.

The tent went up and we moved necessities from the Miata. Steph's were bread, dips, carrots; mine were a flask of whiskey and my lighter. We crawled in and Steph zipped the door shut, kissed me and ran a hand up under my shirt. I removed her top in the darkness. She undid my belt and took me out of my jeans, beginning a slow, dry job. I hadn't noticed the sound of an engine rolling up, coming to a stop and idling outside.

Doors opened and closed, followed by two distinct focal points of torches drawn against the fabric of the tent. 'Shit, maybe it was six-thirty ...' Steph whispered under her breath. I reached for my belt buckle but she stopped me, squeezing harder with her busy hand and cupping the other over my mouth. She pushed me onto my back with her forearm across my chest, pinning my wrist against me. The sharp contour of a rock found its way through the floor of the tent and between two vertebrae in my back. I winced in pain – my shriek muffled to a wheeze through her hand.

'Anyone in there?' asked a man's voice from outside.

The torches bounced and waved at different tempos against the tent, their outlines becoming smaller and more concentrated as they moved closer. Steph's pace and squeeze increased as she chafed her hand up and down me.

'Hello? You need to pay for your night's stay,' said the same voice.

'Maybe they're still out on a trail?' the other male voice suggested.

'This late? Doubt it. Hello, anybody home?'

Steph leant more weight onto me and tightened her grip again as the rock pushed deeper into me. I gripped her wrist with my other hand but had no leverage. Subtle light from the torches came through the fabric, detailing a silent 'shh' on her face that curled into a smile. The burning became unbearable and I tried to roll away, only to dig the rock further into my back. I yelped a muted cry again. The crunching of gravel underfoot circled the tent. A familiar surge started to build and breach the agony. I tried to slow and quieten my breathing through my half-covered nostrils. I imagined myself back to lying on the living room floor, watching the shadow of the turning fan on the ceiling. One torch darted from the tent.

'This thing has New York plates. Come on, let's just tag them and go get a beer.'

'Hmm,' the other voice responded. I pleaded with the faceless man in my mind. 'Alright, tag 'em.'

LIAM MURPHY

The remaining torch wandered from the tent, the crunching moved away, the truck's doors opened and closed and it lumbered away. I came, light taps of me landing on the tent floor and my shirt, set to the backdrop of families laughing and loving. Steph slowed her pace to a stop then brought her hand away from my face, taking her weight off me. I took in a deep breath and groaned as I rolled over to dislodge the rock from my spine.

'That good, huh?' she asked.

I sucked in deep breaths. She left for the site bathroom to get some toilet paper. I reached for my flask and poured half of it into me.

6.

The Appalachian Trail was a twenty-two-hundred-mile trek, spanning from Maine to Georgia. I was four miles into a section somewhere in its middle and my legs were already failing. Steph led, wearing my backpack and powering over steps made of stone and dirt running up the side of the mountain. The trail narrowed as we climbed, soon becoming a path no wider than an arm's span, with a vertical rock face on one side and a fall on the other big enough you'd hope it'd kill you if you went over. People took turns moving across the section in opposite directions, all seeming to feign calmness when passing. Heights never scared me, but somehow the idea of falling always had.

We reached the end of the narrow path, where a leafy summit marked by brown rock jagged from its side to form a cliff. The trail made a swift turn and continued north from there. Hikers stood around eating packed lunches and taking photographs from the safety of the path and a small clearing. A few pointed to an eagle soaring above.

'Come on,' Steph said, moving towards the formidable brown rock.

'What? Where?'

'You can't say you made it until you reach there.'

She pointed to its furthest point hanging out from the mountain.

'Okay. I promise I won't tell anyone I made it.'

'Who cares about that? You won't be able to say it to yourself.'

She hooked her fingers over an out-thrust of rock and began climbing. I didn't move. After she'd scaled out of my reach, she stopped and looked back.

'Don't be stupid,' I said.

'Hey, Mark.'

'What?'

'You know how I offered to carry the backpack?'

'Yes.'

'And you know how this morning, before we left, we put all the food into said backpack?'

'Come back here.'

She smiled and resumed climbing, becoming obscured as she made her way across the rock. I couldn't fathom her motivation. The fall only got larger as the rock stretched further out over the steepness of the mountain. Why did making it matter so much to her? Why had it always mattered so little to me? I lifted my arms and grabbed the same lip of rock she had, took a breath and hoisted myself up.

The terrain was formed like ocean waves frozen still, with the safety of the mountain as the beach. Each wave had a steep face of grooved rock which formed a sharp peak before descending on the other side. It would plunge into a trough too deep to see out from, full of loose stones and barely living plants silly enough to try to sustain life there. Another would begin right after. I scaled the first few by folding my body over their tops, rotating on my chest and walking my legs around. This meant when I reached a peak, I was lying face down, parallel to it. The manoeuvre wasn't graceful, and I could hear comments and laughter from people back on the path, but I was making it. I would reverse the movement

THE ROADMAP OF LOSS

on the other side, walking my legs down, and leaving one hand on the previous formation's peak before stretching my other out to the next.

On the next wave, I turned my head to trace my progress. The gap to Steph was even wider than when I'd started. I lunged for the next, pulling myself up. This time, instead of folding my body, I straightened my arms to place a foot atop the rock, passed my other leg through the gap, and brought it down the other side. It was a much faster technique and instilled some confidence in me. I was halfway now, with each wave becoming narrower than the one before as the cliff concentrated towards a fine point. Soon they'd be no wider than I was tall, and already I could see the mountain range and plunge on either side in my peripheral. I traversed the next few with increasing pace, catching Steph as she neared the end. It could be done even faster, I thought. I launched myself up the next with vigour, driving with my leg to get the momentum needed to swing the other through in one movement.

The theory was sound, but my execution poor. Passing through the gap, my foot snagged the rock. I lost my balance and fell forward, seeing only a blur of blue sky, brown rock and green forest somewhere below. In the chaos, one hand came away from the cliff, passing over my other as it too separated.

For a moment I was hovering in space, detached from the earth, the sky, from everyone and everything. I seemed to hang there for an eternity, unsure if I was falling to my death or had already arrived. I reached out and something filled my grip. I squeezed as tightly as I could – if I was gonna go, I was going out with clenched fists.

My body slammed into the rock face. I looked down as my feet swung across the trough and out over the edge of the cliff, launching a loose stone. It seemed to hang still in the air, its white texture contrasted against the green far below. I watched for a few seconds before the forest cover shivered as the stone was swallowed. 'Oh my god!' a woman screamed from the mountain.

'Did that guy just fall?' yelled a man. I rocked backwards and forwards a few times; the soles of my shoes grazing the dirt below, like a child dragging their feet through the bark under a swing set. I looked up at my outstretched arm; my hand clasped around the tip of the rock I'd attempted to clear, no more than a foot from where it abruptly became air.

'Mark? Mark?' came a voice from the other direction. 'Are you okay?'

I hung for a second, swaying and looking over the mountain range that went on forever, hearing the familiar voice's words but not knowing the answer myself. The sun was warm on my face and a breeze blew. How easy it would be to just let go, I thought. My grip began to weaken. The eagle passed by, turning its head for a moment to study this fool without wings.

Turning my body and gripping the rock with both hands, I shimmied back to its centre. 'I'm alright!' I yelled back to Steph. An echo of collective, relieved exhalation came from the mountainside as I popped my head up.

After the last formation, the land flattened before falling away. Steph and I sat with our backs against the rock, legs stretched so our feet dangled off the cliff's edge. We looked over the range and ate peanut butter sandwiches in silence.

'I'm sorry,' she said.

I paused mid-bite then continued chewing.

'I'm serious; I shouldn't have made you feel like you had to do that.'

'It's okay.'

'No, it isn't. You could've died.'

'Yeah, I know,' I said. 'But I made it.'

Back at the site, we wandered through foliage to the nearby river. The valley was grey – a dense fog blanketing the torrent, making it hard to see, though still churning with violence beneath the small, rickety bridge we trod across with careful steps. Trees grew from each bank to touch in the middle above, forming a tunnel. A small path took us beyond the extremities of the campsite to where the creek became wide and calm. Steph hung our towel over a tree branch.

I stood ankle-deep at the edge on a shallow ridge of pebbles. My body ached, but the place made me feel alright. That cliff hadn't tried to harm me; it had merely presented itself as an unwavering challenge, and if I was to step up to it, it was my duty to overcome or die. The rock and the stone and the sky and the trees didn't care if I'd let go – if their hardness had met my body with such a relentless force that my insides rattled and turned to dust.

There was something so unapologetic about nature that I felt no need to make excuses for myself. I was not the rock. I was human because I hurt, and I hurt because I was human. Small wonder this land was so contested: it affirmed life in such a way people were willing to kill and die for it.

I watched the icy current collide with Steph's naked body as she submerged herself – her nipples upright and hard, water glistening as she shivered and parts of her jiggled. The shape of her, too, was whatever it had to be. She was as brazen as the land. One life-giver bathing in the waters of another. I stood at the bank and lit a cigarette, undeserving to join.

7.

We moved gear from the tent back into the Miata the following morning. Steph opened a small switchblade she'd been using to cut fruit and went at the tent, placing its tip between fabric and stitches and pushing forward, careful not to go through to the other side. The stitches lifted and pulled tight, stretching across the blade before succumbing and snapping in two. She turned to see me watching on.

'Are you as outraged as I am that all these stitches popped the very first time we used this?' she asked.

We moved west, with me taking direction from her. It was beginning to feel like none of my movements in this country were my own – dictated to me by either a father I never knew, or a girl I barely did.

Cades Cove was a large expanse of flat green, surrounded by mountains which seemed to be closing in. Steph took us there because she wanted to. The isolated valley could be viewed from a narrow, one-way loop of road running its circumference, following the edges of its fields and drifting through sections of the surrounding forest. I was beginning to tire of how beautiful everything there was. You can only have your breath taken away so many times before you begin suffocating.

We reached a dirt road meeting the loop. The cars ahead of us all continued past. I turned to Steph, and her to me. We both shrugged and I turned the wheel. At the road's end was a car park and a large, white box with a bell tower. I walked to a stone plaque next to the building: 'CADES COVE PRIMITIVE BAPTIST CHURCH – ORGANISED JUNE 16 1827'. We walked up the building's few steps and were the only ones in there. Its interior was a wooden box with everything at right angles: the corners, the windows, the chairs, the hole in the ceiling and the ladder reaching through it. Steph walked down the aisle and I followed. My boots were loud against the floor, sending a crude thud into the silence. It was the first time I'd been in a church since the day I buried my mother.

Steph approached the altar, but not too close. She moved into the second row of bench seats and sat, resting her head on crossed arms on the back of the seat ahead.

'Hey,' I said.

'Yeah?'

'No sitting. The Lord gave you knees for a reason.'

She ignored me and went back to staring at the altar. I walked there, around its front and up the step.

'What are you doing?'

'I'm seeing how it looks from this side of the lectern.'

'Well, don't.'

'Why? Are you afraid I'll attract a following?'

She stood and walked to the altar, staring up at me.

'Why do you feel the need to make a mockery of everything?'

'Not everything, just the things worth mocking.'

'You know ... you're a real tragedy, Mark.'

'Excuse me?'

'You go around snubbing your nose at everything, mocking it all,

THE ROADMAP OF LOSS

and not realising the only joke you make is one of yourself. It's sad, really.'

She turned and walked out. I stood at the lectern, addressing the empty room.

I approached the gravestone she was examining – one of the more modest in the cemetery behind the church. We stood for a moment before she asked for the keys and went back to the car. The carvings in the man's stone concluded with: '1822 – 1847'. He'd either had one hundred and fifty years of heaven or nothing at all. The worms probably couldn't tell the difference.

We climbed Rich Mountain Road – a harsh, unsealed trail snaking out of Cades Cove towards Knoxville. Shafts of afternoon sun came through the trees above the Miata's open top. Our backpacks bounced in the footwell under Steph's tucked legs while the collapsed tent jumped around in its bag on the shelf behind our heads. The interior rattled and the piece surrounding the gauges dislodged to rest against the steering wheel. I held it back with one hand and steered with the other as Steph placed and lit a cigarette in my mouth. Then we went back to not speaking.

About a mile up, we rounded a sharp turn and saw two cars stopped halfway through the next. Their doors were open, two occupants standing by each, looking up the next section of road. A moustached man beside the nearest car signalled us to stop with a wave of his downturned palm. We sidled up behind them. 'Kill the engine,' he said leaning towards me, but peering down the road. I did and we stepped out. A black figure stood about thirty yards away, ushering another of its shape to follow.

A woman standing behind one of the opened car doors wound the reel of her disposable camera and clicked a photo. Its flash illuminated the road, filling in the tree-traced shadows drawn across it. The light touched the beast and, for the briefest moment, I saw it. Two glowing emeralds within the black mass, staring down the road at us.

'Turn the damn flash off, Susan. You'll spook her,' said the man on the other side of the same car.

'It's a mama bear,' grinned the woman towards me and Steph.

'Yeah, and she'll be coming this way any second now,' added the man.

'How do you know?' Steph asked.

'Because she's got two cubs with her, and one of them is right there.'

The man pointed at the embankment beside us where a cub no taller than your average dog was sniffing the ground, oblivious to its surroundings. It moved past the Miata, retrieving a scent from the rear bumper, almost within Steph's reach. She watched in utter awe, or terror. The mama reared her enormous head.

'Holy shit, that's a female?' I asked, my heart beating in my ears.

'Oh yeah, the fathers ain't shit. It's the mothers that'll rip you to shreds,' stated the moustached man. 'Be ready, because the second that cub's out of her sight, she's gonna be on it.'

The lagging offspring arrived by its mother's side; the more audacious one sniffed the earth behind us, rounded the corner and vanished. The mama lifted onto her hind legs, making the road look like a footpath.

'Okay, everybody in,' the moustached man ordered. Three doors banged shut, then the click and flash of a camera before a fourth. A muffled, 'Goddamn it, Susan!' from inside the furthest car. The mama started walking towards us, her head low to the ground, swaying from side to side. I threw myself into the Miata driver's seat and wound the windows up. Steph stood frozen as the mother halved the distance.

'Grab the roof, Steph. Grab the fucking roof!' I yelled.

She sank into her seat, staring forward in a still, silent trance. I reached for the soft top's handle, eyes trained on the beast. The roof lifted a few inches before snagging on something. I pulled again and again, becoming more desperate each time it stopped at the same spot, the distance between us and the mama bear shrinking. I looked back. The tent had propped itself between the roof's hinge and the back of my seat like a doorstop. With the bear only a few yards from the first of the cars, I wrestled the tent from the nook it had fallen into and tossed it through the open space above. It landed in the ditch by the road as I heaved the soft top over us, reached across Steph and locked the passenger's side latch. I turned back to mine, but it was too late.

The mama sniffed the front bumper of the Miata, working her way up the fender and over the wheel. I saw Susan, turned in her seat to face us, lower the camera from her eye and past her hanging mouth. Towering over the Miata, the mama stretched up the window frame towards the opening above me, effortlessly folding in the side mirror. Claws as long as my fingers scraped along the glass and I wondered what kind of fight the soft top would put up anyway. Moving only my gaze, I watched her nose linger over the gap, pulling air from the cabin through colossal nostrils. She smelled me and I smelled her. She stank.

The sniffing became more intense, and then stopped. She lowered herself back to the ground, our eyes meeting at the same level, staring into each other for a moment before she moved away. In the collapsed side mirror, I watched her round the corner, the second cub waddling in pursuit. I breathed out for what felt like the first time in minutes.

'You okay?' I asked Steph.

'That was beautiful.'

'You're out of your fucking mind.'

We booked into a hotel in Knoxville. Neither of us spoke much on the way. I spent the entire drive using the ember of a cigarette at the end of its life to ignite the next. While Steph showered, I crossed the street to a decrepit liquor store with chipboard sealing up broken windows and bought a flask of whiskey. I sat on a parking stop out the front and sipped until the clerk came and told me I had to go because I was making the place look bad. Back in the room, Steph was lying naked on the bed, with her knees together and bent, swaying left to right.

'Would you like to fuck?' she asked, bringing them apart.

I didn't reply, walking into the bathroom and drinking the rest of the flask as shower water ran over me. She was still bare, but sitting against the bedhead when I returned.

'You know, there's something about you, Mark.'

'Okay.'

'I'm serious. I saw it today. Shit, I think that bear saw it too.'

'Please drop it. I'm too tired for this.'

'See, you had me believing the tough guy act, but it's not that at all. You just really don't care at all what happens to you –'

'I said drop it.'

'It's like you're searching for the end in everything. It's terrifying, because I know you're going to find it eventually and so do you, but you don't know when or how, so you walk around always ready. You only seem excited when you think it's near. I want so badly to know … what on earth could happen to a person to make them like that?'

My grip tightened around the empty bottle in my hand. Before I knew it, I had wound it up to pelt across the room. Steph flinched and I caught myself. I was not my father. I lowered the bottle and placed it on the table.

'Hmm, finally, something real,' she said.

I sat on the end of the bed and told her everything. I didn't just answer her question; I answered every question I could conceive someone asking about me. From the beginning to then. Our abandonment, her death, my fall, the letters so far. Steph sat and listened. I let her read them all from start to finish.

'Ah, well, this explains your obsession with getting to New Orleans. And, to some extent, why you're such an insufferable prick,' she said, sorting back through the pages until she found the next letter and shook it at me. 'This, here, is some –'

I raised a hand to stop her.

'Right, sorry. You haven't gotten to this one yet.'

'And I don't think I will.'

'Why not?' she demanded.

I rolled onto my back and let out a defeated breath.

'We almost died today, Steph. Fuck, I almost died yesterday too. My mother only ever wanted me to be safe and secure, and what do I do after she kicks the bucket? I go and put myself in more harm's way than I ever dreamed of.'

'It's for a good cause, though … Sure, he left and she lied to you, but this is a blessing, whether you choose to see it or not,' she said, after a minute of silent contemplation.

'I don't see how.'

'I mean, in a messed-up way it is. It's sad, what happened, but you've got a chance now to do something most people never get to.'

'And what's that?'

'To really know your parents; to understand your past. How many people get answers from someone after they're gone?'

'I'm not feeling better about it or myself,' I said after a long pause. 'Wherever I go, there's either no answer or one I didn't want. I feel like a rowboat with broken oars being pulled further out to sea.'

Steph sat up and got dressed, took her washbag into the bathroom and began brushing her teeth.

'You know, I haven't known you very long,' she said, looking at me in the reflection of the mirror, spitting frothing toothpaste into the sink, 'but you might already piss me off more than anyone I've ever met.'

I didn't reply.

'What kind of coward only wants the truth if it makes them feel better?'

'I'm just a little sick of it always going the other way.'

'Give yourself and this world some credit – neither is as bad as you think,' she said, lowering the toilet lid and placing her washbag on top. 'What you're doing is ballsy and, dare I say, kind of noble. If you're not doing this for you, then do it for your mother or the man she loved. Jesus, do it for me if you have to, just don't be such a fuckin' cheapskate about everything.'

I closed my eyes, breathed and listened as she began sweeping complimentary soaps from the counter into her bag.

We visited the same Walmart the next morning, and the tent was refunded as expected. Steph even got a store credit for her trouble and used it to buy lunch for the day. Some people are just built to make it.

We drove to a rental car place on the outskirts of town and she hired one. She was going to Charleston, South Carolina. I told her I'd never heard of it; she told me that didn't surprise her. I held her tight as we said goodbye. She wrapped her hand around the back of my neck, pulled me through the open window of her car, kissed me and was gone. I watched her disappear into the distance. To call her a diamond would've been an insult; she was something much harder than that.

I lit a cigarette and extracted a letter from my pocket. 'Where to now, you bastard?'

May 23rd, 1977

My only,

The Mississippi River is unlike anything I've ever seen. She takes her time, turning when it suits and moving straight when she wants. I followed her like a guide, tracing her shape closely as she weaved her way through this country. Oddly, I did not feel alone while moving with her, even though my passenger seat remained empty.

For that time, we were the only constants. The land around us changed dramatically as we moved south, but we remained the same. One ancient and wise, the other fresh and foolish, but both the same days older. Moving with her was like moving along life itself in many ways. I think, sometime, you, Mark and I should trace her together.

I have arrived in New Orleans. This place gave me the strangest feeling in my bones as I stepped out of the car. There is misery in the walls but music in the streets — it is beautiful. The city catches a cool breeze off the Mississippi as she cuts her way through, and the city feels like it is comprised of five smaller ones. Moving away from the town centre is like moving back through time. Black Americans have so little money but they have so much of something else. Something I cannot describe. It is a humility and joy which can come only from the most decrepit of pasts.

I'm a guest in a house with a blue door, yellow walls and a terracotta roof adorned with ornamental doves. It is raised from its foundation, as many of them are, with a porch running the entirety of its front. It is not large, but houses many. How so much living and loving and sorrowing can be contained inside its tiny walls, I will never know. I have learnt more about pain and life from its occupants in a mere evening than I had maybe in all my years leading up to it. There is suffering here, but there was suffering back home as well. I am *beginning to wonder if any place is devoid of it, or if it is the only truly universal language. I think I will stay here for a little while. There's an ease to this place I had become all too unfamiliar with.*

1.

The last hundred miles were rough. My eyes ached and every highway marker ignited like a firework as it caught in the headlights. But I pushed south through the night towards Louisiana with newfound enthusiasm; the Miata's engine blaring at four thousand revs per minute helping me stay awake. A sign read: 'Welcome to Louisiana; *Bienvenue en Louisiane*'.

I took the first exit, soon reaching a back road with farmland running alongside, and pulled over. A silhouetted countryside drew itself in the rear-vision mirror as the day woke. In front, the sky was still dark and starry. I turned the car off, reclined the seat and closed my eyes. As the engine cooled, the time between its ticks and clicks increased until there was only silence. For a moment, I was almost certain it was the beating of my heart.

I drove through piercing morning sun, already beginning to sweat. Rural Louisiana was beautiful, except it stank. I decided driving towards the lush horizon would be worthwhile even without the letters. I pulled into a gas station, the attendant looking me up and down as he handed me the bathroom key. I washed a mixture of exhaust soot and sweat off my face. I looked like I'd aged; contours and lines I'd never seen before framed my face. My eyes stared back at me, but even they seemed older.

Someone beat on the door. 'Come on! Shit and get out!' yelled a man. I dried my beard and face with my shirt and apologised to the truckie as I passed him on the way out. 'Fucking crackhead,' he said. I stopped and turned back. He postured upwards and sunk his thumbs into the front of his jeans, sucking on his gums. I got in the Miata and carried on.

Light skipped along Lake Pontchartrain's glassy surface as I crossed its lonely bridge. The tree line behind receded until water was all that could be seen in every direction. New Orleans materialised ahead. I drove in straight as an arrow with no target.

I got a room in Mid-City. My shirts looked no different after spending four dollars in a laundromat down the street. The attendant didn't look at me as I told her through security mesh that their machine wasn't working. She offered a clipboard through a slit and blew a bubble with her gum. 'How Were We? (In 25 Words Or Less)' headed the small, yellowed feedback sheet. I pushed the board back through and left, washing my clothes in the motel bathroom with hand soap instead. Rivulets the colour of dishwater dripped from them and stained the bathtub.

Late morning drunks teetered down Canal Street as I wandered to the French Quarter. I washed down fried chicken and biscuits with bad coffee in a diner and began walking. A group of old men sitting on milk crates on a corner rolled into 'Champagne and Reefer' by Muddy Waters. I kept my distance, leaning against a street sign. The bassist noticed, reaching behind him and sliding a spare crate towards me. He winked and resumed his riff, the others seeming not to notice his absence. I took a seat and listened.

Soon, my foot was tapping in time. The music and lyrics weren't complex, but they didn't need to be – the arrangement was less

THE ROADMAP OF LOSS

important than how it made you feel. I thought about how easily music creates emotions – shapeless and fluid like water in their essence. Words seemed so rigid and unforgiving in comparison, like coarse stone, yet still we push them down mountains expecting them to flow like rivers. I found myself with an involuntary morsel of respect for my father being able to craft anything with these blunt instruments. The band finished. I smiled, pushed the crate back towards the bassist and began to walk away.

'Spare a dollar, sir?' he asked.

'Oh yeah, sorry,' I said, rummaging through my pocket and handing him a fiver.

'I don't have any change for this.'

The others bobbed in time in a slow, silent fit of laughter.

'That's alright, keep it.'

'Where you from, sir? That sure is an interesting accent.'

'Melbourne, Australia.'

'Well, you have yourself a nice day in New Orleans.'

I moved down the street, turning back after a few steps.

'Changed your mind about the fiver, sir?' he asked, extracting it from his pocket.

'No, no. I was wondering if you might be able to help me find something: a house with yellow walls and a terracotta roof. It's got a, uh, blue door with a porch out the front.'

'Oh, you not gonna have any trouble with that one.'

'Really? You know a house like that?' I asked with a rush of excitement.

'Sure, there's one just like that on damn near every street. You ain't gonna have any trouble finding a house like it 'round here.'

The band bobbed and the bassist counted into their next song as I walked away. I stood on the next corner of the empty street.

2.

With a flask of whiskey and no direction, I boarded a streetcar, thinking I might view the city from its luxury and happen upon the house. Maybe there'd be a few massive neon arrows pointing to it if I was real lucky. I shared sips with an ancient lady seated nearby who corrected me for calling it a tram.

'Sounds like Saint Claude to me,' she returned after my description of the house. I offered to help with her bags when we approached her stop, but was refused. She reminded me of my mother as she walked away with those heavy weights swaying either side of her little frame, so convinced the ground beneath would crumble before her feet gave out.

I stepped off the streetcar and walked to St Claude. Thick clouds obscured the sun, with heavy grey light only interrupted by occasional streaks of yellow that managed to find a way through. The wind was picking up, trees overhead groaning as their branches faltered and collided like drunks. Moving east towards Poland Avenue, I went north a block, then walked west back to Franklin.

I walked for hours as the day became darker. On one street sat an orange house with a green door and a porch. On another, a blue house with a white door. No doves on either, though what looked like an eagle on another. 'It's been twenty years,' I thought, 'would the house even look the same if it's still here at all?' Searching seemed naive, but none of the letters had held such specific detail about a place thus far, so I kept going. I worked my way through the flask and the neighbourhood, wondering why a dog's bark sounded familiar as I passed the same street twice. The wind continued to intensify, spits of rain like needle pricks against my skin in the humidity.

Long grass surpassed the footpath on the next block, with smaller houses more tightly packed together. Occupants of cars bug-eyed me in silence as they rolled by. I passed a picket fence of rotting wood and flaking white paint, giving the house behind the same quick assessment I'd given every other. A fatigued cream colour; its door a mess of rotted wood with pale blue paint pulled into its fissures. The roof was brown but so stained it was almost black. A lone rocking chair sat on its front porch. 'Close, but no cigar,' I snorted between swigs. By the time I'd reached the next block, the rain had picked up. I decided to write the day off, find a streetcar and go back to the motel.

I passed the dilapidated house with the single rocking chair again and paused. If the closest I'd come to closure in New Orleans was pretending it to be the house in the letter, I was going to savour the moment. Standing at its fence, I pictured the place in better shape: sounds of laughter coming from inside its walls; my father bounding up the front steps and being welcomed by its inhabitants. Maybe he spent evenings on this very porch, looking out at a crimson sky.

The more I imagined, the more I wanted to believe these were the walls in my father's letter. I had nothing to lose. The gate squealed open and I moved up the path. Chances were, even if it was the same house, it wasn't the same people living within. A run-down mower sat abandoned on the lawn surrounded by overgrown grass in varying stages of neglect.

The porch's tired boards groaned under my weight. I ran my

fingers through damp hair and knocked on the door. There was movement inside but no answer. I waited then knocked again.

'Who is it?' asked a woman from behind the door.

'Hi. I'm, ah, wondering if you might remember someone who used to live here.'

'Plenty of people used to live here.'

'Well, he was a young man.'

'No young man has lived here for a long time. Bye-bye now, take care,' she said, footsteps moving away from the door.

I knocked again.

'Get lost! You want me to call the cops?' she yelled.

'Please, just hear me out. It was in seventy-seven. There was a young man – an Australian. Now I don't know if you lived here back then, but –'

One lock turned, then another. A door chain slid. The blue mess creaked open a few inches as dark fingers with red painted nails curled around its edge.

'... Dylan?' she asked, her face still behind the door.

'Yes! Dylan, Dylan Ward. So you remember?'

'Of course. How could I ever forget?'

She opened the door and stared out with wet eyes. A dark woman, trim and taller than I, in her early forties, maybe late thirties. She stood in a silk bathrobe with hair in a bun; her lipstick was a few shades darker than her nails. A soft jaw and high cheek bones sat proudly on her face. She would've been young when my father was here. Perhaps he was a guest of her parents'. I didn't want to ask where they were now.

'I was thinking this day might come, and now it has,' she said with a delicate gulp. 'Come in, Mister Ward.'

The house was much cleaner inside than out. Bookshelves stood full and organised. Not a single cup or plate astray on the coffee table.

A sheet covering a television nestled between two large speakers. On the dresser by the door, a small porcelain dove.

'I'd already hung up my drinking shoes for the evening, but I can make an exception for special company,' the woman said. 'Would you like one?'

'Sure, thank you.'

'Heh, how did I know you'd say yes?'

'Safe guess, I suppose,' I replied, offering a handshake. 'I'm sorry, I'm –'

I paused as she reached a hand right past mine, bringing it to my face, a thumb covering my closed mouth.

'Uh-uh, that word doesn't come from you while you're here. I should be sorry for what happened to you. Poor, poor boy,' she interjected, brushing damp hair from my forehead and outlining my face with the tips of her fingers. 'Funny. I tried to imagine what you might've looked like after all these years,' she sighed. 'But there it is; there's that jawline.'

I was taken aback by how little I'd had to say. It seemed enough that my face shared similarities with my father's, and that I was about the right age to come bearing questions. I'd never taken comments about how much I looked like him well, but I did then, even feeling a kind of strange pride that he'd told her about his family in Australia.

She ushered me to the couch and I sat. My father's words began to make sense to me. There was love in this house and in her. Even an unannounced stranger like me, the son of a man she used to know, seemed to be welcomed as if an old friend.

'There are so many things I want to talk about,' I said, looking up to her, experiencing a wash of relief. 'I know it's sudden. If I'd had a number I would've phoned ahead.'

'Don't be silly,' she said, striding around the couch, running fingertips along its top as she passed. 'You coming knocking is no surprise, though I never dreamt it'd take this long.'

'What do you mean?' I asked, watching her move around the room. 'How did you know I'd be able to find you, or that I'd even look?'

She opened the door of her liquor cabinet and removed two glasses, one at a time. Her movements were vague but delicate, as if she were afraid anything she touched might be damaged. She was beautiful and genial; like a warm breeze moving through a room, caressing everything but interrupting nothing.

'Well, I wasn't going anywhere, and I had a feeling you were counting on it. Besides,' she said, filling each glass, 'we can only resist our curiosities for so long.'

'Yeah, suppose I was counting on a lot of things,' I said. 'It does feel foolish to have expected so much to stay the same. Suppose I wanted to believe there was something new to be found about a man I wouldn't even recognise today.'

'Sweetie, I'm sure you're not all that different from the man who sat here all those years ago.' She lowered herself onto the coffee table in front of me, handed me a glass and raised hers for a toast. 'To discoveries, old and new.'

I clinked my glass to hers. I sipped and she slugged.

'Well, after all these years, I'm here,' I said, not sure myself what I had expected. 'Where should we start?'

'Hmm,' she answered, turning her face towards me with a blank yet somehow coy consideration. The gentle hum of a fingertip skirting around the rim of her now-empty glass the only sound in the room. Setting it down, she stood and moved towards me, placing a hand onto my chest and sitting on my lap.

'What are you doing?' I asked, startled.

'Sweetie, I think this would be a fine place to start. I can't be the only one who's been thinking about it,' she whispered. Her hand slid from my shoulder to nape, crushing into a fist and pulling my hair into a ball so tight it hurt. She yanked my head back and brought her lips to mine.

I turned my head away. 'I don't understand,' I squeezed out, but the protest was futile. She placed her hands on my cheeks and steered me back towards her. It wasn't a romantic embrace, the taste of desperation on my lips growing each time she pulled them back towards hers.

Things started to click. This woman was yet another in love with and left by my father. Laying eyes on me had only reminded her of the man who'd walked out so many years earlier. Now, broken and lonely, living in a house that used to be so full of life and love, she was trying to find some warmth in the cold. Another home left in a similar state came to mind.

'Come on now, this isn't necessary. We can just talk,' I said, trying to push her away.

'Please. Kiss me,' she countered, her despair palpable. Anchoring herself to my shoulders, she rolled onto the couch, pulling me on top of her. 'Even if it's the last time, just let me make it better, then we can talk about whatever you want.'

I felt a twang in my gut, the same I used to feel when returning home from school, only to find my mother with that faraway look in her eyes. The more hopeless this woman's efforts became, the more I felt my resolve weaken. Maybe it was the only way I could ease her suffering, even if only for a little while. Maybe, in some strange way, I could help this woman have the goodbye kiss my mother never did. Maybe I'd never made a good decision in my entire life. I stopped resisting, lowered myself to her and our lips began swimming in the ocean of the other.

As she held onto me tight I began to feel ill, whether from the movement combining with the liquor in my stomach, or from the fact this woman was imagining me to be my father.

'Oh, Lord, I've been waiting so long for this,' she murmured, looking through me to the ceiling. 'They all said you wouldn't come back, but I knew. I knew.'

'What do you ... what do you mean, "come back"?'

'There were others. Oh, baby, there were others, but none like you. I waited and wanted and hoped, and now you're finally here.' She smiled and raised a hand to my face. 'And you haven't aged a day. I missed you, Dylan.'

I moved my face away from hers, everything still except our rising chests.

'No, don't stop. What's wrong?'

I withdrew the hand I held the small of her back with, raised and waved it between us, watching eyes that did not react.

'Oh no ...' I said, standing and stepping back from the couch.

'What's wrong, Dylan? I'm sorry I put it on so heavy. I didn't know I'd feel this way.'

'There's been a terrible misunderstanding here.'

'No, there hasn't! You're back after all this time, it can't be a mistake,' she said, reaching out to where I no longer stood.

'My name is Mark. Mark Ward ... I'm Dylan Ward's son.'

'What? Dylan, stop playing. This isn't the time for your jokes.'

'Oh god, oh shit. I wish I was joking.' I became frantic. 'My name is Mark Ward, and, uh, I came here from Australia, because a house just like this one was described in a letter written to my mother twenty years ago, by ... by my father, Dylan.'

She sat in silence for a moment before drawing the shoulder of her robe back over her chest, holding the thin fabric closed in a clenched fist. After a moment, she exhaled a deep breath. I took a step closer, anticipating an invitation to explain. She took another collected breath and began screaming. Feeling around, she snatched one of the empty glasses on the table and hurled it where she thought I was standing, missing me by a few feet. It hit the dresser with the porcelain dove and knocked it off. I watched it shatter against the floor.

'Get the fuck out of here! You're not my Dylan!' she yelled.

'I'm sorry – I didn't know you thought I was – I thought I just reminded you of him. I was trying to help.'

'Trying to help me?! What the fuck is wrong with you?' she shrieked, locating and launching the other glass at me.

'I'm sorry, I didn't mean to, I'm so sorry!' I stammered as the glass shattered around me. I opened the door, ran down the steps and through the gate. Her screams erupted from the house and chased me down the street. Porch lights flickered on all as I ran. I'd never run so fast. The sky was a gruesome chaos of purple and black, swirling and falling to earth. Rain glinted white against its wickedness as it was caught in lightning.

A car's horn blared and tyres screeched, missing me by inches as I ran through an intersection. A few blocks away, already saturated, I stopped and threw up on my boots between breaths. I watched the rain dilute and wash it off the leather and then I ran again. I hailed a cab and went back to the motel. The receptionist asked how I was doing. I stared at her as water ran into my red eyes. 'Okay then,' she said.

I got out of my wet clothes, climbed into bed, turned off the lights and listened to the storm raging outside.

3.

Early the next morning, I packed and checked out. I didn't get much sleep, spending most of the night being jerked awake by thunder. I drove to the international airport, left the Miata in a No Parking zone and walked inside, resolute on purchasing a one-way ticket home with the little money I had left. Washing my face in a bathroom, I stared at myself in the mirror.

Closing my eyes, I began charting my face with my fingers. What could be learnt about another from the delineations of their face? Perhaps they're the truest measure of all. I wondered what the woman had read from the Braille of my years. I walked back to the Miata, ripped up a ticket propped under the wiper, and drove back to the motel.

I walked through St Claude with my hands in my pockets and head down. Reaching the house, I looked around to see if anyone was watching. A woman walking a dog said hello as she passed. I swore she did a double take. A bassline throbbed inside the house, the door swaying open when I knocked. 'Hello?' I said, keeping my voice down. There was no reply. I surveyed the street from the porch again. Broken glass crunched under my boot as I stepped inside. There was blood across the wooden floor.

'Hello?' I said again.

'Who's there?' Her slurred voice emanated from somewhere I could not see.

'It's ... It's Mark – please don't scream.'

'Mark Ward. Son of Dylan Ward.'

'Yeah, that's the one,' I said, following the defined trail of blood with cautious footsteps. It disappeared behind the far side of the couch next to the liquor cabinet.

'You've got some nerve coming back, ya know? My brothers are coming and they'd kill ya. They'd kill ya if they knew what you did,' she said.

I rounded the corner to find her sitting on the floor, propped up against the couch, still in her robe. Her neck, legs and hands were covered in blood; some dry, some wet. She took a sip from a drink.

'Fuck. What happened?' I asked.

'I tried to clean up after the mess that I ... that you made me make,' she chuckled.

'How much have you had to drink?'

'A little.'

'Okay, hold on,' I said. Locating a pair of tweezers in a bathroom, I soaked a rag in the kitchen and returned to her. I knelt down and asked if it was okay to touch her. 'Didn't ask last time,' she snickered. I wiped blood from her neck and it came away with no cuts underneath.

'My name is Felicia, by the way,' she said as I wiped blood from a shin.

'Well, Felicia, it's nice to meet you. I believe we have a mutual acquaintance.'

I removed glass from her hands and cleaned cuts. She tensed when I lifted the robe up her leg. 'It's okay,' I said, plucking a shard from her knee, blood following. I held the rag over the opening of the wound, watching as red seeped up the fabric. She refused to move to the couch, so I cleaned the rest of the blood and glass and sat with her on the floor.

I told Felicia about my life, and how a letter had led me to her living room floor twenty years after it was written. She then told me her story. How lucky a nineteen-year-old girl had felt to get a window seat on the streetcar back to St Claude during a bright and hot May afternoon in 1977. How tired she was after a long shift at the theatre. How a cool westerly breeze arrived to usher humidity out of the city. The man's voice that roused her from a daydream to ask if the seat beside was free.

'He just ... sat down and started talking. Charming in an infuriating kind of way; I couldn't stop smiling,' she said, shaking her head with tight lips before taking in breath through her nose. 'Insisted he come over for dinner. Ended up staying for months. But I knew he was something special right away.'

'Surely not,' I said, already feeling a stab of anger that Felicia, like my mother, seemed only to hold on to good memories of the man.

'Mhmm, I did. The kindness your father showed me and my family was something I don't think I'd ever experienced. We were still at the back of the bus not long before that. Lot of people still thought we should be. Some still do. Dylan might not have seen my colour, but I sure saw his. He just seemed to see ... me.'

'Were you two in love?' I asked, wincing at myself at how blunt I'd managed to be.

'I believe so, even though the word was never said. Ha, I didn't even let him kiss me the one time he tried. Thought I'd received my second chance last night,' she laughed before her tone turned cold. 'It was a dark little dot wherever I looked at first. Had been with me for years, then one morning – few weeks after Dylan had arrived – it was suddenly just ... bigger. Seemed to grow every day after that; a little less of the world getting in around it when I woke each morning. Got the diagnosis shortly after. Nothing they could do, they said.'

'I'm sorry,' I managed, gulping down the lump in my throat. 'So, what? He left you when you told him?'

'Dylan? Lord, no. No, he pleaded to stay even though I demanded he go. I told him I didn't need his damn pity, but really I just didn't want him to see it happen to me,' she said with the calm intensity of someone who'd long ago made peace with an imperfect world. 'So, in a desperate moment of weakness I will never forgive myself for, I told my brothers he'd forced himself on me. They sent him down those front steps so hard I'm surprised his bones didn't break. Yelled he was dead if he ever came back. I'll never forget that look on his face as he threw a bag over his shoulder and backed down my path for the last time.'

I breathed in deep, steadying myself. Felicia reached a hand to me. I met hers with mine and felt the strangest sensation of sadness draining from both of us as she squeezed it.

He'd written to her as well after that, albeit with a fake name, she told me. Even said he'd come back to her when the time was right in one of the last she read. The hardest part, she told me, was watching the paper of his letters slowly become as dark as the words written upon them. Felicia had truly believed with every part of her being that my father would return to her one day. A tear ran down my cheek. Her pain was so akin to what I'd grown up watching my mother endure.

'I wonder what he'd be up to now – if he's still out there, I mean,' she said.

'Probably more of the same. Men like him don't tend to change.'

'Do you hate him? You speak like you do.'

'He didn't give me many reasons not to.'

'Nothin' good ever came from hate, Mark.'

I didn't reply. I'd been given this lecture too many times. She sighed.

'You ever cut open a bit of fruit that looked good from the outside, but once you were in there you realised it was all spoilt?'

'Yeah, I guess so.'

'Sweetie,' she said, searching for my face with an unfolded hand. I leant forward to help her find it. 'That's hate. Hate rots. A man ain't all that different from a piece of fruit, really.'

'I don't follow.'

'What I mean is a man can look real fine on the outside, but he can be rotting in there. What I'm saying, Mark, is be careful. Because sometimes, if you get into that fruit too late – if you judge it from the outside and let it go rotting too long, pretty soon you'll find none of it can be salvaged. Pretty soon you'll find none of it can be saved.'

'I didn't have a choice,' I said with a lump in my throat. 'My mother never had the strength to hate him. So I had to; enough for both of us.'

'It takes more strength not to hate, Mark, and there's always a choice. Your father was a wonderful, loving young man. He knew anger and sorrow, but didn't live with them. They were guests in his home, but did not choose the carpets or the drapes or the colour on the walls. They visited occasionally, to sit and talk, but always left the place how they'd found it. They were familiar company, but he did not let them furnish his soul.'

I sipped from her glass.

'You know, Dylan was only about your age when I met him on that streetcar. Just another lost boy trying to piece it all together. Maybe you two are more alike than you realise ... Ah, what I would give to be back at that window seat. To turn around and see him again for the very first time,' she said, with a smile. I watched as the richness of the slideshow of her memories played behind eyes that no longer worked.

There was a knock on the door before it swung open. Three enormous Black men entered the house.

'Who the hell are you?' one of them asked, stepping towards me, covering almost half of the room with a single stride. I stood up in a panic.

'Christopher, it's alright,' Felicia said, craning her head around the side of the couch, 'he's a friend.'

The men approached and saw Felicia's legs through the bottom of her robe.

'The fuck happened?' asked another, looking at me.

'Nothing, Landon. I dropped a glass and tried to clean it up myself. Mark here was tending to my cuts,' Felicia countered.

'Well, why he look like he been crying?' he asked.

'Because I'd been telling a sad story. Now come, help me up.'

Christopher rushed to her.

'Come on, girl, stop being so stubborn. Like that damn lawn, just let me mow it,' he said as he sat her on the couch. I felt the floor buckle as he moved past me.

'Hush,' she said. 'Chris, Landon, Cyrus, meet Mark. Mark, meet my brothers. Mark is an old friend passing through town. He stopped in to see how I was doing.'

'Alright, man, that's good. Good to meet you,' they said, all shaking my hand and nodding. Their sister's word was final.

'But I'd say we're all caught up now, and Mark is a busy boy. I'm sure he has many places to be. Wouldn't you agree, Mark?' Felicia asked, not looking at me but smiling.

'Yeah, right. I, uh, I best be going.'

She extended an arm in front of her. I moved to it and leant in. She hugged me tight. 'Good luck. Go find what you're looking for,' she whispered in my ear. The brothers wished me well. I opened the door and began closing it behind me.

'Hold up, sweetie.'

I stopped and turned back to her.

'Yeah, Felicia?'

'Is it sunny out?'

The street was still drenched from the morning rain, but the sun had come out and everything glistened. I opened the door, filling the room with light, and spoke back into the house.

'It is.'

'Leave it open, dear. I love the sunshine after a storm.'

I smiled at her, nodded and walked down the steps, along the same path my father had.

'Man, that dude looks real familiar,' said one of the brothers.

'Don't be ridiculous,' I overheard Felicia reply.

August 2nd, 1977

My love,

It has been too long since I pushed pen to paper and reminded you that everything reminds me of you. I'm sorry. Do you ever feel some people are born with poison in their veins where there should be blood? That their hearts become blackened by some toxic sludge as it courses through them? You said, time after time, things were not like that. That I was not like that. But the irony is not lost on me; I was abandoned and now I have abandoned you and Mark as well. My father was a despicable man and I am glad you never had to meet him, but I am beginning to see his face in mine. I seem to only steer myself towards it the harder I try to pull away.

Surely there is more to this life. There has to be more to it all than merely repeating the same mistakes over and over. The bombs get bigger and the guns get more powerful and the only thing remaining the same, it seems to me, is how willing we are to use them to hurt each other. Maybe that's our ultimate punishment: to watch our sins be passed down to our children and the cycle we were not good enough to break, continue in them.

This life is a difficult thing for me. I often look at others and wonder how life seems so easy for them. What does it take for a man to make it? I am less sure of the answer than I am that, whatever it is, I do not possess. I miss you and Mark so much that I feel sick, but I am not worthy to come home yet. I have left New Orleans because I was not good enough to stay, and I stayed so long because I was not good enough to leave. I have love for everything other than myself. I believe in you and I believe in this world, but I don't believe there's a place for me within it for me to rest my head.

I have sold my car and moved east by train, so I am comfortable with money for now. Expect transfers more regularly. Savannah,

Georgia, has welcomed me, but I will not stay here very long, that I can already tell. It is nice, though, to sit by the water and watch the boats drift by.

1.

The Miata started losing motivation as I followed the Gulf of Mexico east. The clunk was worsening and a whine had developed after driving at highway speeds for extended periods. An auto store clerk told me the differential fluid was toast and sold me two quarts of the stuff. I managed to squeeze them into a nook in the boot.

I stopped for the day at a motel outside Mobile, Alabama. The carpet was damp from a leak in the air-conditioning unit and the room stank. I walked to the payphone out the front of a bar across the street and fed in all the coins I had. It rang and rang.

'Hello, Linda Crawford speaking.'

'Hey, it's Mark Ward.'

'Mark,' she somehow whispered and yelled at the same time, 'where have you been? I've been trying to reach you for a month.'

'I'm in Alabama.'

'You're fucking where?' she said, then apologised to somebody in the room.

'It's not important. Why is my bank saying the money still hasn't arrived?'

'The buyers fell through. There's no money coming, Mark.'

'Fuck me. What happened?'

'They couldn't secure the loan – it happens all the time. I called you the same day, but evidently you're not listed in Alabama.'

'What happens now?'

'I've contacted other bidders to see if they're still interested, but I can't sell the house on your behalf again without permission and a signature.'

'Okay? You have my permission, forge the signature.'

'You know I can't. I'll send you a new contract, have you sign and send it back.'

'That could take weeks.'

'Yes, it probably will.'

'I don't have weeks. You don't know how much I need this money.'

'Well, this is what happens when you disappear with unfinished business.'

I drummed my forehead with the palm of my free hand then ran it down my face.

'You know what you can do for me, Linda?'

'What's that?'

'Forge it, then put in right above that your commission's been tripled.'

She cleared her throat but didn't speak.

'I'm glad we've reached an agreement,' I said, gently placing the handset down then smacking the inside of the booth until I'd lost count.

I stepped out and held a cigarette between throbbing fingers. Waves crashed like laughter on the other side of the indifferent interstate. I blew smoke towards the rouge sky then headed back to my broken air conditioner and damp carpet.

2.

The drive from Alabama to Savannah could be done in a day. I squeezed myself between towering trucks on the wide highways cutting through the timberline and shooting off in all directions.

A staircase from Emmet Park on the Savannah River led me down to East River Street. I browsed trinkets in a marketplace and felt patches of sun on my skin from a bench beside a path lined with willows. The city was quiet, and I got the feeling that's all it was. My funds were dwindling and the cost of accommodation was exorbitant. One receptionist told me they had a sister motel just out of town and wrote the address down for me. I drove south to the place – there was nothing more I needed to see in Savannah.

On a road off the highway, I passed through a small town. A Black teenage boy walked onto the road ahead of me, moving towards a corner store. He strode like all his weight was a few feet in front of him and he had to lean back to counterbalance. When almost across, he stopped in my path and looked towards me. I changed to the other lane and he took a few steps back to place himself ahead of me again. I moved back to my original lane. He stepped forwards. I wasn't sure if he wanted me to stop or to run him down. He stared with fire in his eyes. At the last second, I pulled the steering wheel onto the wrong side of the empty road to go around him. His head craned on his neck, following me as I passed. He stood unmoving in the middle of the road as I rounded the next bend. He seemed disappointed.

It was hardly downtown anymore. Just fifteen miles south and marshland surrounded the motel. I showered and drove to a bar a few minutes away, pulling off the highway onto a small side road running parallel with it – a strip of grass separating the two. Parking the Miata on a quiet, suburban street a few blocks from the bar, I decided to walk the rest of the way. Yet another brilliant, southern sunset formed above me. The road opened into a parking lot with a row of shops – the bar the last of them.

I walked in and took a seat. The place looked rough, but most of the patrons were laughing and talking. A few of us sat in silence.

The bartender was a peroxide blonde, as wide as she was tall, placing enormous faith in the stitches of her denim shorts.

'What you after, honey?' she asked.

'A Bud, thanks,' I said, using the neutral accent I'd learnt in order to avoid attention.

She smiled, turned and bent over to retrieve one from the fridge. I tried to look at anything else as her shorts pulled into a thong. A man on the stool next to mine stood on its footrest, gripping a beer bottle by the neck, and flung it behind the bar. It soared over the bartender, meeting with the wall beside her and shattering. Shards fell around the bar, about half landing in the bin below.

'Goddamn it, Marty!' she yelled as she straightened up.

'Zero for three!' echoed from across the bar.

The man clicked his fingers and sat back down.

'Ah heck, Charlene, thought I'd have it that time,' he said, looking at me and shrugging.

Charlene placed a beer down in front of me. I sipped and smirked as she went at the floor with a broom and dustpan. A few of the others hollered and pretended to throw their bottles. She scowled and pointed at them, then laughed.

My cover was blown when I ordered a water. A 'wor-tah'. Two locals shifted closer and started quizzing me. I told them I hadn't seen much of Savannah, then lied and said I couldn't wait to see more. I mentioned the boy crossing the road.

'Did you hit him?'

'No, I drove around him ...'

'You said this was a Black boy?'

'Yes.'

'Ah, well, should've hit him.'

'He did seem like he wanted me to.'

'You should've hit him.'

I went out the side of the bar for a cigarette with the two men. A car in the lot belonged to one of them. It was long and wide, low to the ground. Jet black and shiny, muscular and poised, like an animal ready to pounce. It was a Corvette – I'd never seen anything like it. The locals peppered me with free drinks. I was a novelty, but I was welcomed. We laughed and joked, threw back shots and slammed the glasses down onto the bar. Charlene always in wait to top them up. I tried shooting hoop with an empty bottle at their request. It landed on one side of the bin's rim, bounced, kissed the other side, then fell to the ground, breaking.

'Shit! Someone get this boy in the NBA!' a woman yelled as the room erupted.

I stood outside alone in the warm night a few rounds later, smoking a cigarette and swaying, thinking it wasn't all so bad – that life doesn't have to be so hard. You just need to keep it simple, and a drink and a smoke was about as simple as things got. My mother and I weren't so different after all; I'd just opted to find my comfort in more dangerous places.

In the distance, a growl grew louder until it was all I could hear. A large pickup truck pulled into the lot, the vibrating earth I stood on becoming still as the engine shut off. A guy got out, his chunky, slick black leather boots hitting the ground with a thud. They shone like the Corvette. He walked over and stood on the other side of the door that led into the bar and lit a cigarette.

'Hey,' I said.

He looked over as if he hadn't noticed me standing there. Scanning me up and down, he ran a palm over his shaved head.

'Mark,' I said, pointing to myself.

'Ray.'

'That truck sounds pretty mean.'

'Sure is. She'd kick the crap out that pissy little Corvette there, that's for sure.'

He spat on the ground.

'You not from around here are ya?' he asked.

'No, no I'm not.'

'Well...?' he asked, drawing a circle with his hand, ushering me on.

'Australia. I'm from Australia.'

His eyes lit up. He stepped closer. From afar he'd looked young, but up close there were wrinkles covering his face. He could've been fifteen or fifty. It made me uneasy.

'You a long way from home.'

'I guess so.'

'Hey, man, that's cool. That's real cool. The hell you doing here?'

'No idea. Not sure there's anything to do here.'

'Well, depends. You looking for some trouble?'

'Heh, that seems to be about the only thing I don't have to look for. Have any suggestions?'

'Well,' he said, stepping closer, making sure we were alone and composing himself. 'You can kill a Black fellow.'

THE ROADMAP OF LOSS

'Oh yeah? That a hobby of yours?'

I waited for a sign that I'd called his sick bluff, but he only moved closer again; unblinking, unaffected.

'I do it for fun,' he said through rotten teeth with rotten breath.

And then I no longer felt alright. I went back inside. A minute later, Ray came in and I saw some of the regulars react in uneasy ways. He moved to the stool beside mine and ordered me a drink I didn't ask for. As Charlene bent for the bottle, Ray leant in close and pointed to her denim floss.

'Don't get any ideas. That pussy belongs to me.'

'Wouldn't dream of it.'

'Hey, you and I should hit a titty bar tonight.'

'Sorry, I'm not a huge fan.'

'Alright, then we'll go to the whorehouse, don't bother me none. I know a great one.'

'It's okay. I don't have the money.'

'Well, shit, I'll cover you, buddy.'

'Still can't.'

'Y'all can't afford free?'

'It's not really my scene. I'm not that kind of guy.'

'Hey now, hang on. Got no money or not that kinda guy? Because you've told me both now, so which is it?'

'It's both.'

'Nah, nah. I don't believe that for one second. I can see it. I can feel it. You as fucked up as they come. One sick puppy.'

'I'm not.'

'Yeah, you are, it's in them eyes. Hey, it's alright, I'm the same,' he said, slapping his chest with both hands at the same time. 'Some of us just born that way. Ain't no use trying to fight it.'

Some of the locals watched on with sideways glances.

'See, I don't know much, but I know a few things. And one of them is that people, them other people, they look at guys like us and they think they're something better.'

'What? Guys like us?'

'Yeah, guys like us. Men who don't shy away from what they are. Men who wear it proud like a badge of honour. What I know is that it don't matter how much money you got, how many women you got, how much you think you got. What I know is that all it comes down to is how you wear your leather.'

'Your what?'

'Your leather. This shit,' he said, pinching the pale, thin skin on his forearm and letting it snap back like a rubber band.

'Only matters how you wear that. Don't nothin' else matter. Because at the end of the day, nobody gonna give a shit 'bout what you *think* you got over another. At the end of the day, there ain't a man alive whose leather is too thick to be sliced through or too tough to be dissolved in the stomach acid of another.'

'Ray, man, come on,' said the guy with the Corvette.

'Come on what?' Ray growled back at him.

'Just, uh, shit ...' the man retreated.

'I'm educating the boy.'

He stared at me, waiting for acknowledgement. Maybe he'd eaten a man alive and that was the rotting smell of his breath. I looked forward and sipped from my bottle and didn't want to be there. He was crazy, and what's worse, he thought me his alumni. Maybe I was, a little. But there had to be more than one way to be crazy, and I wasn't like him.

I suggested a cigarette outside and Ray agreed. 'Gotta piss,' I said, deviating from our path and towards the bathroom. I moved slowly. When the door closed behind him, I paid my tab with haste. 'Good thinking, sweetie. He's a little intense,' said Charlene. I walked out the front and across the car park, obscuring myself behind the buildings

THE ROADMAP OF LOSS

until I reached the side road. The night was alive with moonlight.

My thoughts rumbled and rattled inside my head as I neared the Miata. The road began to shake and then everything was bright. I looked back; I knew that sound. I picked up my pace as floodlights moved up the road behind me. Then Ray rolled past, turned his truck and blocked me.

'Get in. I decided for you. Whorehouse it is,' he said, looking down from the driver's seat.

There was nothing in his voice. Real rage is pure, absent of all other emotion.

'No, really, I'm alright. Gonna call it a night.'

'You coming?' he asked, the night turning cold around him. 'Or you want to see how I put them Blacks away?'

He reached for something in the cabin and I froze. I peeked sideways; the street with the Miata was a stone's throw. I could make a dash; somehow beat Ray's truck there, fumble the key into the ignition, start it and go. I'd never make it. I could try running back to the bar. Forget about it. Ray hoisted something onto his lap. He looked at me. His patience was just about gone.

My mouth opened before I had words to fill it.

'Hey, Ray, I've got a better idea,' I stuttered. 'Before we go, why don't you show me what that truck can do?'

His mouth bowed into a snarl. That was it. I was going to be shot and left to bleed out in some street in bum fuck Georgia for that line, and I'd deserve it.

'Well,' he said. 'You asked for it.'

He looked at me, grinning as he reached again for something in the cabin. Crunching it forward, he gave the truck a rev which shook the ground and then the rear tyres started spinning – smoke glowing in the moonlight. He did a U-turn over the grass divider, spraying dirt and ending up on the highway, almost hitting another car as he roared into the distance. He was too dumb to pass up a challenge. I stood there, everything around me still and quiet, and then I was sprinting. I reached the Miata with such speed I couldn't pull up in time and bashed into the door.

I twisted the key in the lock, pulled the handle and felt a familiar lack of resistance. Fuck. Running to the passenger side, I opened the door, leant across and pushed the driver's door open from the inside, ran back around, got in and sat in dark silence. Only the sound of my staggered breathing filled the cabin, and then the roar. I looked in the rear-vision mirror, recognising the outline of headlights as he came back down the highway on the other side, veered, and disappeared into the grassy valley between the directions of traffic. The glaring lights shot up from the side nearest me, like some demon clawing its way out of hell. Ray crossed the highway with complete disregard for oncoming traffic. Driving over the grass divider onto the side road where he'd left me, he stopped.

'Where are you, Mark? Where the fuck are you?' he shrieked from his open window.

He crawled onto the same street as me, the burble of his truck getting louder. I slunk lower in my seat as the shape of the Miata's rear window was drawn in light over the dash. I had maybe thirty yards on him and he didn't know where I was, but he could at any second. Starting the engine would give me away. I eased the key into the barrel as if Ray might hear it, feeling the pins of the lock tuck away one by one. Readying myself, I rotated it to one click before ignition.

Red, green, blue. Red, green, blue. Red, green, blue. The cabin lit up from the inside, projecting colour from the Miata's footwells, over me, out the windows and onto the street, pulsating to the blaring bassline of Queen's 'Don't Stop Me Now' on the radio. The disco lights. Those fucking disco lights. *Carl, you little son of a bitch, you've killed me,* I thought.

THE ROADMAP OF LOSS

Ray pounced – the shine of his headlights shifting up the tree line above as the truck's body tilted. I twisted the key and the Miata hummed into life. I pushed it into gear, brought the revs way up and let the clutch go. The tyres squealed and the car shuddered so hard my vision blurred and teeth rattled. I took it up to sixty-five-hundred revs down the narrow suburban street, planted my left foot to the floor and yanked the gear shifter back into second. The plastic surround came free from the dash with a bang.

Thirty-five, forty miles per hour. I hit a speed bump, lifting from my seat and becoming airborne in the cabin before returning to earth with a crash and a bellow of sparks from the tailpipe. Floodlights closed in, filling more and more of the rear-vision mirror, blinding me. The Miata was no match for Ray's truck. Up ahead, a street intersected the one we rocketed down. I had to try something. Afraid to slow down and lose precious distance from Ray, I kept the throttle down, yanked the wheel and prayed.

The Miata dug in and swung through the corner, missing the kerb and a parked car by mere inches. Ray attempted to follow me, but locked up his tyres and missed the street entirely. I turned another corner and floored it, blinded for a moment as I passed the next intersecting street. Ray emerged from it behind me, his truck closing the gap on the straight road again with ease. It had to be done in the corners.

The next intersection approached: a right-hander. I moved the Miata so far to the left it threw up dried leaves from the gutter and turned with more speed than the first time, clearing the corner so fast I thought one of the wheels was going to come off. Ray tried to match my speed but couldn't, careening onto somebody's lawn and taking their letterbox out before returning to the road. I'd easily tripled the gap with one movement.

I sped through the neighbourhood, my confidence growing after each corner. The time between me straightening up and Ray's lights filling the street behind increased with every turn, and soon there was no sign of him at all. I figured, the more turns I made, the greater my chances of ending up face-to-face with the mammoth truck became, so I pulled over in the shadow of a tree and turned the radio, headlights and disco lights off.

Somewhere in the distance, circling like an enemy chopper, I could hear Ray pacing. I kept the Miata's engine idling in preparation for another bout with the heavyweight, but soon there was silence. After a few minutes, I started moving, keeping the revs low. I came to the highway and stopped, waiting for a break in traffic. Then that hum, again, increasing. I looked around frantically, but saw no headlights behind me. The volume grew to a roar and then a flash as his truck flew by on the highway. I caught a glimpse of Ray's confused rage as he recognised me and the Miata, but he didn't slow down. A second later, two police cars with lights and sirens on flashed by in pursuit.

I accelerated out behind them and hooked a U-turn as soon as possible, almost getting taken out by a minivan. I rowed the Miata through its gears down the short stretch of highway between the bar and the motel, pulled up in the darkest corner of its parking lot, and ran upstairs to my room. Turning both locks, I sat on the bed with a cigarette, fell on my back and began to laugh. I laughed so hard my eyes teared up and my cheeks ached. I laughed and I laughed. I didn't even think it was that funny.

3.

In the morning, I returned my room key to the office, hesitating as I left. 'Would you happen to have any scissors?' I asked the receptionist. Tentatively handed a pair, I walked to the Miata and snipped every wire attached to the controller box for the footwell lights.

I took the letters from my bag and scanned the first few lines of the next. My father went south from Savannah, so I decided to go north. 'Fuck you and your letters,' I growled, butting a cigarette out.

Knowing next to nothing of the East Coast, I looked through my maps and recognised Charleston, South Carolina. Perhaps Steph was still there. I would find her if I was meant to, or she me. Taking off towards the highway, the Miata bucked so violently the engine almost stalled. It had not coped well with the abuse of the night before. We were both being ground down by our travels. I wondered who would give out first.

A bridge lifted me over the Ashley River and I descended into downtown Charleston. The streets were clean and calm. I waited at an intersection as a horse-drawn carriage swept past – its passengers bringing champagne glasses to their lips. A hostess outside a fancy restaurant smiled and nodded as I ambled by. I felt an unusual sensation wash over me. Comfort. I decided if there was a city where

I had to run out of money and take refuge on its park benches, then Charleston was it.

That evening, I laid all the cash I had left out on a motel bed. Never do that. If you're going to lay it all out, do it on something small so it looks like you have more. I could pull the last few hundred remaining from the house deposit from an ATM, but otherwise, I was about dry. I called Linda. She wasn't happy, acting as if I'd grabbed her hand, squeezed its fingers around a pen and forced the dexterous movement of my signature onto the page.

'And did you up the commission as well?'

'Yes, like you told me to.'

'Then you can't feel all that bad.'

I walked the streets and did not meet an unkind face. Buying a six-pack of beer, I went back to my second-floor room. It had a narrow window that could be unlocked and swung out over the sidewalk. If you tucked the room's wobbly chair tight up against the wall, you could look east along Spring. I watched people walk below as the light turned peach and their shadows became long. The radio was on and when I finished a beer, I'd reach for another, crack it open, return my foot to the sill and lean back on the wheezing chair. In that moment, I owed nothing to anybody. I did not want and was not wanted. I did not pursue and was not pursued. My father had gone one direction and I the other. It felt good to know he had never sat where I sat.

It was dark when I woke underneath the turning fan. The sound of faraway revellers crept in through the open window. My buzz was gone – this wouldn't do. I picked up and smelled the folded bath towel on the bed then put it back. I showered in my floor's shared bathroom with sandals on and walked back down the corridor to my room, naked and dripping, with clothes bunched under my arm. I sat exposed on the bed in the darkness, smoked a cigarette and dried off in the lingering heat the fan pushed over me.

Following sound, I found a bar full of people – rambunctious and arrogant. I took a free booth and looked at the menu. Dinner could be skipped again. I got a lot more from a few drinks than I did from a meal.

I had often thought I had much less will to live than the average person. Growing up, everything felt like a chore to me. Eating, shitting, going to sleep, waking up. Sometimes it felt like I had to will the very process of taking in and exhaling my next breath. I looked around the bar at the loud men and the confident women. A chubby young guy stuffed his red face full of wings with glee. He snorted at his friend's shouted story and a chunk fell from his mouth, which he picked off the plate and shovelled back in. He looked like he was about to come.

How did they all do it so easily? I didn't want death; I just wasn't so enthused by living. Somewhere between the two, I'd become stuck.

Blowing smoke up into the warm night, I went through yet another budget in my mind, thinking of dollars falling away like autumn leaves. Then she walked by. Heels didn't seem to come naturally to her, and she concentrated with absolute intent as she stepped over a crack in the sidewalk. I tried to catch her eye as she passed and entered the bar.

A gap at the bar presented itself. I stepped into it and then she was beside me. Her lips curled downwards, disappearing into deep dimples. Very feline. She turned her head to confirm I was looking before turning back twice as fast.

'Trying to get a drink?' I asked.

'I'm standing in line at a bar, so, yes,' she said, looking forward.

I could barely hear her over the crowd.

'Don't worry; I'm not trying to take you home. I'm just warning you it might be a while.'

I pointed down the bar to its only tender as he continued high-fiving and laughing with a bunch of college kids, oblivious to the queue at its other end.

'That's quite rude of him,' she said.

'You're telling me. I was but a boy when I lined up at this bar,' I said, scratching my beard.

'That's funny.'

'You think so?'

'Yes.'

'You're not laughing.'

'I don't think I should have to,' she said softly. 'I don't cry just because I find something a little sad.'

'Oh, so now it was only a little funny?'

She smiled and nodded short, snappy nods.

'Can't argue with that, I suppose. Mark.'

'Hannah.'

I reached out a hand and she put hers in mine. It was soft and untainted, as though it'd never seen fire or a blade or even been pulled into a fist. We ordered and I suggested we sit together. She agreed, to my surprise. I paid the price of the drinks and not a cent more.

'Really? No tip for me, guy?' the bartender asked.

'Oh,' I said, turning back, 'yeah, yeah, I got one. Maybe stop circle jerking with your buddies when there's a line of thirsty people waiting.'

I saluted with the bottle. Hannah and I walked to a booth.

'How can you talk to someone like that?' she asked as we sat.

'Sometimes it comes easy. Does it upset you?'

'No, I just think I could never speak to someone like that, even if I really wanted to. Thank you for the drink.'

'Yeah, well, enjoy it. It's the last I'm gonna be able to get in here, I think,' I said, looking back across the room to the seething bartender.

I blew him a kiss and he shook his head like his neck was going to burst, then went back to wiping down the bar. Hannah got another round from him.

'How'd you manage that?'

'I told him you're not well, mentally.'

'And he believed it?'

'With very little convincing.'

The drinks kept coming. We talked about everything but ourselves and whatever had steered us into the bar that night. It was nice. She ran fingers across the fringes of her dress, as if reminding herself where it ended, and then her hand was on my thigh. She gazed at me with coy guilt.

'Hannah, I have a confession to make.'

'Oh? You do?' she asked, pulling her hand away. I placed it back on my thigh.

'Mmm, I do. I'm a liar.'

'Really? What do you lie about?'

'Many things, but tonight, only one.'

'Yes?'

'When I met you just before, I lied. I said I wasn't planning to take you home.'

She gripped tighter. I squeezed that soft hand in mine. Then I got us out of there.

4.

An abundance of brightness worked its way through the shitty motel room's narrow window the next morning, penetrating my closed eyelids as I enjoyed the few seconds of blissful numbness remaining before the hangover consumed me. I turned over and it arrived right on cue. I stretched an arm across the bed, reaching for a warm body next to mine, but sensing only the touch of sheets and familiar mixture of relief and loneliness. Everything about the bed felt nicer than it had the day before as I worked my eyes open and shifted my weight around. The room even smelled nicer. I decided I would spend the rest of my life there.

I sat up. Through blurred vision, I saw the green of treetops against a sapphire sky, framed by a large window carved out of a white wall; a desk with a computer; a bookshelf; drawers and dressers. I gave up the search for my underpants and walked towards the quiet sound of music making its way through the closed door.

'Mornin',' I croaked, stepping through into a living room.

She looked up from a book, cross-legged on her couch.

'Good morning. Oh, wow. Could you please put some clothes on?'

'Really?'

'It's a little ... much for the morning.'

'That's fair enough, uh –'

'Hannah.'

'Hannah! Yes.'

I raised my fingers to my chest, opening my mouth to speak.

'Mark. I know.'

'Right, of course. Sorry.'

'There's coffee if you want. Toast too,' she said, nodding her head towards the kitchen, scanning me then turning back to her book.

I looked down at my vulnerable manhood. It'd looked a lot better to me the night before as well.

We sat and talked in her apartment. She explained we were on Johns Island, the second of three barrier islands between Charleston's downtown and the Atlantic. I didn't remember getting there, but I believed her. I smoked on the balcony. She asked for a drag and coughed, sniffling and shaking her head. The balcony overlooked a service road of dirt running alongside the row of apartments, lined with ancient oaks. They reached past the third floor we stood on; spaced far enough apart that one's branches would embrace another's without feuding for the air in between. They came together and swayed.

The road's end was obscured as the gaps between the trees closed off to nothing as you peered down, like posts of a fence. A few feet of grass beyond the oaks on the other side of the road met dense forest, forming a barricade and tying the whole scene neatly. My hangover was no match for the beauty of the place. I couldn't feel bad while here. My idea of paradise had always been palm trees, white sands and turquoise water, when maybe all along it should've been oak trees, some dirt, and a girl I could make smile.

Hannah drove us back downtown from the island, eager to show me as much of Charleston as my body would allow in the sweating humidity. We walked Rainbow Row and Waterfront Park hand in hand. She pointed out things of cultural and historical importance and I vomited into a bush. She doubled over in hysterics, then almost did the same. Neither of us was going to rest on the pages of history, but then neither of us really cared.

We spent the night together, then another and another. Before long, we were retrieving the Miata to bring back to Johns Island. As I pulled my duffel bag from the boot, its underside dripped with what smelled like gas. I had forgotten about the bottle of differential fluid wedged in the corner of the boot. The hinge of the boot's lid had pinched splits into its plastic, and now the contents were pooled on the floor where I had, a lifetime before, neatly placed a leather jacket I'd bought in New York City. I heaved it out, heavy with the weight of oil held in its pores, crammed it inside a garbage bag and carried it upstairs.

'It's ruined,' I said, scrubbing with a sponge to no avail.

'Only if you give up trying to fix it,' Hannah retorted. I immersed it in the bathtub – the water turning a lighter shade of brown with each plunge. Draping the leather over the balcony's handrail, I went inside and tried to forget about it.

Hannah was unlike anyone I'd met. She had moved from the chaos of New York City about as far as possible, if you factored in everything except distance. Staying on with a law firm in the city, she now did freelance contract editing. It meant that a few hours of work each week more than covered the time spent reading or sipping drinks, walking or sleeping.

There was an ease to her and everything she did. I would seldom return to a room to find her in the same position as when I'd left. She shifted around the apartment like a cat tiring of its position every time the clock's hand moved.

One afternoon, I passed her lying on her back, head hanging off the edge of the couch, as her eyes drifted over a book she clasped. I leant over to read its upside-down cover but couldn't. Her legs were apart with knees bent over the back of the couch and her dress fell around her thighs. Without hesitation, I unzipped my jeans, removed myself and took the weight of her head in my hands. She kept the book between her fingers, resting it against the carpet and took me in her mouth. Licking me off her lips, unfazed and without a word, she lifted the book from the floor and resumed glancing across its pages. She wasn't like me. She didn't have to make sense of everything, so everything made sense to her. The book only looked upside down to me.

5.

Hannah hadn't asked for a cent except to help cover groceries. She knew I was from Australia and knew I'd been moving around, but didn't know why I was in Charleston with a beat-up car and no real plan. She asked nothing and I told even less. There was an unspoken understanding that any conversation like that would only hinder the comfort we had found in not knowing.

We spent our days together walking and talking, and our nights drinking and fucking. I could've repeated the cycle indefinitely. Being around her didn't bring some immense, overpowering joy, but the thought of being without her made me feel unwell. I wondered if that's what it was to truly make it with someone. My money was lasting, but I didn't have enough of it to trace the letters anymore and soon wouldn't have enough to live, even with Hannah's seemingly endless hospitality and patience.

One evening, she drove us to a bar at the far reaches of the next and final island between us and the Atlantic: Kiawah Island. I watched as the private land's manicured golf courses and colossal, exquisite homes passed by my window. After a drink at the clubhouse bar, we wandered the green of the final hole down to a beach. The tide had receded enough to expose a small sandbank about forty feet out – a thin walkway of exposed dune leading to it with silty water either side. We stood in the middle of our tiny island and I moved in close, looking into her squinting eyes, and kissed her. The sun was setting behind me. I was a silhouette to her – whoever or whatever she wanted me to be in that moment.

I smoked a cigarette out the front of the clubhouse and waited while she used the bathroom. It was a beautiful corner of the earth and there were worse places a man could find the end. I perused a noticeboard next to me and saw a posting: SUMMER WORK AVAILABLE: CONTACT PAMELA IN LAND MAINTENANCE.

The following day, after Hannah went for groceries, I drove back to Kiawah. The road leading towards it was magnificent, with oaks either side forming a tunnel disappearing into the distance; trunks so close they'd take your side mirror off if you weren't paying attention. Even the brightest daylight only just worked through their branches to illuminate the road in small spits of light.

I arrived at the island's security checkpoint – the second of its two guards turning away from paperwork towards me when he heard the tone of the first. They looked over the Miata with scornful eyes, filled out and handed me a guest pass, and waved me through. I thanked them and pulled away with a clunk and a bang.

'It's hard work, but it's a job,' Pamela told me, leaving her sunglasses on as we spoke in the lobby of the office. She looked like a tough woman, with skin so tanned it had become the same sandy-brown as her hair. 'Monday through Friday. Start at seven, clock off at three-thirty. Half-hour break in there for lunch. Shirt, hat and safety equipment is provided but you need your own pants and shoes. That's really all there is to say.'

'Not an issue at all. I'm willing to work.'

'That's good, but you need to understand the line is long in this town for people looking for work. There's no sense in me bothering with all that paperwork if it turns out you're not fit and able.'

'Yes, I understand. I am, I promise.'

'We need more than your word.'

She paused and waited. I looked around then dropped onto my hands and began pressing out push-ups with moderate difficulty in the middle of the lobby. The receptionist peered over her desk.

'What the hell are you doing?' Pamela asked.

'Showing you I'm fit and able,' I answered, masking my exertion.

'Get up, Mark. A drug test. Are you going to pass a drug test?'

'Oh. Yeah, I could do that.'

I followed Pamela's directions to the island's medical centre. 'Hi there, I'm here to pee in a cup,' I said to its receptionist.

'Oh, you must be the boy Pam called about,' she announced with delight. A room became free and I was sent to it. The doctor was a stumpy Black woman with breasts so large they swallowed her neck.

'Do these take very long?' I asked.

'Few minutes,' she mumbled back, writing my details onto a sticker.

'That's pretty quick.'

'Uh-huh.'

'You do a lot of these?'

'Uh-huh.'

'Pretty amazing we have this kind of technology.'

'Uh-huh.'

'Be honest, did you dream about this moment in medical school?'

'Uh-huh.'

She laid the sticker around a jar and handed it over. I went into the bathroom, filled, and gave it back. She pulled opened the machine on her desk's tray, retrieved a dropper resembling a turkey baster, sucked up a portion of my sample and squirted it in. Closing the tray with a click, she pressed a button labelled BEGIN. The machine whirred to life, producing a hum that kept growing. Then the room went dark – the sound of fluorescent globes ticking off throughout the building echoing around. A blackout.

'Shit. That bad, huh?' I asked into the pitch black.

A sigh returned.

'Uh-huh.'

6.

My first day was a Wednesday. It was still dark when I closed the door of the apartment and walked down the stairs. I'd set the alarm for 5.40 a.m. and had, somewhat miraculously, woken up by myself a few minutes early. Hannah's gentle snoring continued as I pulled pants on and closed the bedroom door as if defusing a bomb. I reached the end of the complex's driveway, and joined Maybank Highway to a sea of head and tail lights in both directions. How was the entire county already awake?

Joining the flow of traffic, I followed country roads to Kiawah as the sun rose. I'd watched so many sunsets in this country and the south, but this was my first sunrise. I found the land maintenance base after a few wrong turns. It was a large compound with a courtyard in its centre, an office building shaped like a U, a shed to store equipment, another full of boats and trailers, an expanse with the fleet of trucks parked throughout, and a dilapidated greenhouse in the back corner.

I walked through the compound to the office. The receptionist was a stout, older woman named Betty. She had a smile that made you smile even if you didn't want to, and the skin on the underside of her arms jiggled as she typed.

'You'll be just fine. The work can be pretty tough, but the guys are all great.'

'I've had some pretty wicked hangovers. This should be a walk in the park.'

'Oh, Pamela said you were funny!'

I wasn't sure what she meant.

I was introduced to my boss, Dale, one of the only other white guys working in a labouring role, with skin that wore years of blistering days in the sun in a way that didn't quite match the more youthful features of his face. He puffed his chest and raised his chin when speaking, seeming to hold the job and its variations in much higher esteem than anybody else there – especially more than the only other member of my new team, Benjamin.

'Come on, work started two minutes ago,' Dale yelled to Benjamin as he strode across the courtyard towards us, his hand slapping familiar greetings against the hands of all the other young Black workers he passed.

'Fix that watch of yours, man. Thing runs fast every morning,' Benjamin replied as he finally arrived. Dale shook his head, adjusted his hat, and continued gathering equipment.

The island, as far as land maintenance was concerned, was split into four zones, ascending as they moved away from base. Dale's team was tasked with the fourth and farthest zone.

'It's the best zone because we get the least amount of people and it requires the most amount of work, so we get to show up all these lazy fuckers,' Dale told me.

'Nah, it's the best zone because it's far away and your ass can nap on the way,' Benjamin chuckled, using all of his gangly frame to launch a leaf blower into our truck's tray when Dale was out of earshot. I already liked Benjamin.

We drove down the main road to the other end of the island.

THE ROADMAP OF LOSS

Walking paths ran alongside, sometimes disappearing behind a wall of foliage, sometimes tucking up close when the land rolled away into one of the lakes covering the island. The ride-on mower rumbled to life and Benjamin drove it down the trailer's ramp before disappearing around a corner. 'He likes working alone. That area takes about two hours to do properly, so we'll see him in three and a half, I reckon,' said Dale.

The leaf blower was heavier than it looked as I threw it over my shoulders. Dale and I were doing a section of road leading from a golf-course car park back to the main road. It looked fine to me – who expects a road to be spotless? We put earplugs in and started the blowers. Dale's fired up with one yank of the cord. Mine let out a few feeble gurgles before firing up on the fifth try. I followed as Dale showed me the proper technique for what he referred to as 'blowing'.

'Would you say you're a big fan of blowing?' I yelled over the noise as we walked and he forced debris off the road ahead.

'Yeah, because I'm good at it,' he said, turning his head side-on without looking back. 'It's all about patience, especially when you're working a big spot with someone else. I've had to show a lot of guys here how to blow properly.'

'That's real good, Dale.'

'Hey, I like that you're asking so many questions. I think you're gonna be a good addition to the team.'

'I'll do my best.'

The sun climbed over a fairway – the dew on each blade of grass shimmering. There was method to our movements. You'd hit roads early because they had the least shade coverage and traffic was minimal, and move to sections with shade when the heat was up. We blew a few roads then walked back to the truck. My shoulders and back already ached and I wanted a drink. I looked at my watch: it was 8.47 a.m.

The work was hardest in summer, I was told, as things grow rapidly during those warmer months. We spent a lot of time driving loops of our zone to check the condition of places. I had to keep my gloves on and seat belt off in case Dale saw a piece of rubbish by the side of the road. It was always the same: 'There's some trash over there,' he would say as he flicked on the hazards and pulled over. I would have to jump out of the truck, locate and snatch the rubbish, run and throw it into a bin in the tray, and get back in so we could keep moving. He'd get mad if I took too long, even though he never told me where the rubbish was. The switch for the hazards was worn down.

I ate lunch by myself in the corner of the breakroom. There were about twenty-five labourers – Dale and I two of only five who weren't Black. It was hard not to notice that all the people working inside air-conditioned offices were white. It was the first time I'd seen all the staff in one room. Many looked me over, but very few spoke to me.

One who did was an old Black man named Rupert. A big guy – wide and tall, but also frail, like an aged bear. He had a grandfatherly quality to him. A little hard of hearing, but a soft soul. I sensed there was a pack mentality among most of the staff and clear allegiances when Rupert stood up for someone bearing the brunt of insult, only to have it turned on him. He waved the comments away like flies buzzing near his head, and walk on with little steps. Dale told me there used to be a lot of fistfights until a one-strike policy for violence was introduced. 'These kids all think they're rappers about to make it,' he said. '"Keep pushing your mower, asshole," is what I think.'

My team went out again after lunch, and I fought the urge to fall asleep on the way back to Zone 4. We cleared fallen palm fronds from a roadside, throwing them behind bushes. It didn't matter where they went, as long as they couldn't be seen from the road. They had to be launched like a javelin, with the stalk facing forward, to get any distance. If you did it the other way around, the leaves would catch in the air and the frond would fall into a slumped heap a few feet in front of you. The sun was intense and the humidity inescapable. Every movement took a little more out of you. Soon you wondered if there was any more left to take, and somehow there always was.

I found myself panting, not because of exhaustion, but in some instinctual attempt to cool down. But it was no use. The air coming in felt even hotter and heavier than my insides, each breath making the overheating more intense, and giving the sensation my lungs were filling with steam. I began to appreciate Dale's strategy of getting work done in the early morning. He told me discomfort was something your body adapts to. I disagreed, and said it's something your mind does.

I sat in the lunchroom with the rest of the staff, waiting As the clock struck 3.30 p.m., a line formed around a small keypad on the wall, where staff clocked in and out. Each would reach the front of the queue, enter their code with four accompanying beeps, and walk away happier than before. I walked to the end of the other wing.

'Hi, Betty, I forgot to punch in this morning.'

'That's alright, darling. I'll get your hours from today over to payroll.'

'Thanks, Betty.'

I turned and walked down the hallway, stopped halfway and went back.

'Hey, Betty, you reckon we could do this every day?'

'Ha, yeah, right! You're a riot! Have a good night, Mark.'

'You too.'

Betty's arms resumed their jiggling. I went home with a feeling I was going to spend a lot of my life waiting for that machine.

7.

Thursday was more of the same, but there was energy in the compound come Friday morning. After another week of breaking their backs for $5.50 an hour, people were still excited about the weekend. I wondered how they managed either.

Dale sent me to the boat shed to fill a fuel canister. There was a rusty barrel with a pump on top resembling one side of a bicycle's pedal assembly, with a loose, splintered wooden handle. The pump's hose and nozzle were too heavy for an empty canister to support, so had to be held in place. The handle was hard to turn, and would only deliver fuel at a certain rate. Rotated too slowly, it couldn't work the stuff up the hose; too fast and it would collect pockets of air that spluttered as they passed through the nozzle, coughing fuel onto your skin and clothes. I wrestled the pump for five minutes and finished with a tired arm and a mostly full half-gallon canister.

We drove to Zone 4 and unloaded the trailer. Dale took off to tidy another spot with the ride-on. Benjamin and I started on an area consisting of eight lawns. 'Ain't no wrong way but the long way,' he explained. The technique was simple: trace the perimeter of a lawn counter-clockwise until you got back to where you'd started, then bring the mower's right wheels to the left of the mowed grass, go around again and keep doing it until you reached the centre. If done properly, even a convoluted shape could be trimmed without missing any spots.

The most complicated of my lawns was dotted with palm trees and curved from the road's edge to disappear into a lake in a steep descent. I traced along the top of the lawn, banging wheels into its bowed kerb whenever I added too much throttle. At one end of the edge, I turned to trim alongside a garden bed in a more or less straight line descending towards the lake. Reaching the bottom, I made another sharp left, tilting the weight of the mower onto its rear wheels and pivoting around. A few plants in the bed were crushed under my Chuck Taylors during the manoeuvre. The lake's edge had a vertical bank of mud which dropped about six inches from the grass into its cloudy water. I kept the right wheels as close to the small cliff as I could.

The further along the lakeside I moved, the steeper the hill rolling down to it became – soon angled enough that I had to place my left foot up the hill and lean away from the water. At the other end, I faced the mower uphill and placed myself between it and the lake. Opening the throttle, the front wheels lifted. I hadn't been emptying the mower's bag often enough and now there was too much weight behind its rear wheels. The handle plummeted, taking me with it. I lost my balance and slipped back – my leg plunging into the water and muddy bank underneath. The mower stalled and locked its rear wheels in place. I froze, positioned like a sprinter at the starting line, with hands stretched out ahead on the mower's grips, one leg bent underneath and the other extending into the lake behind.

There was silence without the mower running. I took a few deep breaths of relief but then, even through my foam earplugs, the sound. Pockets of air, held in perfect spheres by the pressure of water surrounding them, reaching its surface and bursting from their grimy shackles with distinct pops. I looked over my left shoulder and saw it; a still, matte shape interrupting the glossy surface of the lake, no more than an arm's reach from my sunken foot. I'd have thought it a moss-covered stone if it weren't so close. A dark red groove ran along the figure and up a ridged bump holding two slippery orbs, which disappeared for a moment as their stony surrounds swallowed them then retracted. I looked into them as they looked into me.

My right leg straightened beneath me, pulling the other from the water and launching me up the hill. I fell over, turning onto my arse and scrambling backwards up the hill on hands and feet. I stopped, too afraid to breathe, both of us motionless. I waited an eternity for it to burst from the water, launch up the hill and take me back in. But then, in an unrushed way, the rim of water surrounding the thing rose until it wasn't there anymore.

I finished the lawn but kept away from the lake, looking over to it every few seconds. 'Ah, you missed a few spots down by the water, but not bad for a first try,' Dale said as we all walked back to the truck. Benjamin pointed to my brown shoe and pants' cuff.

'You go for a swim, dude?' he chuckled.

'Almost. It's pretty slippery over there.'

'Be careful, there's 'gators in those waters,' Dale added.

'Yeah?'

'Yep, there's thousands on this island.'

'I saw one earlier.'

'Really? Was it close to you?'

'Kind of, why?'

'How close? You gotta tell me if one ever comes up to you. I'll have the boys put one through its skull. They can't become socialised.'

'Not very close.'

'Okay, good.'

I got home that afternoon to Hannah asleep in bed, painted by sunlight making its way between drawn blinds. I stripped off, put my clothes in the washing machine and rinsed mud from my sunburnt skin. Crawling into the bed beside her, I ran the backs of my fingers along her body outlined in sheet, and then I fell asleep.

8.

On the Saturday night, Hannah furled up beside me on the couch like a kitten. I stroked her hair and continued watching television and nursing my exhausted body. She brought a hand up my thigh and began trying to rouse me. When I declined, she got stroppy, responding with a locked bedroom door between us. My apology through the wood only resulted in her turning the music up.

Crossing James Island, the only one between Johns Island and downtown Charleston, I passed a bar recessed into a dirt parking lot. The gaps between trucks parked in its lot were too small to fit another, though I squeezed the Miata into one with ease. The courtyard at the rear of the place was like a large deck with no roof. It had a tree in the middle and a stage in the corner. The band played under fairy lights running throughout the tree and reaching out to meet the tops of the mural-covered walls and stage. On the opposite side was the bar; I took a seat and lit a cigarette. The scene gave me the same sensation I'd first had when I arrived in Charleston. The bartender drummed his fingers against the bar top in time with the music. He saw I was wanting and came over, flashing a smile through a perfectly sculpted goatee. He had the eyes of a child. His face could've wrinkled and decayed around them, but nothing was corrupting those eyes.

I ordered a beer, a shot of whiskey and we shook hands.

'Australia, eh? How'd you end up in Chucktown of all places?'

'It's a long story, Mick. But don't worry; there'll be plenty of time to tell it.'

'Yeah?'

'Yeah,' I said, feeling good, looking around as the band finished a song to the applause and whistles of their audience under the hanging lights. 'I think I'm gonna be here for a while.'

Hannah's car was out front when I returned to the apartment. I opened the bedroom door to find her sitting up against the bedhead with a lace top on and a book in her hands. The covers were draped over bent legs and a half-empty wine bottle sat on her bedside table.

'How was your night?' she asked.

'It was alright. And yours?'

She took her glasses off and put them next to the bottle. Then closed the book and did the same.

'I have a question, Mark.'

'Shoot.'

'Do you think I'm an idiot?'

'Excuse me?'

'Do you think I'm another one of the "dumb fucks" you talk about so often?'

'No, I don't.'

'Do you think I took you in off the street so you could use my bed and my body and then ignore me?'

'No. You're right, I'm sorry. I've just been exhausted.'

'I haven't asked for anything from you. Not even rent.'

'I know.'

She pulled the covers off and brought her legs apart. Her exposed carnation was in full bloom.

'Now this, I am not asking for.'

I scratched my beard, slipped my boots off and crawled onto the bed up to her. She reached down between her knees, ran her fingers through my hair and squeezed. Her head pivoted back as she bit her lip and ushered me downwards. I looked into her, took a deep breath, and paid what I owed.

9.

My days didn't get easier, I just became better at the processes. I mastered the early wake-up, pumping the fuel, locating the trash, steering the mower, when to cut myself off at the bar with the strung-up lights, and sensing what Hannah needed before she had to tell me. I drove across the bridge onto Kiawah Island while the radio played and light worked its way over the trees at the far end of the marshes.

It was Friday and the week had been even hotter than the one before. I pulled the cord and the mower sprang to life. Already I could do my area in just over half the time it had taken me the week before. I reached the lawn by the lake, emptied the bag and began. When I was finished, I shut it off and sat on the grass a few feet up from where I'd fallen, obscured from the road by a garden bed of tall ferns. I smoked a cigarette while the sky turned a lighter blue. Grass reflected the yellow of the sun and shadows moved in the cool air. I tilted my hat down to cover my eyes. After a minute, the figure rose, facing me – the movement so gentle the water around it did not wrinkle, nor the light skipping along its surface flicker.

'Mornin',' I said, blowing out smoke. 'How you going today?'
Nothing.
'Yeah, I hear that. Excited for the weekend?'

A blink.

'Oh, yes, sir, me too. Hey, you got a lady 'gator in another pond you go visit? What? Really? A few of them? Oh, you sly dog. I bet they like that scar, huh? How'd you get it, anyway?'

A bird landed on the branch of a tree in the distance and was chased away by another.

'Probably from making this lake *your* lake, I reckon. Well, don't mind me. I'm just keeping it nice for you. Besides, I already live with something that wants to bite my head off.'

It drifted a foot towards the bank.

'No, no, no. I wouldn't get close if I were you. That only ends badly.'

Another foot, now only four or so from the lake's edge. I stood.

'I'm serious, get the fuck away.'

Stepping towards the lake, I stomped so hard I almost slipped. It blinked again then retreated, disappearing into the water.

My chair in the lunchroom was always empty. People either respected it was mine or left it free because they wanted me in the corner. I didn't know most of the workers, but I was on friendly terms with more of them each day as word got around about where I was from. Groups would yell as I passed, 'Yo, Aussie!' or 'What's happenin', Crocodile Dundee?' always followed by laughter. I was a spectacle to them, but at least I wasn't getting in any fistfights.

One morning, the wipers of the Miata smudged rain across its windshield as I drove the dark, oak-lined road towards the island. I'd been working for weeks, but this was the first rainy day. The idea of working in drizzle wasn't appealing, though I thought it might be a nice change from the heat and humidity, and I needed the money. I arrived, went into the equipment shed and wheeled a mower out.

'No, no. None of that today,' Dale said, manhandling it from my grip.

'Why's that?'

'Can't mow wet grass.'

A few teams went out to clear fronds and debris from roads and paths. I'd hoped to get picked so I could sleep in the truck on the way out, but Benjamin, Dale and I were told to help in the greenhouse. It was a tired-looking thing, like an ancient temple held up only by the mildew clinging to its windows. The inside was configured like a classroom without chairs: a doorway at the front and walkway running its length with rows of benches extending to walls on either side.

We were to separate stacks of plastic pots and fit them into trays for growing seedlings. The pots were smaller than a handspan, pressed into stacks about two feet high. Each one stuck to the next – glued together by months of humidity and dirt since they were last used.

Rain tapped against the dirty roof as we worked in silence. It was an oppressive silence – the kind that makes you think even if you wanted to scream, nothing would come out. After a while, Benjamin threw his hands down against his bench across from mine at the back of the room.

'This shit is too boring. I'm losing my damn mind,' he growled.

Half of the room looked to him, including me. Benjamin unhooked the portable CD player from his belt and opened it to remove a disc. He walked to the front of the room to a dusty stereo sitting on the shelf. He ejected a CD and, without even a glance, tossed it like a Frisbee into the corner of the greenhouse to replace with his own. A loud bassline began thumping from the speakers – the badly produced demo tape of some not-so-talented rapper. I preferred the silence. Benjamin strutted back down the aisle to the hollers of his friends, pouting his lips and high-fiving each of them as he passed their bench. He spun on the spot, dipping the visor of his cap with one hand and tucking the thumb of the other into his belt as he thrust his hips and came up onto his toes. A little Michael Jackson. Reaching his bench, he looked at me. I bumped a fist into his waiting one. We smiled and I went back to my pots and trays.

'Boy, turn that shit off,' Rupert said from his bench nearest the front.

'Na-uh! I can't hear you!' Benjamin yelled back, still dancing.

'I'm sick of this Black trash.'

'Old man, you is Black!' yelled one of Benjamin's friends.

Half the room laughed.

'Yeah, but I'm the good kind of Black!'

The entire room laughed.

'And this shit's getting turned off right now,' he added.

'Don't do it. Don't you dare stop the music, old man. I'll kill your ass,' Benjamin said as Rupert approached the stereo and lowered the volume. A few of his allies stepped out from their benches with chests puffed towards Rupert.

'Oh, that so? That's the way it's gonna be? Alright then, I got something for you.'

Rupert turned from the stereo, and passed through the doorway at the front, his figure becoming distorted and blurred in the dirty glass as he walked away from the greenhouse. Nobody spoke as Benjamin's CD quietly segued onto another track. The tone had seemed light-hearted to me, but now tension filled the air. I looked to Dale. He shrugged and shook his head, returning to his work. After a minute, Rupert returned with a damp hat and shoulders.

'Here, told you I had something for your disrespectful asses.'

He reached a hand around to his back pocket and pulled it out. The room halted. Between his fingers was a case with a tape inside.

'The hell is that?' a squinting Benjamin asked from the back of the room.

'Ha! It's a cassette! Dude's got a cassette!' yelled one of the others, holding his gut, almost toppling over in laughter.

'Yo, why not grab a vinyl while you at it?' quipped another.

'You a fuckin' weird dude, Rupert, you know that?' from a third.

He ignored them, waving a hand by his ear as he shuffled to the player and pressed 'STOP'. He opened the cassette tray, slid his in and pushed it shut. The room was silent in anticipation. Even the rain seemed eager to know what was coming. I heard a guitar, strings, a drum beat, and then a piano that sounded soothing and familiar to me.

'Oh. Oh, alright, grandpa,' Benjamin said, getting into it, smiling and rolling his shoulders in circles alternating left to right. 'Not bad.'

The others who'd ridiculed Rupert also started swaying at their benches.

'Now this some real music. This here ... this gold ... this black covered in gold!' Rupert yelled to Benjamin, cranking the volume and clicking his fingers as he walked back to his bench.

It was coming to me. I'd heard this from the speaker of my mother's record player as a child. The bars of music repeated themselves a few times, and then a voice:

'Me and Mrs. Jones ...'

A trumpet came in during the first line and filled the room, sending a tingle down my spine that shot to every corner of me. I turned to Benjamin as the second line arrived, to see him serenading the lyrics towards me, his head ducking left and right in time with the beat.

'We got a thing goin' on ...'

The song caught on and spread, one by one. Soon we were all swaying in unison. I even saw hard-arsed Dale bopping his head. It was like a rehearsed performance I hadn't been told about. I smiled back at Benjamin, copying his head movement, swaying left to right as I clicked another pot into a tray.

'Yeah, get it, white boy,' he chuckled.

'*While the juke box plays our favourite songs . . .*'

The song built in me and I let it all go, joining in with the rest at the top of our lungs for the chorus, so loud we could've been heard all the way from the office.

'*Me and Mrs. Jones, Mrs. Jones, Mrs. Jones, Mrs. Jones*

We got a thing goin' on . . .'

I didn't have a family anymore, though I came pretty close to feeling like I did, that day inside a run-down greenhouse in South Carolina as rain tapped against the roof.

10.

The weeks fell away in a pleasurable way. Hannah and I began learning each other's rhythm. Soon there was a balance between us, with the days returning to the way they were in the beginning. We'd talk for hours, discussing everything under the sun. She was thinking about writing a book. 'They say everyone's got one in them,' she insisted. It seemed a bizarre sentiment to me; just having one in you wasn't the same as having a good one in you. Did everyone have one space expedition or brain surgery in them as well? Maybe I had a mass murder in me by the same token. I sipped my coffee and nodded.

My life there was peaceful. Soon I didn't worry about how much money I'd put aside, or the house in Melbourne, or anything at all. I stopped counting the days since I'd left home, or the days since I'd taken my stand of defiance against my father's route and his pointless letters. A drink and Hannah's touch felt better when I could enjoy them for what they were, and not just use them to forget about something else. I felt calmer in my own skin and safer within my own soul. And then came the hurricane.

Pamela and the rest of management sat us all in the lunchroom and laid it out. It was meant to hit the coast on the Saturday morning at around 2 a.m. 'Eh, a category three on the news always ends up being a one, maybe two,' Dale leant in and whispered to me. Management recommended evacuation, but also tempted us with a day of penalty-rate pay on the Saturday to help with clean-up. I asked for and was given the shift. Hannah was staying with a friend in Columbia for the weekend, and pleaded for me to go with her. I declined, stayed and went into work on the Friday feeling uneasy.

'How about you? You think it's gonna be that bad?'

A palm frond fell from a tree in the distance and landed in the garden bed below.

'Eh, what am I talking about? Of course you're not. Look at you – you're probably not afraid of anything. Alright, I'll see you next week, assuming I'm not killed later tonight.'

I stood and walked back to my mower from the lakeside.

After work, I showered, napped and scooped another boring meal into me before heading to my bar. It being open seemed a little optimistic but, when I arrived, the parking lot was so full I had to fold the Miata's side mirror in against the bumper of a truck to fit into a space. The place was overflowing with revelry and laughter – even more than on a regular Friday night when there wasn't a potentially fatal natural disaster rocketing towards us.

I nudged through people and up to an empty stool. Mick was halfway through taking an order from another group, but stopped when he saw me. He poured a harmful amount of bourbon into a cup, cracked open a PBR and slid them over without a word, then resumed the other order. I threw the shot down, gulped the beer and lit a cigarette. The buzz was comfortable and immediate, like getting into bed with someone who's been waiting for you – their warmth already spread throughout the sheets. I combed my hand through my hair and pushed it behind my ears while the band led into their next song.

THE ROADMAP OF LOSS

The air was electric, and the large trees in the parking lot could be seen through the courtyard's open top. They moaned and wheezed, trying to fight back against the mounting winds above. I was just one of the little beings below. A whole place full of them, who weren't just ready for the end, but were inviting it to sit down and have a fuckin' drink. Maybe it was the need to be around others. Maybe it was something else. It could be that fear is divided, not multiplied.

The wind was overbearing as I returned home, the Miata bullied across lanes as I drove past the golf course and over the bridge back to Johns Island. I walked up the stairs and unlocked the door. Lying in the bed, alone, I stared at the ceiling through the darkness while the wind howled and screamed all around. The storm seemed like a wild animal circling me. Each crescendo becoming more intense than the last, as if it were sniffing out my scent and closing in for the kill. The branches of the oaks banged against the bedroom window. I expected shards of glass to be shot into me at any moment and I waited for it. I longed for it. I wanted the roof to be ripped open. For the sky above to be exposed, wicked and laughing, or maybe wailing in sorrow. Whichever it was, in that moment, I wanted nothing more than for it to reach into the room, pull me out and destroy me.

I opened my eyes to the sound of talkback radio and a familiar number illuminated in green on the bedside table and was disappointed. It's funny. Sometimes, just when you think you can't surprise yourself anymore, you do. I thought I'd found peace, or it me, but something menacing had begun clawing at its cage inside me again.

I drove to the island, over fallen branches which snapped and banged against the floor of the car. There wasn't a lot of damage I could see, but it was still dark and the Miata's headlights only worked if you had a relaxed definition of 'function'. A thick, fallen branch blocked part of the oak-lined road ahead. The driver of a truck with orange, flashing lights waved cars heading to or from Kiawah through a few at a time. Passing, I saw the blinking hazard lights of a car – its rear end crumpled around a tree's trunk just below where it had snapped. The windshield was badly smashed. I couldn't tell if there was anybody inside.

At the compound, Dale was nowhere to be seen. I searched until someone told me he hadn't taken the shift. It was the first time I'd worked without him and I felt anxious when I was partnered with a guy I'd never spoken to. Trey was his name, a black kid, tall as a tree but skinny as a twig. We were given a section of the main drive through Zone 2 and a pickup. We drove in silence. I looked around. There was damage, sure, but not complete destruction.

'You lived through many of these hurricanes?'

He ignored me, staring down the drive.

'Trey?'

'Trying to listen to my music, dude,' he murmured, not breaking eye contact ahead.

'Okay.'

I looked back at the passing gardens and thought it was strange. The radio wasn't on.

We gathered fallen branches into piles, threw them into the truck's tray, drove back to base and pushed them into the wood chipper. The mess was never-ending. I took to throwing piles onto front laws when Trey wasn't watching. There was next to no traffic. I assumed most of the island's residents had fled.

We worked. I tried to make conversation but was always countered by apathetic dismissal, finding myself wanting to punch Trey in the head a little harder with each non-response. He acted like he was better than me and I didn't like it. 'What makes you such hot shit?' I asked him in my mind. I kept reminding myself it would be the last time I'd work with him and relaxed clenched hands. At the end of the day, the eight of us who'd come in clocked off.

THE ROADMAP OF LOSS

I walked back to the Miata and saw Trey getting into his car.

'Yo, Trey!' I yelled to him.

He turned towards me. I'd intended to tell him to fuck himself, but there was the strangest glimmer in his eye.

'... You have a good night, alright?' I said.

He nodded, got in his car and was gone.

I arrived on Monday morning like any other, walking into the compound, smoking a cigarette and spinning keys around my finger. Someone I usually spoke to stared in silence as we passed each other, then so did another. Dale walked over – a change from his normal morning routine of pretending he was the only person there – and patted me on the shoulder.

'Pam wants to see ya.'

'Oh. What about?'

His face was blank.

'Just get up there.'

I was fucked. Just my luck a driver of the one or two cars that passed me on Saturday had seen me hurling shit into people's yards. I was more afraid of Hannah's reaction than dealing with Pam. I stepped into her office and she gestured that I close the door and take a seat.

'How are you, Mark?'

'I'm okay. How are you?'

'I could be better.'

'Yeah, me too.'

'You worked with Trey on Saturday, correct?'

'Yes, that's correct.'

'And did anything seem out of the ordinary to you?'

'Not really, no. Just piling all the debris I saw and bringing it back here.'

'I see. Well, uh . . .' She breathed in. 'Most of the other guys already know, but, Trey was found. By his mother. On Sunday morning.'

'I wasn't aware he was missing.'

'No, Mark. Trey was . . . *found*. He took his own life on Saturday.'

'Fuck me.'

'I know, it's awful. We're shocked, and trying to understand what happened here. Did he say or do anything that seemed unusual to you? Anything out of the ordinary? I only ask because, well, you may have been the last person to see him alive.'

'No . . . I don't know him. I mean, didn't know him. Not one bit. I wouldn't know what was usual or unusual.'

I kept talking as the alternative to vomiting.

'It's okay, Mark. I know he kept to himself; you couldn't have known. If anything does come to mind, feel free to reach out. If you're not okay, we've organised counselling for some of the others. You're more than welcome to attend.'

I left the office and walked back to the yard. More people had arrived, which meant more eyes on me. I pushed the mowers onto the trailer and filled the canister. Benjamin wasn't there. 'They were pretty close,' Dale told me in a monotone as he heaved a blower into the tray. The truck hummed across a paradise Trey had decided he wanted no part of anymore. We did our regular day's work, but Dale didn't comment on my technique or anything else. We headed back to base. There was a piece of trash on the side of the road. We drove right past.

After the shift, I went to the Miata, leant against the fender and smoked. Three guys walked over.

'Hey, man, how you doing?' one asked, his head slouched.

'I'm feeling pretty fuckin' shitty. I can only imagine how you guys are feeling.'

The three nodded and the same guy stepped closer.

'Did he ... did he say anything to you? I mean, why would he do this? He was so young, man.'

His words were laboured, like he was choking on pain.

'No, he didn't. Seemed like a quiet guy. I couldn't even get small talk out of him.'

'And did you say anything?'

'What? What do you mean?'

His tone changed.

'Did you say something to him? Put some fuckin' idea in his head?'

'Of course not.'

'He never would've done this. That wasn't him, man. The fuck did you do?'

He started moving towards me. The other two held grabbed and him back.

'The fuck did you do? Tell me! That wasn't Trey, man! That wasn't Trey!'

His screams became cries. Tears ran down his face as he matched the strength of two men. The friends clutching him began crying too, and then I almost was.

Finally exhausting himself, he slumped over, struggling to get air in. The others helped him back into the compound. A few workers watched from afar. One was Rupert, who let out a long, sad breath, shook his head, got in his car and left. I started the Miata, drove straight past the apartment and to my bar.

'Ah, shit, man,' Mick said, sliding me another drink. 'Don't beat yourself up. He probably made that decision long before turning up to work that day. Those guys was just upset and looking for something to blame.'

He moved to the other end of the bar, picked up a glass and began polishing it.

'I guess we all metabolise pain differently,' I mumbled into my glass.

'What's that?' Mick asked.

'Nothing.'

I threw down my shot and wondered what the point of my hurting had been if I couldn't recognise it in another. I lit a cigarette and looked up at the golden trees swaying in afternoon sun above the courtyard. They looked peaceful, now that the storm had passed.

11.

Things were never the same for me on the island after Trey's act. A lot of people kept their distance, whether out of resentment or fear, I wasn't sure. I remained close with staff I spoke to often, but there'd never been such distance between me and the rest.

'There's something about that guy,' a friend of Benjamin's whispered to him as I passed them sitting on a bench.

'Nah, man, come on. He's cool,' Benjamin muttered.

'Nah, man, he ain't,' he refuted, hiding his mouth behind a cup. 'Dude's cursed, like a bad omen or something.'

'I can fucking hear you,' I said, stopping and turning towards them.

The guy got up and walked away quickly. Benjamin shrugged. 'Man ... I'm sorry,' he said.

He meant it, but it didn't mean a whole lot to me.

I didn't tell Hannah what happened. I'd wanted to, a few times, to confide in someone about how I felt, but always found myself changing the subject. Part of me thought it was none of her business. The other part didn't want whatever curse I carried around with me to spread any further.

'I keep thinking it's like he was on a tightrope, and I could've been the hands that balanced him or the winds that blew him off. I didn't make him do it, but maybe I didn't do enough to stop it either.'

I sat right at the edge, skimming the soles of my shoes along the surface of the lake.

'Mick's right, though, I guess. The guy fought and lost the battle in his own mind. Nothing I or anybody else could have said would've changed it.'

He floated a few feet from the bank. I could've reached out and grabbed him, and he me.

'Ever get the feeling nobody's life has ever been better for having you in it?'

I butted my cigarette into the mowed lawn and threw it into the garden bed.

'I'm running out of places to hide.'

Neither of us moved. We each looked at the monster in front of us.

12.

The final weeks before the mercury dropped were the worst of them. Another area was added to Zone 4 in preparation for house construction and we weren't given extra team members. Foul water sat still in deep, dirty puddles all around the new area, attracting mosquitoes and other bugs as big as your nose. They would fly close to your face, landing on and irritating you, if not worse. A decision had to be made each morning as to whether you'd coat yourself with the oily bug spray required to stop the buzzing onslaught. You could have your peace, but the stuff was so viscous it sealed in heat. A one-hundred-degree day felt like one-twenty with the stuff on.

Days of ruthless sun and heat without rain would pass, but those goddamn puddles never seemed to dry out. You could be collecting fallen fronds from dry earth one moment and be submerged in filth the next, stepping through what looked like long, dry grass. If you fell for one of the island's booby traps, you'd be able to smell it emanating from your sock for the rest of the day. If you didn't, then someone else surely would and the truck would stink all the same.

I stood on the balcony one evening and smoked a cigarette. Hannah joined me as I looked out listening to the oaks brush against each other in the breeze. That road, that little section of dirt running between trees, had never failed to soothe me somehow. And on that evening, under a pastel sky, it still managed to, the same way it had when I first looked out over it.

'Have you walked to the end yet?' Hannah asked.

'No, I haven't.'

'Do you want to?'

'Yeah, I do.'

We strolled with an arm around each other as light left the sky. The road was straight for maybe two hundred yards, oaks lining both sides. The end was marked with a swinging gate the width of the road, no higher than my waist. It was locked – a sign indicating private property lay beyond. I leant onto it, wondering why I'd taken so long to walk down that road, why I always preferred to appreciate things from afar. Maybe it was because they couldn't disappoint you in the same ways. Maybe it was so I couldn't disappoint them.

The road continued then circled around on itself, with smaller trails darting off and disappearing into forest at thirds of its revolution. On the inside of the loop stood an oak. I'd never been stunned by a tree before, but this one was something else; similar to the others, yet more mature, somehow wiser. Deeper fissures sat in its bark and its trunk was thicker. It didn't move in the breeze, the air not worthy to disrupt. I felt sheepish in its presence, as though my being there was something this tree had allowed. The thing had just seen so much time. So much more than I had, and so much more than I ever would. We could both age another day and it would mean a lot more to me. Maybe its pollen had laid birth to the oaks lining the road some centuries ago and now they looked towards it like a father.

'You never did tell me what this forest is,' I said.

'What do you mean? It's forest.'

'Yeah, but who owns it? It must be whoever put this sign and gate up.'

THE ROADMAP OF LOSS

'Oh. Yeah, there's a story about it. You want to hear?'

'Sure.'

'Okay, well, this land was plantation. All of it. Proper plantation – they held slaves here,' she said all too casually.

'Right.'

'And the owner, he had a young daughter who became ... close with one of the slaves. They had to keep it secret and sneak around, because the father would have lost it if he found out. So they had this affair. It went on for months – they were very much in love, apparently. Then, one night, they're caught. The father is furious, not just with the slave, but with his daughter and anyone who knew it was happening. So, I guess as punishment for the lovers and a message to the rest, he has the slave hanged and doesn't take him down for weeks. He wanted everyone to know the consequences for that kind of behaviour.'

'Jesus ...'

'It gets worse. So, the daughter is mortified, as you would be, and then a month later, realises she's pregnant with the slave's child. She knows she and the child will never be accepted by her father, so –'

'No ...'

'Yep. She hangs herself as well. Right from the same place her father had her lover and the father of her unborn child hanged.'

'That's awful.'

'I know, it's messed up. And,' she said, pointing to the father oak, 'you see that branch in the middle to the left? The especially flat one?'

'Yes.'

'That's where the rope was tied. Twice.'

I stared, almost seeing the scene play out ahead. The oak was wise only because it had witnessed things it never should have – its trunk thick because it had supported the burden of dead bodies and tired souls. Night had arrived. I turned and began walking back to the apartment.

'Hey, where are you going?' Hannah asked, running up beside me.

I didn't reply. We walked along my paradise road that had been an artery of pain for so many and it no longer soothed me. It didn't matter if the story was true or not. Maybe there was good reason things always looked better from afar.

13.

'You ready?' Dale asked, smiling.

'For the last six weeks,' I said, launching a blower into the tray.

It was a Friday and our last scheduled day on the new area. Consistent with the rest of our luck in the area over the last month, Benjamin had been called in for a random drug test which would take most of the morning. The weather was cooling off and most of the hard work had been done in the previous weeks. No more felled trees, chainsaws and splinters. No more dirty, stinky puddles. No more bugs the size of small dogs. Even I found myself a little excited; I could almost taste Hannah and a beer in the air.

Dale drove and I napped with my cap tipped down, waking as we passed my lawn by the lake. The outlines of trees were drawn in shadows across the water in the morning sun. I smiled and gestured a lazy wave towards it.

'What are you doing?' Dale asked.

'Just saying hi,' I answered.

We arrived at the new area and began laying hay in its garden beds. Benjamin arrived when the sun was sitting high in the sky, dropped off by two guys in management, Rodney and Matt. I found it strange they'd tasked themselves with dropping him off at the furthest reach of the island and had used Rodney's blue Toyota Tacoma to do it, but it was Friday and I felt good, so shrugged it off and continued.

Dust billowed from the hay when you patted it against the earth. You either worked slowly enough for it to not reach your nostrils, or held your breath and laid the hay in fast, aggressive bursts. Both were exhausting in different ways under a blistering sun. We began on the final garden. Already I was starving from all the running around, finding myself daydreaming about chicken and biscuits. A branch gave way and fell somewhere in the distance with a deafening, echoing crack, pulling me from my trance. I kept working, clawing handfuls of hay, throwing it down, patting and moving forward, one foot at a time.

We arrived at the fork in the road just before base. Right took you up a side road where the labourers parked; left took you into the compound via a small parking lot with reserved spaces. We turned left as we always did and the trailer wobbled and banged over the speed hump. Rodney's Tacoma was parked in one of the spots with a group huddled around the tray, blocking it from sight. Dale drove into the compound and parked near the greenhouse. I reached the steps leading up to the lunchroom at the same time some guys who'd been standing around Rodney's truck did.

'Mark, dude, you gotta check that shit out,' one said, pointing back to the Tacoma.

'Why? What is it?'

'Go see for yourself,' said the other with a grin as they went upstairs and disappeared through the flyscreen door.

The few still loitering around the truck started heading for the lunchroom.

'Ooh, that boy got it,' one said as they passed.

'Wish I had a camera!'

I crossed the now quiet, empty parking lot towards the Tacoma.

Its rear suspension was riding low, the sidewalls of its tyres bulging. With caution, I peered into the tray and my heart stopped. More scaled spikes than I could count ran back and forth inside. Two times it had to be folded to fit – so much bigger than I'd ever imagined. I reached a hand in, slowly halving the distance over and over until I made contact. It was coarse in a way that made me struggle to believe we were both flesh.

I ran fingertips up a ridged bump, alongside a familiar, dark red shape. Opposite it, a dime-sized hole tunnelling deep and disappearing into darkness – some dried blood streaking away from the opening. There was a lump in my throat. I stroked lightly as if to not wake him, though I knew those eyes would never open again.

'I'm sorry. I told you not to get close. You weren't afraid of anything ... but you should have been afraid of me.'

14.

Summer was almost over. Hannah steered conversation like she normally did, but this time it was about moving somewhere, perhaps back north. I could tell she wanted to know, without asking, if I'd go with her. I feigned naivety to avoid the subject, certain she would never come out and say it straight, and she never did. She wanted all of me and I only ever gave her crumbs. I was the biggest coward on the planet.

I went into work each day as usual, but there was less and less to do. They would downsize the staff soon. I sat by the lake with my feet at its edge and looked over the still, empty water. Nothing was growing with the same tenacity as before.

I began to feel like a guest in the apartment and then realised that's all I ever really was. 'Home' was just a term I'd all too vaguely used to feel like I belonged to it and it to me. None of the furniture was mine, or the framed pictures, or the vacuum cleaner. I didn't own the forks or the spoons, the mugs I drank my coffee from or the glasses I tipped whiskey into. I was a fraud.

Weeks slipped by and then we were all seated in the lunchroom again. There was another hurricane forming near the gulf. It was a big one – even Dale looked nervous. 'This is a legitimate category four, people,' said Pamela. Kiawah Island was being evacuated, not at the choice of its residents but by decision of the governor, and so too was the entirety of Charleston County.

The land maintenance team spent the next few days preparing the island for the worst. Any branch that looked susceptible to coming down was sawed off and put through the chipper. All debris was cleared. Bins were collected and placed inside buildings before they could become projectiles. On the final day of work, the fleet of trucks was moved to a section of higher ground on Johns Island, and with that, an uncertain, 'I'll see you when I see you,' was shared between all the staff. I shook Dale's hand and left.

When I got back to the apartment, Hannah and I began preparing. I found it a little exciting, but Hannah looked sunken. We were packing her life away to protect it from a storm that didn't care. Her reflection sat in a framed photo of her parents held in her hands. They were up in Virginia and worried. The phone hadn't stopped ringing. I watched as she rubbed her fingers against the glass of the frame and held it to her chest. She had no idea how lucky she was to be able to feel that kind of sad.

We filled every pot and pan to the brim with water and placed them in the bathroom next to the filled tub so there'd be drinking water even if there weren't working taps. I packed everything I had into my bags, not knowing how long we'd be gone for. We carried the mattress into the living room and laid it next to the sliding doors to the balcony, ready to be propped up against the glass come morning.

I stepped out onto the balcony to collect candles then lit a cigarette in the wind. My jacket was still there, hanging limp over the railing around the corner with a light coat of moss. I lifted it by the collar. The right side looked decent, but transitioning across the back in splotches which became the entire surface, was a darker shade of

THE ROADMAP OF LOSS

wrinkled brown. By the time it reached the left sleeve, the leather was stiff, with a tough, scaly surface. I brought it inside and showed Hannah. 'Are you going to get rid of it now?' she asked.

'Not now,' I said, putting it next to my bag on the floor.

That night, Hannah slept with her head on my chest. I listened to her gentle breath as I looked up through the branches of the oaks and tried to catch a glimpse of the moon and stars. A familiar nausea was growing in my gut.

Hannah left for Columbia the next morning. I slept for a few more hours, then loaded my bags into the Miata, a task I had not missed. It was late when I left. The evacuations had been taking place for the last three days, and the hurricane was due the following. I drove across James Island and through downtown Charleston. The winds were savage and the only other cars on the road were the occasional emergency service vehicle flying past with sirens blaring. It felt like the end of the world.

I arrived at Hannah's friend's place in Columbia that evening. His name was Chris. He had a modest apartment and a good heart. The three of us went drinking. Hannah checked out first, slouching over in the booth while Chris and I went toe to toe. He darted to the bathroom after a few more. I declared me the winner and raised a toast to myself as Hannah snored against the table.

We returned to Chris's apartment, and Hannah and I collapsed onto his inflatable mattress. Hannah reached back and squeezed my hip, pulling me in close. Our bodies rolled and gyrated on top of the compressed air without finesse or rhythm. Two drunks holding onto each other for dear life. We both tensed with everything we had as I came deep into her then relaxed. She turned her head back to me with sad eyes.

'Mark.'

'Yes?'

'I don't love you.'

'I know.'

We stayed another night and kept an eye on the news. A low-pressure zone in the Atlantic had steered the storm out to sea one hundred miles south of South Carolina, and roads were being reopened. We packed the cars and said our goodbyes to Chris. I kissed Hannah before she got in her car. 'I'll see you soon,' she said, as our interlaced fingers pulled apart. I followed her along country back roads to avoid flooded interstates and traffic, but as we hit congestion near Charleston, I could no longer see her. At some point, we had lost each other.

I drove through downtown and onto James Island in the early afternoon sun. Traffic lights were down at all intersections – police officers standing by their cars waving me on. I drove the empty roads alone, past my bar with the strung-up lights, and over the bridge to Johns.

Pulling off Maybank into the complex, I saw my paradise road. It was carnage. Huge branches hung by threads of bark from the oaks, those with less grit littering the road below. I pulled up on the dirt, shut off the engine and then it was silent. Hannah was still stuck in traffic somewhere. I leant against the fender and looked up through the damaged oaks. The sky was tired now, only able to muster the palest of blues like a sigh. There was no rage left and the air sat still, without even the energy to move a leaf.

Everything around me was too still and quiet. The place was a photograph and I was just in the way. The storm had come and, like everything must sooner or later, passed. Had it gotten what it wanted from this place?

I put my apartment key in Hannah's letterbox and breathed the fragrance of the oaks one last time. I started the Miata, dropped the top, spun the flint and threw up dirt as I bucked through a U-turn. Weaving through downtown Charleston, I headed south. A hurricane can be steered, but it can't be stopped.

August 17th, 1977

My dear,

I have been wrong about many things, but not Savannah. I left the city a few days after my last letter and headed south, staying in Miami but finding myself underwhelmed. I feel it's taking more and more to keep me away from you and Mark, and one day soon there won't be anything in this world that's enough to. Perhaps I've finally cured the itch and am ready to come home. Or maybe all of this just feels wasted because it's not being experienced with the two of you.

    I am tiring of all this movement. My body, my mind and my soul have stayed strong for longer than I ever expected they would. Now I think they remain strong only to find a place to rest and be soft for a while, like a hunter exhausting a last shred of will to catch prey. Could a hare spell the end for a lion? There's a distance between us which can't be measured in miles, yet I feel is becoming wider and wider. I'm not sure I have the energy to traverse it

    From Miami, I've gone much further south – a feat I didn't know possible until I was told a few weeks ago. I have trekked the Overseas Highway across the Florida Keys. They are a series of islands extending from the southernmost tip of Florida into the Gulf of Mexico like a wasp's stinger, all connected by a single road spanning some huge distances of the tropical water. Each of them is beautiful. Stress is not in the language here. I was spending a day or two on each key and then going onto the next, but have now reached the final land, Key West, where I've remained for a week.

    Key West seems like the edge of the earth in many ways. The highway steers you here, guiding, lifting and ushering you on, and then, before you know it, it's finished and you have nowhere else to go. This island feels very much like the end. But what does one do when they reach the end? I suppose you either keep going and fall off *or you turn around. Could one stay there indefinitely – teetering on the edge of the end? Well, I guess that depends on how you got there and what you've got coming up behind you. Seems silly not to think a man always has the chance to turn back around.*

1.

I reached Miami in eight hours. South Beach was a grid of flickering neon, expensive cars and even more expensive women. A multistorey car park with a boom gate and unmanned booth sat a few blocks from the beach. I stopped across the road from it and got out of the Miata. Bringing a pointed finger from the highest point of the windshield's frame to my ribcage in a straight line, I held it there and walked to the boom gate. The underside of its arm touched the top of my knuckle. With my other hand, I pushed up and felt some give in the mechanism. I drove the Miata over, lifted myself out of the seat, pushed the gate up and drove underneath with an inch to spare.

I filled my backpack with essentials and wandered until I found a room, then showered and walked to Ocean Drive. It was a zoo. A man asked if I wanted to make my night a whole lot better. I wasn't sure if he was a pimp or a drug dealer, but I declined and kept moving. All of the bars had loud scenes I didn't care for, but one had women in bikinis out front handing people free drink vouchers. I took one and entered.

There was a stage inside with dancers straight out of a thirteen-year-old boy's imagination, shaking and jiggling for an eager audience.

I liked the Latin music. I didn't understand a word but it made me happy. I tried to redeem my voucher.

'Only valid for a third drink after the purchase of two,' the bartender told me through his dead face.

'Okay, can I start a tab then?'

'No tabs, cash upfront.'

I pulled a ten-buck note from my wallet, ordered two beers and redeemed the voucher for a whiskey. I smiled at two women sitting nearby. They arched their brows and turned away before asking the same bartender to close their tab, which he did. I said hello to a woman in a red dress who looked me up and down, scoffed and walked away. Everyone in the place was an asshole. I would've fit right in if I'd had the money.

I went to the bathroom and caught myself in the mirror. My shirt was tattered, dirty and unironed. I was as brown as some of the Latinos in there, but it was from pushing mowers in the sun, not from any shared heritage. My hair was getting long, with streaks of sun-bleached blond. My beard was thick and now covered half of my neck.

Crazy blue eyes stared back at me through the mess. I was having an identity crisis, stuck somewhere between cartoon character and serial killer. This was the part of being on the road I had not missed. The isolation, the loneliness, the feeling you were a pinball bouncing between places you didn't belong. The woman in the red dress may have had a brick where her heart should've been, but she also had a point.

2.

Miami was too big to wander on foot and South Beach was a much nicer place to be during the day. I had no need to explore – being there was just more box-ticking. I walked Ocean Drive in the sunshine to the faraway sounds of waves crashing into sand. The bars made their trade at night. If they were open during the day, it was to cover the lease, and they took what they could get by offering cheap drinks. I stopped at each and had one or two. I floundered past a homeless man who asked me for a cigarette. I took one out for him, one for me, lit them and we smoked together. He complained about America, as most Americans do.

'All I'm sayin' is,' he said, dragging through the cigarette and putting his other hand on the hip of his shit-stained camouflage pants in a very sophisticated way, 'if you're gonna wear your Nazi uniform, then you have to wear it above ground as well as below ground, ya know?'

'I think so.'

'What's the use in wearing an ideology half of the fuckin' time?'

'There isn't one. You're damn right.'

'People just got no class; changing their values to suit a crowd like they change clothes. Bunch of animals if you ask me.'

'Amen.'

We parted ways. I liked the guy. He may have just been the sanest person I'd ever met.

I returned to the motel that afternoon after another tour of the bars. I struggled up the stairs to my floor and heard music echoing from a room, and the laughter of girls. The floor's bathroom door was open and two Latinas were doing their makeup with a portable radio on the sink.

'Hey there. Are you gonna be much longer?' I asked.

One of them froze with a mascara wand to her eye while the other looked at me, chewed her gum and sulked.

'Okay, I'll come back in five.'

I went into my room and closed the door. It didn't block out the music. I thought about Hannah. Did she sit on that couch with her legs crossed, waiting for me to come back until reality seeped in? What did she do then? Did she flip the mattress back onto the living room floor, beat her fists into it and use it to muffle a scream? Or did she pour herself a drink, turn on some music and dance through the apartment? Leaving like I did was rotten, but I was rotten; so maybe leaving her was the least rotten thing I could do. Shit. I didn't know. Where was my homeless friend with the camouflage pants? He'd know.

I needed to piss. I walked back to the bathroom and got the same reception of repulsion.

'I really need to use the bathroom.'

They looked at each other and whispered something in Spanish. I couldn't understand a word but the tone said enough.

'Hello? I need to piss. Me es, ah, need'a to piss'o. Pronto.'

They ignored me and went back to the mirror.

'Alright then.'

I stepped past and lifted the toilet seat. One of them started yelling and the other screamed when I pulled it out.

THE ROADMAP OF LOSS

'Sorry, me no comprende,' I said over the noise, opening my tap onto the floor and steering it back towards the bowl.

They screamed in disgust and ran from the bathroom. A moment later, one leant back in, grabbed their radio off the sink and spat on me.

'Gracias, really,' I said.

I went back to my room, locked the door and listened to the sounds of the street below as the sky turned dark.

The next morning, I walked back to the parking lot. The booth was manned now by an old security guard. He had black skin and a white beard. He watched as I passed him and headed towards the lifts. There was a sign with a list of rates. A lost ticket was $15. Still less than the cost of the two nights I was there, but $15 I couldn't spare.

'Hey,' I said, turning to him. 'You look like you could use a coffee.'

'Do I?'

'Absolutely. Must get boring sitting in that booth all day.'

'It does.'

'Come on, let's go get you a coffee around the corner then.'

'I cannot leave this post during my shift, sir.'

'Really?'

'Really.'

'Even to shit?'

'Even to shit.'

I started the Miata, dropped the top and negotiated ramp after ramp. I didn't know what I was going to do when I reached the bottom. The guard was still in the booth. I pulled up and he looked down at me from his window.

'It's the darnedest thing, but I think I've lost my ticket.'

'That's alright, happens all the time.'

He reached behind him towards a clipboard covered in registration numbers and dates. He struggled with it until the clip cleared the head of the nail in the wall it hung from.

'Reckon we could let it slide this one time?'

'No, sir, that's not possible.'

'Come on, man. Look at me. I'm not asking you this from a Porsche.'

'Not happening, sir.'

He wasn't budging. That's what happens to a man's humanity when he's not allowed to take a shit. He gets filled to the brim with it for five bucks an hour and then there's no room left for an imagination or a soul.

'Oh wait, I know where it would be,' I said, fidgeting through the glovebox and my pockets.

He blew out air between his lips and turned to face the wall behind him. The clipboard tapped against the head of the nail a few times until it found its way through the hole. I pretended to search a little longer, then threw my hands up and slapped them down against my thighs.

'No luck. Well, shit, I guess those are the breaks. Write me up, sir.'

He turned and reached back for the board again. I pushed the shifter into first and rolled forward a few feet. The head of the nail caught against the edge of the clip like it had before. I reached past the windshield and pushed against the exit gate. It lifted. Not as much as the other, but it lifted.

The guard turned back. I brought the revs up and let the clutch out. The arm banged against the Miata as I forced my way under. 'Hey! Stop, now!' he yelled, opening the door of the booth and running out after me. I turned onto the street and punched it. Another driver slammed their brakes and horn as I took off down the street. The guard made it all of forty feet before he stopped, panting, and threw his hat to the ground. I swung a right through a red and was gone.

3.

The problem with a map is everything looks so small. The problem with a letter is you only ever know what the person who wrote it wants you to. My father didn't write about things that weren't pretty. He didn't write about the traffic jams or sunburn or the mindless ticking of a million gas bowsers or the dark thoughts one has while being on the road. I suppose he wrote for a particular audience. It sure kept my mother believing the fantasy.

Ringing echoed for what felt like minutes as I tapped my foot against the floor of a roadside phone booth, then it stopped.

'Hello?'

'Hey. It's Mark.'

Silence.

'Claire? Are you there?'

'Yes.'

'How have you been? Is now not a good time? I have so much to tell you.'

'Where are you?'

'Southern Florida, on my way to the Keys from Miami,' I said at pace, feeling hopeful for the first time in days at the sound of her familiar voice. 'It's beautiful. You should see the car I got. It's an absolute heap – you'd love it.'

Silence again.

'I figure I can probably make it to Key West by lunchtime then read the next letter and figure out where to go after – it's only ten in the morning here.'

'Four months.'

'Four months?'

'Four months since I last heard from you.'

'Shit ... I just got swept up, I'm sorry. Things, and this place, have been a little crazy, and I was meaning –'

'Fuck you. I didn't know where you were; I didn't know if you were safe; I didn't know if you were alive. Do you know how many calls I made trying to find out where you were? I've gone to bed feeling sick every night for the last four months, for what? Just to find out you've been perfectly fine, gallivanting around the United States like some cowboy?'

'I'm sorry.'

'No, you're not. You're never sorry, just out of luck. You know, for a guy who's so pissed off it happened to him, you're pretty good at abandoning people.'

'Claire, please –'

'No. No more. I'm glad you're alive and well, I really am, but I'm not your doormat. I hope you do find whatever the fuck it is you think you're going to over there, because god knows you're going to deserve whatever comes your way.'

'Wait, I just –'

'Goodbye, Mark. Don't call me again.'

The line went dead. I slowly returned the handset to its cradle as trucks and cars roared by the booth, pushed my hands into my jean pockets and walked back to the Miata.

THE ROADMAP OF LOSS

It hit 10 a.m. as I reached the southern tip of Florida's mainland and was thrust above the water by the Overseas Highway. Dark grey and uninterrupted blue traded the sky as I drove past Key Largo and headed to the sea. Something about the drive reminded me of being a child at the beach. I was not a strong swimmer, never having the confidence to join those bobbing heads further out. Each time a bridge took me aloft from an island – and I watched it disappear in the rear-view mirror – I felt the same pinch in my gut I had as a child when lifted over a wave but not able to feel the sea bed as I came down on the other side. Those little slices of dread when my mouth and nose and eyes would go under even though I had my legs stretched out, desperately reaching for something to stand on. 'This is it,' I would think as the unforgiving water surrounded me. Then the next island would arrive like sand against my toes and, with a push, I'd be able to breathe again. The Keys were paradise, no doubt, but I had an unshakeable feeling of vulnerability and hopelessness there.

More islands and bridges – all larger than I'd anticipated. I filled the tank halfway across one of them. A woman had her photo taken beside the Miata while I paid. I came out and said she could sit in it. She looked over the interior and declined. I kept moving. Claire's words ricocheted in my head. The sand, water and trees were so beautiful, and in their company I'd never felt uglier and less deserving.

I neared the end of the next bridge and again felt the sand against my toes as Conch Key appeared. I moved towards its centre on the thin tip of land poking out to meet the bridge. To the right of the road ahead, where the land widened, was a motel – a building of pale yellow and blue with a swordfish on the side. A sandy car park and beach lay between it and the sea. Mesmerised, I almost drifted off the road. Traffic slowed me to a stop near it. I stared and felt ease. An oasis thirty feet from an interstate. 'That would be a nice place to die,' I thought aloud. Then the traffic started moving.

I reached Key West with no idea what to do. I parked in the lot of a small Irish bar, went in and had lunch. Flyers of companies operating on the Florida Keys were littered about. Snorkelling, fishing, water skiing, happy faces doing happy things. I couldn't even imagine mine contorting that way anymore. The bartender told me she'd just moved to Key West. I asked why.

'Just to get away.'

'From what?'

'I don't know ... life, I suppose.'

'The whole thing or just a bit of it?'

'I guess a bit of it.'

'Which bit?'

She poured a drink for somebody else, not resuming the conversation but standing close enough I knew she wanted to.

'What was his name?'

'Miguel.'

'Death or a break-up?'

'Jesus. You don't fuck around, huh?'

'I got no time to fuck around, lady. None of us do.'

'A break-up.'

'So what's here for you?'

'You already asked me.'

'No, I asked why you're here. Now I'm asking what is here.'

'I don't know ... I guess what's not here are all the things causing me trouble in the first place.'

'Except for you.'

'Except for me.'

I bought us a shot. Why couldn't I just talk about sports like everybody else? We raised our glasses and I left her looking sadder than when I'd walked in. I drove around the boundary of the island

and stared out to water in all directions. Then I was back at the highway that brought me in. Key West was a dead end sending you back where you came from. Not a good place to find anything, an even worse place to run from something.

I headed towards the Florida mainland. My father had found a reason to stay there for a week and I hadn't lasted an hour. Did he see some light in everything that I was blinded to? I guessed the biggest difference between him and me was that he lived for himself, while I was always living in emulation of something. I didn't know what I was supposed to be. I'd grasped at meaning in this world since childhood and never found enough to justify the pain caused. Happiness was just dirt in my palm, and the harder I squeezed to hold onto it, the more I lost.

I didn't hate my father for what he'd done; I hated myself for letting it turn me into what I'd become. After twenty-five years of clenched fists and staring into mirrors with disgust, I was tired. So tired it hurt in my chest. I reached Conch Key and saw the motel with the swordfish on the side. 'That would be a nice place to die,' I thought again. So I decided to die.

I got a room with a view over the water for one night and took my bags inside. The décor was like the living room of a home and it was a nice place to be. I removed two full bottles from my bag and placed them on the table, one of bourbon, the other, sleeping pills. Enough of each. I looked at them sitting there and let out a breath. Water folded over itself in a gentle way down on the beach and cars disappeared into the horizon over the bridge as others appeared and came closer. It seemed like a waste to not enjoy the scene, even for a little while, so I wandered down.

Floating on my back in the clear water, I watched as a few faint, white clouds moved against the clear sky.

'Get outta there, you imbecile!' a man exclaimed from his parked push-bike at the side of the road.

'Why would I want to do that?' I yelled back.

'Because you'll get caught in the current and pulled out to sea.'

'Sounds like a plan to me!'

He palmed me off and got back on his bike.

I went back to the room and showered salt off my body, got dressed in some of my nicer clothes, sat at the table and looked out over paradise. I opened the bottle of pills. There were thirty of them. I organised them into triplets across the table. Ten groupings in a row. A few swigs to accompany each. Something about organising them neatly made the whole thing seem less depraved. Extracting the letters from my bag, I stacked them on the table, arranging them to be found. The cigarette burnt to its filter and hissed against the side of the ashtray.

Then, sitting alone in that room, I realised the end – when you're willing to accept it – isn't an explosion, but a fizzle. We don't accept fate on our knees with arms spread and chests thrust towards the sky; we accept it sitting in armchairs watching television, or at desks assessing bills, or in cars stuck in traffic. The end is not some firework lighting the sky, but an ember becoming the darkness surrounding it. I collected the first grouping and played with them in my palm. 'See you soon,' I said under my breath as my vision became cloudy.

My hands were shaking. I threw them back and washed them down. Then I had another three and another gulp. Before I knew it, fifteen pills had left the table. Something about the scene felt lacking – and there I was, curating my death for others just like I'd done with my life.

Reaching into my pocket, I removed my wallet and pulled out a folded piece of paper. Another came with it and dropped to the floor. I unfolded and held the scrap. A photograph: my mother and father standing behind their son on his fifth birthday. No longer protected by a plastic sheet, it was worn at its edges, with splits at its folds. I put it on the pile and looked through the rest of my wallet for anything else worth adding. There was nothing. I was ready now.

I threw down another two triplets. It was still bright outside, though the sun was losing its anger, succumbing to the late afternoon. I was beginning to feel the same. Soon it would be evening and then night and the moon would reflect against the ocean and, if everything was still enough, it would look like there were two of them and it would be hard to tell which was which. I slapped another set of pills at my mouth and missed with two. They hit against my cheek and fell.

I slumped in the chair and found them on the floor next to the paper I'd dropped. Retrieving and swallowing the pills, I opened the note and studied it. It made no sense to me. Oh, upside down. I turned it between my fingers. Tatty blue ink was scribbled onto it, smudged where the felt tip had been too eager. A phone number. Above the digits: DANNY.

Remembering where, and then how it felt when I was handed it, I picked up the room's phone and tapped numbers as if I'd only have one shot. I expected nothing, but it felt wrong not to try. A last shred of hope, I supposed. It rang and rang as I felt myself tire.

'Hello?'

'Hi, yeah. Is Danny there?'

'Speaking. Who is this?'

'It's Mark. We met in that hostel in New York City.'

'Oh, snap, yeah! How you been, buddy?'

'I've been better.'

'That's no good. Anything I can do?'

'Well, I was just calling to, uh ... '

'Yeah?'

'Would you happen to have a bed for me? Just for tonight?'

He didn't reply. He wasn't going to reply. There was rustling in the background from his end. I prepared myself for the disconnect tone of the conversation and of me.

'It's alright, don't worry about it. I was thinking there might be a place for me, is all. Have a good night.'

I moved the phone towards its hanger then heard a tiny voice.

'Yo, sorry. You still there? Don't hang up. I'm raiding the linens for you.'

'Really?'

'Yeah. Are you in Orlando already?'

'I'm in ... Miami.'

'Oh, so you wanted to stay tomorrow night?'

I looked down at three pills in my hand as I rolled them around with my thumb.

'No. It has to be tonight or it's not happening at all.'

'Ha, alright, man. You're lucky I don't have work.'

I jotted down his address, hung up and went to the bathroom. Cupping hands under the tap, I funnelled water into myself until I thought I'd burst, forced fingers down my throat and vomited into the toilet. I tried to count, but most of the pills had turned to congealed fairy floss. When I felt there was nothing left, I repeated the process again. And again.

I checked out, much to the confusion of the receptionist, and floored the Miata out onto the Overseas Highway. It was five in the afternoon; Miami was four hours from Orlando; Conch Key another two from there. I pulled the shifter into second and planted my foot. If I made it, I'd make it by nine.

I cut west at the mainland, then north to trace up the middle of rural Florida. Soon I was doing ninety down dark, winding country roads. Interior panels shook as the Miata attacked illuminated tarmac ahead. The road burning red behind as it caught in the tail lights. I passed a truck on the wrong side of the road, around a blind corner, just missing the front of another oncoming as I swerved back onto the right side. The Miata's speakers were popping from the volume of the radio and I banged my hands on the wheel in time. I couldn't go fast enough.

I'd never feared death so little because I'd never wanted to live so much. This must have been how my father felt.

I realised, somewhere on that sprint north, that you do not live alongside life; you are at odds with it. It is not your friend; it is a guard holding the keys to your cell, and it will hand you over to the reaper when the time comes. Too many people ask it for permission in the interim, trying to appease and negotiate terms, when they should be wrapping their hands around its neck, digging their thumbs into its throat and telling it how things are going to be. If death was coming, I wasn't going to allow life to let it find me sitting in some motel room under a slow-turning fan. I was going to barrel into it at one hundred miles an hour while the tarmac sizzled behind. The fucker would fear my hand reaching out for it.

I pushed the shifter into fifth and planted my foot again. I had a devil on each shoulder and they were both blocking their ears.

I punched a number Danny had given me into a keypad and was buzzed in as large metal gates slid away. It was just after 9 p.m. I drove into the gated community past a small lake and through the blocks of homes. Shutting off the engine out the front of Danny's, it let out a wheeze that lasted the time it took to carry my bags up his path and ring the doorbell.

He greeted me, looking at my face with horror and wonder. I wouldn't have let me in, but he did, and he did it with that smile. He opened two bottles, handed one to me, and we sat down.

It felt heavier in my hand than usual. I could feel the beer washing around inside – its weight swaying when I brought it back down after a sip, cold through the glass against my hot skin. Even light wrapping around a chair in the room's corner cast a beautiful shadow. Everything in the place seemed so delicate and temporary that I struggled to take it all in at once. I felt a fragile strength that night.

'You look a bit out of it.'

'It's been a strange … life.'

'You want to go downtown?'

'Not really.'

'That's a shame. There're always some beautiful girls out.'

I finished my bottle.

'Danny?'

'Yes?'

'I think we should go downtown.'

Danny wasn't wrong. Downtown was something special. We drank and laughed and it seemed hard to believe where I had been mere hours earlier. No one had ever found what they were looking for at the bottom of a glass, but it wasn't a bad place to start. I got drunk much faster than Danny, managing to have the same amount of success with the girls. I wasn't sure how. He had that smile, and a nice home. The girls could tell he meant his smile. What did I have? A wheezing shitbox and a crumpled shirt.

I'd almost always found my gold with the sadder-looking girls. Anything else just seemed like a matter of circumstance to me. I'd spent so long convincing myself it was romantic; this idea of people recognising a reflection of their unhappiness in the face of another. But it isn't, and doesn't lead to happiness for either, just like rubbing two ice cubes together doesn't create a fire.

THE ROADMAP OF LOSS

I looked back at a girl as she perused me from across the bar and curled a finger through hair cascading around her shoulders. She walked towards me and I kissed her before she could say a word. I listened to her pull and push breath through her nose as our lips danced over each other's. It didn't matter what was waiting behind her little smile. For once I didn't want to know if we shared the same pain. It made no difference whether they were spoken or written or read; words just ruined the wonder in things. I kept drinking. I had to keep drinking. The only thing maybe worse than the words was the silence.

4.

I was in hell, and if this was hell then they had a table ready and all the bartenders knew my name. I lay with my eyes shut tight. There was ringing in my ears echoing the calm water surrounding Conch Key rolling over itself. Through it, though, the faint sound of humming. A woman's voice. It broke on the higher notes, but hitting all the notes wasn't the point and she lullabied all the same. It was perhaps the nicest sound I'd ever heard.

I was in a small room on a small, collapsible bed. My bags were on the floor and a glass of water sat on the counter. I swigged it and got to my feet. I pushed blinds and a sliding door open and walked into the living room. A toddler playing with a toy truck on the other side of the door stopped and stared at me, then got up, ran down the hallway and disappeared around a corner.

'You must be Mark,' said the humming voice.

I turned towards the kitchen on the other side of the room, for a moment convinced I'd gone out in that motel room. That I'd never even made it to the phone, and the manic night of driving and drinking were just malfunctions of my synapses shutting down. I looked at her and couldn't speak. She wasn't some gatekeeper of heaven, but heaven itself. And how unsurprised I was that the place had the shape of a woman.

'Don't mind Aaron. He's a little shy with new people,' she added, with a smile which made me feel like I'd never know another day of pain.

'That's okay.'

She wiped her hands on a cloth and came over to me.

'Hi, I'm June.'

'Hi, June. Did we meet last night?'

'Oh, wow,' she laughed. 'Dan said you liked a drink. Now I believe him. No, we didn't.'

'Yeah, I think I'd remember something like that.'

'Why's that?'

'Doesn't matter. Where is he now?'

'At work. He said you would be staying with us though. He said you guys met in New York?'

'We did. In a hostel in Chelsea.'

'That's pretty cool. He's always making friends.'

'He sure is. Are you his ... partner?'

'No, no, just a roommate.'

'Oh, yeah?'

'My partner Jamie's at work. We live here with Aaron, and Dan.'

'Oh. Yeah. I can pack my stuff and get out of your hair now.'

'No. You're not allowed.'

'I'm not?'

'Not until you've let me make you some breakfast.'

She prepared eggs and toast, juice and coffee. Aaron studied me from the other side of the table as he chewed on a novelty-sized plastic key. It was my first meal in more than a day, and I think they could both tell as I gulped it down.

June had been to Melbourne, once upon a time. She spoke about it with love, much more than I'd ever had. Hearing her talk about the place made me miss it. There had been moments I'd wanted to go back, but it was only ever because I recalled the loneliness not being as great there. It was the lesser of two evils and just because the hurting is lesser somewhere, doesn't make it your home. But in conversation with June, I longed for Melbourne – truly, madly, deeply longed for it. Though I did think I'd miss any place she spoke about in such an impassioned way, even if I'd never been there. She threw a red ball down the hallway that Aaron chased after with a scream of joy, retrieved and brought back. 'He thinks he's a dog, I swear,' she said.

In the back of my mind, I knew I wasn't free from the day before. Deferral isn't a cure, and there was still more than enough sickness in me. Even if I'd fended off the end for a little while, I was sure if I'd left Danny's house that morning, I would end up in another motel room, sitting at another table, with my belongings organised in front of me by nightfall.

June asked what my plans were and when I couldn't give an answer, she looked at me with a tilted head. I was hungover, but I think she saw something else as well. 'You should stay a bit longer,' she said, giving me ten minutes to decide while she walked to the front gate to check the mail. I could have my bags in the Miata and be gone in a few minutes. Surely she wouldn't take it personally. We'd just met.

I envisioned finding a local radio station and steering back out onto another indifferent road. I could shoot blindly at the horizon or steer towards wherever the next letter took me. Neither had brought much of anything good and I knew it didn't matter which direction I headed or how far I got. Another few interstates, another few tanks of gas, another few beers and another few women. What was the point? I'd end up where I was the day before, just in a different town.

Any asshole can drive across a country. It takes something more to span the distances in your own mind.

I sat on the couch with my head in my hands, trying to decide if there was a decision, and then there was a press against my knee. Aaron was standing there. June had left her infant son alone with me in the house. I looked around to make sure her leaving wasn't something I'd imagined. What had compelled the woman to show this kind of trust? I looked like a six o'clock special. Aaron stared at me with big, curious eyes, then offered up the red ball resting in his upturned palm towards me. 'Yeah?' I asked. He elevated his chin away from me and then gave a timid nod. 'You're sure?' Another nod.

I lifted the ball from his palm, drew my arm back and launched it. It bounced along the floorboards of the hallway with a clattering echo, off the front door and disappeared around the corner. We looked back to each other as the sound of the bouncing rang out and stopped. He looked down the hallway and back to me. Then a smile appeared, growing until it had consumed most of his face. He squealed with glee and darted off, pursuing the ball with heavy, clumsy footsteps that beat through the house. He brought it back and gave it to me with less hesitation than before. Each time I threw it, Aaron's laughter would grow and I soon found myself smiling. June arrived back at some point. I was too invested in the game to notice.

'Wow, you two are getting along.'

I stopped myself from smiling and stood there. I felt embarrassed and wasn't sure why.

'I guess so.'

Aaron walked up to me, tugged on my shirt and handed me the ball.

'He gave you his ball?' she asked.

'He did.'

She stared like it was news she didn't know how to take.

'Is that alright?'

'It's fine. He just never gives it to someone he's just met.'

'Well, that's nice then.'

I took the ball, straightened my elbow, and catapulted it down the hallway. It bounced away with Aaron's clunking footsteps in pursuit and I tried not to look like I enjoyed it as much as I did.

'How strange ...'

'I get that a lot.'

'No, not that.'

We looked at each other for a moment and I felt very small in the room. When June looked at something, she did it with no excuses. If our stares had been armies, hers would have defeated mine on the first day of the campaign and been home in time for lunch. She told me to get ready while she got Aaron showered. I conceded I wasn't leaving that day and watched as they left for the bathroom. A mother, carrying the child she'd left alone with me, who had surprised her with his trusting intuition. It seemed a bizarre irony to me, then I realised where he'd gotten it from.

The three of us spent the day running errands. I met June's partner, Jamie, when he returned from work that afternoon. It was more of the same from him: a brilliant, honest smile, friendly and almost sickeningly welcoming. Danny was like a brother to both and an uncle to Aaron. I wasn't sure where I fit into the dynamic other than as a guest, though they had a strange way of making me feel they thought themselves lucky for having me around.

I wanted to find something ugly in all the niceness like I always did, but couldn't. Maybe I was going soft or maybe I'd just gone too long without it. Whatever it was, it was wonderful to feel like I deserved the air I breathed. I was invited to stay another night and then another – every insinuation I would head off the next day met with polite outrage.

One afternoon, Jamie and I were alone in his car, driving back from a park. I tapped my foot to the radio and felt light and air caress my arm as it hung out the window. It had been one of the nicer days in my life. Jamie had insisted he and I travel together while June took Aaron and Danny in her car. He wasn't as eager to talk as he had been earlier. We rolled to a crossing as the light turned red. I was going to be asked to leave, I could feel it. He let out a long sigh and turned to me.

'Can I ask you something, Mark?'

'Of course.'

'I don't want any of this getting back to June, okay? Not under any circumstances.'

'Ah, goddamn it. I know where this is going.'

'Surely not. I can't be that predictable.'

'No, but *I* can be.'

'I don't really know what you're talking about, Mark. Just shut up for a second.'

'Okay.'

Jamie tapped a rhythm against the steering wheel took in deep breath.

'You said you used to work in music?'

'A while ago, yeah.'

'Did you work with singers?'

'Depends on your definition of a singer, I suppose.'

He stared at me. His brow was low and his eyes serious.

'Yeah, Jamie, I worked with singers.'

'So you could pick a good singer if you heard them? I mean, you know what makes a good singer, right?'

'Shit, maybe. I was just the hack working the switches and the dials. Who am I to judge?'

'You're a friend. I trust your judgement.'

THE ROADMAP OF LOSS

He changed the player in his Mercedes from radio to CD. It proceeded onto track one.

'Please bear with me here.'

A basic, electronic-sounding drum held a beat and then a badly recorded guitar played chords over the top. The mixing was rough but I recognised the melody.

'Is ... is that Frampton?' I asked.

'Shh, shh.'

'Hey, yeah, it's 'Baby I Love Your Way'.

'Mark, shut up.'

The music continued. Jamie tapped the top of the steering wheel and sucked in a breath before exploding. He worked the lyrics out. I mean really worked them out. I looked around. I didn't know what was happening, but he wasn't half bad.

People walking the sidewalks turned their heads with curiosity. The lights turned green ahead. A woman behind us blew her horn after the car in front pulled away, but Jamie was somewhere else. I watched a single tear squeezed from his closed eyes make its way down his cheek. I'd never found the song very powerful at all, but he made it seem like it was.

The woman blew her horn again. 'Move it, asshole!' she yelled. I put half my body through my window and screamed back to her.

'Go around! Can't you see we're having a fuckin' moment here?'

She drove past and glared, but Jamie didn't notice. We'd reached the second verse before he snapped out of his trance. He took deep breaths and collected himself then switched the player back to the radio and got us moving again.

'So, what do you think?' he asked me.

'What do I think? I think we need to have you institutionalised.'

'I mean about my singing.'

'It was fine.'

'Fine?'

'It was good.'

'I'm going to propose to June three weeks from now.'

'Shit. And the song...?'

'I'm going to organise a group of our friends by this fountain downtown. A surprise thing for June. And I'm going to sing it to her. Then I'm going to get down on one knee and ask her to be my wife.'

'And you think the answer will be "no" if your voice isn't up to par?'

'I think it wouldn't be worth the woman's time if it wasn't as close to perfect as I could make it for her.'

Fuck me. The man had a point.

'Well, it's good. It has... promise.'

'You really think so?'

'I do.'

'Then I need you to help me get it all the way. Stay as long as you'd like. I want you to be there when I perform and propose.'

I went to a neglected sports bar by myself that night. I both drank and thought heavily. People speak of the dangers of mixing drinks, when it's really those two in the wrong ratios that'll do you in.

I didn't trust myself around precious things. The last time I'd stayed somewhere because someone wanted me to, I'd left both of them in worse condition than when I'd arrived. I couldn't justify making the same mistakes over and over. I lit two cigarettes, handed one to the dark, older bartender, then ordered another drink from him. We were laughing and getting along just fine. It seemed I was getting along just fine with a lot of people in that town.

'You married?' I asked as he put another glass down in front of me.

'No, sir, I cannot say I'm marr–'

Two college kids with backwards caps arrived at the bar next to me and interrupted him to order.

'Why not?'

'Never really saw the point of it all,' he spoke, pulling on a tap handle.

'So you stay alone then?'

He pushed the register closed, handed back change and smiled.

'I'm never alone. Just don't want to get married, is all.'

'Yo, what's with the twenty questions about the dude having a girl?' asked one of the kids. 'You hoping he's gay or something?'

'Pardon me?'

'I said what's with the interrogation, faggot?'

His friend stood behind him, smiling, rolling gum around in his mouth. The bartender looked tense. He'd seen this play out before, but he'd never seen anything like me. My nerves had been hardened or killed or discarded.

'Oh, that ...'

I stood and faced them. They recoiled and puffed their chests a bit.

'Hey now,' the bartender said under his breath.

'That's because I'm gonna suck his dick,' I said in my best Clint Eastwood, stepping closer to them. They stepped back. None of us were sure what I was doing.

'Yeah, guess who's drinking for free tonight? And I'm not talking beer. I'm gonna suck that thing right off him. And you know what, pal? You're next.'

I pointed a finger gun at him. They stood still.

'Fuckin' queer,' the kid retorted after consideration. They backed away from the bar and towards their booth. I blew a kiss to them. The bartender snickered.

'Well, shit. Never seen that one before.'

'Wasn't sure how that was gonna go,' I said, sitting back down and picking up my cigarette.

'Coulda gone a lot worse. Talking like that'll get ya into trouble someday, son.'

'Eh, maybe, but not tonight. Hey, you ever been in love?'

'You a weird fellow, you know that?'

'Yeah, I do. So tell me.'

'Hell. Sure. Few times. But who even knows what that means.'

'You're sure you have, but you're not sure you know what it means?'

'Yeah. Love to me, it's a bit like ... bit like stubbing your toe.'

'Fuck, that's romantic.'

'No, man, listen. I mean, I can stub my toe. And I know what it feels like to stub my toe. And I could tell you I stubbed my toe, and you relate to a time when you stubbed your own toe. But you don't know for certain I'm describing the same thing.'

'Ah, so you think love is like a, uh, impossibility of shared experience kinda thing?'

'No, I think it's like a stubbing my goddamn toe kind of thing. Man, I'm with dumb and dumber now. What's with all the questions?'

'Fuck, I don't know. Listen. You have the chance to help someone who's in love, but you know you also tend to fuck up everything you touch, do you do it?'

'Yes.'

'Yes? Simple as that?'

'Yes.'

'Why?'

'Because love's the finest thing around and Lord knows we could do with more of it. It's the only thing I've ever found where there ain't such thing as "too much". And nothing done in the honest efforts of having more of it in this world can be held against ya, even if it all goes south.'

I bought him a shot and we toasted. After another few rounds, I staggered out to the Miata.

There were other footsteps nearby.

'Oh, this is perfect,' a voice from behind announced.

I turned around. The two kids from the bar.

'The queer drives a little convertible.'

They stepped close.

'Hey now, let's not take what happened before so seriously. Call it a joke,' I said, displaying open palms as a peace offering.

'Little late for jokes. Now you're gonna get it,' the other friend finally spoke.

Something about the whole routine stank of rehearsed bravado, like they'd been preparing for this in that shitty parking lot for half an hour before I'd arrived. They'd have been pacified by seeing some legitimate fear, but I had none to offer.

'Just tell me something, please. I've always wanted to know.'

They paused.

'Do you guys spin those caps around backwards so you don't tickle your buddy's belly button with the visor?'

There was a flash of colours. The kids, and the ground they stood on, rotated in front of me. I folded the side mirror of the Miata in with my body as I slipped down the fender and onto the pavement. A pair of running footsteps moved away and then it was quiet. I climbed back to my feet, lit a cigarette, adjusted the mirror and drove home. I made a bee-line for my bed through the dark living room.

June saw me, but I didn't see her as she sat at the dining table in the corner.

'Boo!' she whisper-yelled through cupped hands.

I jumped. A lamp cast warm, glowing light over her collection of open books. Some of it reflected off them, irradiating her face. I moved closer.

'Jesus, you scared the shit out of me.'

'Serves you right for sneaking through my house, you creep.'

I shouldn't have said anything. Now she was smiling and I couldn't leave.

'Where is everyone?'

'Sound asleep.'

'Why are you still up?'

'I have a midterm soon.'

'Ah, yes.'

'Remember those? Back when you were a contributing member of society?'

'Hmm, I remember the exams. Not so much the latter.'

'You're a tough guy to make smile, you know that?'

'I do,' I nodded. 'Feels like it gets a little harder each day.'

'Well, can I say I was relieved when I heard the front door open just now?'

'Why's that?'

'I don't know,' she bluffed. 'Earlier, when you said you were going out by yourself, I wasn't sure if you'd be coming back.'

The smile faded from her face.

'You had that look in your eye. That same one you had when we first met.'

'And what look was that?'

'Restlessness. Like you were already gone.'

She wanted to be wrong but I couldn't help her with that, so just stood there trying not to sway. I felt like a schoolboy being told off and it was humiliating. I yearned to be getting punched in the face again instead.

'Goodnight, June.'

'Goodnight, Mark.'

I went to my room, closed the door and blinds to the living room and crawled into bed. The sky was full of stars, and the backyard shone a cool blue through the window. After a few minutes, I heard June stacking books away. Gaps between the blinds turned from yellow to grey as she clicked the lamp off. I listened to her footsteps disappear down the hallway towards her bedroom. She'd learnt all she wanted to that night.

5.

I was on a constant rotation. Jamie went to work in the mornings before I woke and I was poached by June or Danny. Mostly June. Days were spent running errands or being shown around Orlando. Americans are so proud of their cities compared to Australians. I guessed it was because they had so many to choose from and with so much choice you were bound to find a place just right for you. Hell, even New Yorkers loved New York City in their own strange way.

In the afternoons, Jamie would return from work and we'd head out. 'Mark wants to go to a bar,' he'd say. It was a believable story. Nobody ever got suspicious of that. We'd get into his car and drive for hours with track one of disc one repeating over and over. By the end of each session, Jamie had improved and I wanted to throttle Frampton a little more. I was no singer and certainly no singing coach, but I knew enough, and it felt nice to see his trust in me paying off. There was a return for both of us on those drives while the sun set, but mine was in a way he would never understand. After our cruising, we'd get dinner at a bar and Jamie would pay.

'You sure that's a good idea?' he asked one night as I tried to flag down the bartender again.

'Jamie, June thinks we've been here for three hours,' I said through tight lips as I lit a cigarette.

'Uh-huh, your point being?'

'Do you have any idea how much damage I normally do in three hours?'

'I don't follow ...'

'If I walk into that house of yours even remotely sober, then she's gonna get suspicious and know something's up. I'm doing this for you, really.'

He pondered for a moment, stood up from his stool and waved a hand towards the bartender.

I'd been their guest for two weeks before Jamie's job sent him to Atlanta – it was only for three days, but he saw each as invaluable. He suggested lessons over the phone. I told him there'd be no point if the acoustics weren't the same. It wasn't true, but I needed a break from him and Frampton, so it felt true to me.

June and I went to a restaurant with Aaron and she insisted on paying. I didn't know what I was to her, or she to me. Her kindness was unconditional, though it made me feel like a charity case. She would remark how impressed she was by me and then push my wallet closed a few minutes later, as if I was a child trying to spend his pocket money. The most infuriating thing about June was the impossibility of disliking her. She was energy emanating in all directions and missing nobody. She was light.

Through all the tenderness, though, was an almost overpowering sexuality which seemed to come as naturally as breathing for her. I'd met plenty of women who relished their beauty like it had an expiry date, not realising it only does for those who make no investment in the other myriad, intangible beauties that could exist in them as well. June seemed immune to such things. She would flick her hair or bite her lip, handing out glances and smiles like candy but never tossing them about in vain. All hit their mark, and if someone was bitter enough to bat one away, then her spirit and mind followed like a boxer adapting to any style and pushing forward unaffected. There was no compromise in her. If she wanted you wrapped around her finger, you would be. I watched people succumb to it and wondered if I'd looked the same.

She broke a long silence. 'How much longer do you think you'll stay?'

Her eyes weren't fixed onto mine as she spoke to me, for maybe the first time I could recall. I sipped beer and watched them wander. Aaron kept colouring-in on the back of his menu.

'A week or so. Why? Do you want me gone sooner?'

'No, not at all. I was thinking maybe you should stay with us.'

'I have been staying with you.'

'I mean long term. I have friends. Between us, we could find you work. That room can be yours for as long as you like.'

'I can't.'

'Why not? You get along so well with all of us, even Aaron.'

The boy recognised his name and looked up. June pointed to his colouring with a feigned look of amazement. He laughed and clapped then resumed his work.

'Because this isn't where I should be.'

'Then where should you be? Where is home for Mark Ward?'

'I don't know.'

'You know, you only ever seem certain about things when they involve you not being good enough. You've got a kind face, but it's always scrunched up in a frown.'

'June, people always talk about finding a place for yourself, but nobody ever talks about what it's like when you can't. To see so much and not feel like any of it belongs to you, or you to any of it.

Everyone needs to believe there's something better just beyond the horizon because it keeps them going, but it's bullshit.'

'There is a place for you, and you'll find it. I want that more than anything for you. And I know that when you do find it, you won't want to wander anymore.'

'And how could you possibly know that?'

'Because I think, someday, you'll catch your reflection in a mirror or a shop front or a car window ... and you'll lean in to make sure it's you because you won't recognise yourself, and you'll find you don't have that look in your eye anymore.'

Her voice was breaking. She excused herself and went to the restroom. An older couple glared at me from their table. It was a sin to make a woman like that upset. I sipped my beer – there was nothing else to do. The truth doesn't always lift you to the heavens; sometimes it straps you into a chair and beats you.

Aaron lifted his completed colouring page towards me. Lines of crayon darted in and out of the shapes' black outlines. His big eyes waited on my approval. For whatever reason, he thought it mattered. It was shit, but it was his and he was proud. I smiled.

'That's real good, buddy.'

Jamie returned and our lessons resumed. I still spent most of my time with June, but it was different. She managed a distance even when right beside me. I was unlike anything she'd seen and it confused her. The day before the proposal, Jamie called into work sick. Under the guise of going to a doctor, we had an all-day lesson. Under the guise of protecting his voice, I suggested we wrap up early.

'You guys had a fight?' he asked me from the other side of a bar booth.

I paused mid-bite then continued.

'I'm just wondering. You guys are close and she seems off. What was it about?'

I gave myself time to think as I chewed and swallowed.

'She just sees things, is all,' I mumbled,

'What things?'

'Things you didn't show her.'

'She can't help seeing what she sees, and she cares too much to ignore someone who's hurting. I'd say it's one of her best qualities.'

I looked up and saw concern on his face.

'I'd say you're right.'

We continued eating in silent appreciation of the woman Jamie had made a mother and was about to make a wife. All I'd ever made a woman was upset.

6.

The day arrived. June was in the kitchen when I rose. She offered to make me breakfast and I accepted. It felt just like the morning I'd first met her, except her humming did not spread through and warm the house.

Jamie headed downtown early to set the scene. The proposal was happening at 6 p.m. under the pretence of a dinner. If I knew Jamie, which it seemed like I was beginning to, everything would happen right on schedule. I went to a nearby park, sat on one of its benches and retrieved pages from my pocket as the tinny sound of a baseball meeting an aluminium bat rang out in the distance, followed by cheering kids.

Taking in the words, I felt a dread build I couldn't explain away to myself. Returning home not long before June and I were meant to leave, I sat alone on the couch in the living room while amber sunset traced the shapes of windows on the floor. Specks of dust shimmered as they danced and turned in the light. I felt like I was floating with them.

A squeal of turning taps came through the wall, June humming as she showered. I got up, walked to the Miata with my bags and forced them into the boot. Up the path, Aaron's curious face stood in the open doorway. Walking back, trying not to meet his gaze, I pulled on the door handle to close it between us. It fought back. I didn't look down, but I could feel sad eyes burning a hole through me. He knew. He'd never been walked out on, yet somehow he knew.

I pulled the handle a little harder. Aaron stepped around and braced himself against the door with open palms; the entirety of his diminutive weight leant into it like someone push-starting a car. He was groaning with exertion and desperation. I let my fingers relax, then walked back into the house with him and sat on the couch. I closed the door of my room before June came into the living room a few minutes later. She was dolled up and my lungs failed for a moment. She noticed and smiled at me for the first time in days. I decided right then there has not been, and never will be, anything as beautiful as a woman who feels she is.

'Are you ready to go?' she asked, looping an earring through her lobe.

'Yes, but I'm going to take my own car.'

'Are you sure?'

'Yeah. I've got a date right after.'

'Oh, really?'

'Mhmm, a hot one too.'

She scanned me with narrowed eyes.

'Eh, warm. Okay, tepid,' I said with a shrug.

'You're an idiot.'

We stood facing each other. She knew, and she knew I knew it. Neither of us was good at covering up to the other anymore.

'Well ... that's good. I'll see you soon?'

'I hope so.'

We hugged. She squeezed tighter than I thought her frame was capable of. Then I felt it all rushing back. I was inviting loneliness back into my life just like I had time and again. Running from the safety

THE ROADMAP OF LOSS

of those who cared for me; making room for emptiness. Its company was so familiar I almost felt a sick longing when it wasn't around. I hugged Aaron and lifted him into his seat in June's car.

'Drive safe. There'll be a seat at our table whenever you decide to join.'

'Thank you.'

I followed them down to and through the security gate. June put on her right indicator and I put on my left. Aaron waved with delight as I pulled up beside them. I waved back to him as June looked on with a smile and wet eyes. She nodded, pulled away and was gone.

I went the other direction and headed north. The clock ticked over to 6.01 p.m. as I worked the Miata into fifth up the interstate. Jamie would be rolling into the first chorus any second now, while the band played and June lit up with that smile. My absence would make sense only to her.

I hummed a melody and tapped the wheel. The family I'd found with those people was the type you take with you wherever you go. I lit a cigarette and clicked the lighter shut. The day was crouching behind the horizon. It would be dark here soon, but I didn't feel alone. The sun doesn't abandon anyone. It wanders so no corner goes without light.

September 2nd, 1977

My only,

I have moved some great distances these past few months, but none further than these past few days. There is an insatiable hunger in me that can only be fed with mile after mile of black tarmac. I have taken seats in cars whose drivers trusted my raised thumb enough to pull over, trekking from the east all the way across Texas to the mountains of Colorado and the deserts of Utah. I was lost for a time as to why this country is divided into so many smaller states, though passing through them one after another, I see they all have a unique beauty, whether it comes as snow-capped mountains or dusts that have never known rain. These words are coming to you from the balcony of a motel in the small town of Holbrook, Arizona, so who knows when they will arrive. I did not plan to come to Holbrook; however the man kind enough to offer me a ride west from Flagstaff had some matters to tend to here for a few days, and a man can wait an eternity for something he believes is a sure thing.

Night is coming. I can see the head and tail lights travelling Route 66 from where I sit. They say all the stars in the sky are already dead; it's simply that their light only reaches us now. Do you believe that? Do you ever wonder what the stars might say if they could speak? Do you think they'd mind only being seen for how beautiful they are so long after they've perished? Do you ever worry we may be destined for a similar fate?

The air is different here – the light, too. The desert land is vast and vague, with an abundance of life that can be sensed but not seen. I feel closest to you in the nights, when I can look up and know those emerald eyes of yours see the same beautiful, dying lights as mine. I worry one day Mark will look to a sky very different to the one we do. That all the beauty we've known will have faded; that he'll never know it was there at all.

    The future is certain; it is we who are not. I don't know what I'm doing. One foot lands in front of the other again and again and I wonder if there's any purpose to it besides preventing myself from tumbling. What if I just stopped? If I let all the momentum, the pain and the longing topple me. Let myself fall and see where I end up. I have been drinking heavily tonight, my love.

    I often worry about the time between running my tongue along these envelopes and them reaching your hand. I have had times of doubt, that these letters may not be reaching you or are simply thrown into the rubbish when they do. But I know you're still reading them, because if you weren't, I would be looking to an empty sky right now. The stars still shine, which means there is still hope. A gentle breeze is pushing me west, back towards your arms. I will write again when I reach California.

1.

I drove and drove. I went further in a day than I thought any man could, then went a little further. Mornings were crisp and new when the Miata and I left some faceless, forgettable motel, night setting in long before we pulled into the parking lot of another. The country was covered in them, all full of people just trying to get someplace.

I covered the twelve-hundred-mile distance from Tallahassee to Amarillo in one stint, leaving at 7 a.m. one morning and arriving at 2 a.m. the next. Driving west felt like running in an unwinnable race: it didn't matter what lead you had on the sun when you set out, it always beat you to the horizon. Mornings were spent watching it come up behind as you swallowed tarmac in front. It would shift higher and higher in the side mirrors to disappear and hover above. For a few hours, you'd be tricked into thinking you were neck and neck. Then it would drop below the roofline ahead, filling the cabin and your eyes with its blinding, condescending wake, the gap widening until it was dark. The whole thing played tricks on the mind. By all accounts, I was moving forward: the land would change, the odometer would climb, the gas tank would empty over and over, and I would fatigue; but watching the sun coast above to disappear again in some faraway place without sound or effort, gave me the strangest feeling I was going backwards.

Denver appeared the following evening. I went towards the mountains on its western side and into the reception of the first motel I saw. Walking back to get my bags, I heard the Miata start wheezing.

'Might want to get some water in that thing,' a passing man said.

I looked over the car.

'... Do you need some help?'

He opened the bonnet, propped it with the stay and asked if I had a shirt I didn't care for. I retrieved one from a collection matching the criteria. He bunched it in his hands, placed it over a cap on top of the radiator, and pushed down with straightened arms.

'This is under pressure and molten hot, so, nice and slow.' He twisted with caution, the wheeze turning to a hiss. A gurgling sound followed and I watched the shirt darken as invisible steam caught its fabric. The gurgle stopped and the man used the shirt to remove the cap.

I handed him my one-gallon drinking bottle, about half-full, and he emptied it into the radiator. 'Gonna need a bit more,' he said.

I filled the bottle in my room and handed it over again. Another third of a gallon went in before dribbling from the opening. 'Your heater – you know, on the dash – it takes heat from this,' he said. 'Long as hot air comes outta those vents, there's still some water in here.' He screwed the cap back on and dropped the bonnet with a bang. I asked if I could buy him a drink. He declined then was gone.

I wandered alone to a bar down the street. It was dead; a few men scattered throughout, none speaking to each other. A whole room full of nothing. No women, no loving, no hating, no dreaming. Nothing doing. I drank a few beers, went to my room and crawled into bed.

2.

If local knowledge in the motel's breakfast room was anything to go by, the journey to Arizona via Utah wasn't easy on driver or car. I wasn't sure what the fuss was about as I began driving through chilly air towards the mountains, shivering for maybe the first time since Pennsylvania. The climb up Interstate 70 challenged the Miata's puny engine. It screamed through its rotted exhaust pipe as I held it in third gear at five thousand revs to match other cars' pace. The water temperature needle began to rise. Accepting I wouldn't be able to keep up with faster traffic, I shifted into fourth and moved along with the trucks and caravans.

After the initial ascent, the road became marvellous, carving and undulating through the range like a needle threading tarmac into the fabric of the land. I entered a tunnel piercing mountainside at a steep descent, and was soon unable to determine the gradient by anything other than load on the engine. The passage ran for miles and only halfway through, when I had to shift down a gear, did I realise I was climbing again.

The tunnel lifted in a crescendo towards a wall of light pouring in at its summit. I burst through and saw it all. There were few points higher than I was, the range unfolding in stunning, endless alps. I thought I'd become immune to that dumb awe caused by things between me and the horizon, but there I was again, jaw drooped, trying to take it all in.

The road descended and the temperature needle followed suit. Beyond the small towns of the valley, I entered a canyon tracing alongside a river, the highway elevated halfway up the corridor of rock, with blue sky above and the flowing artery of water beneath. I had no interest in any god, though I did concede there, as the river carved through to massage the pebbles and banks below, that if they did exist, it was in every drop of water and grain of dirt, every leaf and every stone.

Colours transformed as I moved west. The land traded its greens and greys for reds and browns, the changes so swift that by the time I'd processed one abrupt shift in the environment, the next had already arrived. Before long, I had left the lush forest of Colorado and entered the arid bowl of Utah. The sun took the lead, its rays too intense to have the roof or windows down. Rising and falling in bursts, the temperature needle mirrored the highway's undulations.

Soon, the cabin became unbearable and sweat dripped into my eyes. Each gear change seared my palm as the shifter gathered energy from the sun. I removed and used my shirt like an oven mitt when the Miata had to be worked up and down the hills. Within a few crests, the engine could only manage thirty miles per hour uphill before the temperature needle swung towards the ominous 'H'. Large trucks with trailers blasted their horns as they overtook me, their echo like the desert's cackle.

I remembered the man from the motel's advice. Turning on the fan, I slid the temperature toggle into the red. Warm air blew from the vent, though no warmer than what my dangling fingers swam in through the small gap in the window. I pulled over. Sun beat down

THE ROADMAP OF LOSS

on my face and neck, shoulders and arms, evaporating sweat as fast as my body produced it.

Taking my shirt from the gear knob, I laid it over the radiator cap and mimicked the movement I'd watched the night before. The hiss came and went. Lifting the cap with care, I poured in most of what remained in my drink bottle, though it never reached the brim. I began driving, the needle staying put for a while before moving again. I didn't have enough water for a second top-up. I looked at the fan vents. I was no physicist, but if heat was energy, then maybe the heater could be used to extract it from the engine. It was worth a try; I had nothing to lose but my life. Switching the fan speed to max, I turned the temperature all the way up. Transparent fire erupted from the vents and the cabin turned into a sauna.

For a brief eternity, I struggled to breathe, not able to comprehend the heat. It didn't feel real. Working on Kiawah was a winter's morning in comparison. I passed a sign for a rest area fifty miles ahead. The needle still danced about, but didn't approach 'H' with the same persistence as before.

Forty miles. The road began to flatten out, the Miata capable of fifty miles per hour. I somehow needed to piss. I waited for my body to reabsorb it.

Thirty miles. Visions of the rest stop's faucet spitting out that miracle elixir consumed me. I was Moses in a Miata.

Twenty miles. The needle started soaring. I became delirious and suddenly very tired, no longer able to discern temperature with my hand raised to the vent.

Ten miles. My armpits were bone-dry and a salty crust sat in my eyebrows and beard. The Miata began backfiring as the engine lost power. I tried to swallow saliva but there was none – my tongue just a piece of bark jammed down my throat.

I almost missed the rest area's entrance, swerving in and banging a tyre into a kerb. My legs gave out as I laboured from the driver's seat, bracing myself against the door. I was all alone. The swelter of the tarmac pierced my thongs as air swirled above in the heat. Even with unrelenting sunlight thrashing my body, the desert somehow felt frosty compared to the cabin. Its great flat nothing reached from the rest area towards mountains in the distance either five or fifty miles away. I grabbed my jug, swishing the precious little remaining water against its insides like a snare drum.

I trudged towards the shelter with heavy steps. I would cup water in my hands and pour it into me. Handful after handful. Gallon after gallon. I would empty a lake with my thirst. I pushed the wooden shack's door open and stepped inside. It stank with the rancid stench of super-heated shit, the toilet just a hole in a bench disappearing into a pit. No pipes ran to or from it. No handle to flush. I looked around the room for a basin and tap that wasn't there. It was a dry rest area. There was no sense trying to irrigate a place like this; I was fucked.

I'd have cried if my body had the moisture to spare. It was two in the afternoon, which meant at least another five hours of this sun and even more of this heat. I could take refuge in the shade of the room with the faecal air, or I could push on. I wasn't sure the Miata would make it, and was even less convinced I would. A decision needed to be made fast; every minute wasted was one less my body would last.

I pulled myself from my shorts over the hole in the bench. Right before the flow came, as I felt it surging through me, I stopped. I walked out into the heat and propped the bonnet. A hiss evacuated from the cap turning under my bunched shirt. With lips almost too dry to seal against the bottle, I poured the remaining water into me in little gulps. Hovering my hand above the opening to make sure it was safe, the engine let out an almighty belch, and with it, a

THE ROADMAP OF LOSS

cough of steam from the radiator. It singed my wrist from the thumb up, a pink shape like licks of a flame forming within seconds.

I screamed, cursing the desert as I cradled my hand and kicked the front bumper. I settled, checked again, and then removed myself from my shorts. With bent knees, I lowered my tip to the radiator's opening and relaxed with a sigh. Resting my head against the edge of the bonnet, I closed my eyes and listened to the tinny echo of my stream. I'd never been so grateful for a good, long, uninterrupted piss. Every drop of the stuff would be a little further the engine could make it.

A door slammed and broke my trance. I looked over to a van parked a few spaces up and the faces of the family it had ferried in. They were mortified. A man stood by his closed door, his wife and son staring through the windshield towards me, a young girl frozen with her mouth gaping open and one leg reaching out of the van's sliding door to the ground below. I stood before them, shirtless, half-squatting, drooped into my radiator.

'Howdy,' I said.

'Howdy ... Car troubles?' the man asked.

'Yes, among others.'

We looked at each other, my trickle the only thing filling the silence.

'Okay then,' he said, turning away.

The family went about their business as if I wasn't there. I wondered if this was what Claire was referring to when she said I'd deserve whatever I got. The mother took her daughter to use the bathroom, the father did the same with his son. I emptied myself, but the radiator wasn't nearly full. The family gathered around their opened sliding door with a large container sitting on the floor, condensation collected on its exterior. The woman brought a bottle to its tap.

Salvation cascaded from the nozzle, clear and pure, kissing the inside of the bottle and streaming to pool at the bottom.

I wanted it more than I'd ever wanted anything. I looked at my own empty jug, bulging with expanded air, splotches of moisture dotted about from the atmosphere boiling inside. I wriggled my shirt on and combed a hand through my hair. The family looked wary as I approached like a lame beggar.

'Would, uh, I be able to trouble you for some of that water?' I asked.

'Sorry, we don't –' the woman began.

'Of course,' the man interrupted.

'I don't think we have enough to be giving it out like that.'

'There's another drum in the back.'

She pursed her lips.

'I can give you some cash,' I said, stepping forward and opening my wallet. We all looked in. It was empty.

'Come on, let's get you filled up.'

He took the bottle from my hand and filled it.

'That enough?' he asked.

'Yeah, I think so. Half for the car, half for me.'

'No, no. Fill the car, come back, fill it for yourself.'

I did as I was told. The radiator took almost a gallon before diluted piss began overflowing. The man filled my bottle again.

'Thank you. Thank you so much,' I said to them.

He smiled. Even the woman seemed kind when she saw how much I meant it. Maybe she saw the bigger picture, understanding that someday her son might be stuck pissing into his engine at the side of a highway in need of a friend as well.

The family left, disappearing into the churning heat. I started the Miata – the temperature needle pointing to 'C'. I got moving straight away to take advantage. Keeping the heater on, I managed sixty-five as the road smoothed out in sections. The chilled water was ecstasy as I glugged and poured some onto my head, letting it trickle down my face, back and chest.

A solitary building appeared on the horizon. I leant against the Miata as the bowser ticked and pumped. Even forty feet away, under the shade of the gas station's roof, I could feel heat radiating from the lone strip of tarmac reaching towards each horizon. There was nothing else around. I went into the bathroom and washed sweat and dirt from my face and arms. Brown water splattered across the sink. I binned my bottle and pulled another two gallons of chilled water from the fridge. The clerk ran up the bill and looked to the Miata.

'That thing overheating or the air con ain't working?' he asked.

'Two for two,' I replied. He shook his head, pushed glasses back up his red nose and resumed tapping keys on the till. He told me scorching days like this were great for business. That the gas in the underground tanks heats up, causing it to expand, and a gallon of it on a hot day has fewer hydrocarbon atoms in it than on a cold one. Fewer hydrocarbons meant less combustion in the engine, which meant fewer miles out of a tank. A more frequent need to stop meant a higher chance of people stopping there and filling up with gas that wasn't going to get them as far anyway.

He sniggered to himself as to why the common consumer hadn't caught on it should be sold by weight, not volume. I forced a smile and nod of concurrence then asked what the hell he was doing in a place like this. 'I love gasoline,' he deadpanned. 'Where else would I be?'

The sun took a substantial lead, sitting lower in the sky as I turned south onto Interstate 15. The valley was still drowning in heat, but at last I could drop the top. I extended an arm to the atmosphere above.

Warm air pushed up the windshield and into my palm. I squeezed it into a ball and let it go over and over.

The radiator needed to be tended to a few more times but covered more miles between each refill. Crossing from Utah to Arizona, I put the Miata into neutral and gave us both a much-needed break. We weaved the Virgin River Gorge – a steep, winding descent with tall, unforgiving rock on either side. Walls of it drew back like curtains as the road snaked around to reveal the next, each making you feel smaller than the last. Without touching the brakes, the Miata sailed to ninety miles per hour, pushing me sideways in the seat as we rounded bends and flew past every other car and truck on the road.

Now I was making good time. The engine idled and for a while all I could hear was radio static, air rushing overhead and the whoosh of other cars as I sped by. It was peaceful. The gorge's end arrived, its rock changing from brown to nearly pink as it fell away. Flat desert with a cool breeze stretched in all directions. I heard a familiar bassline as the radio caught a frequency. The Miata seemed happy, coming back up to seventy without issue. A deep breath felt like my first in hours.

Turning the song up, I lit a cigarette, sucked in deep, and felt profound relief as tears began to run down my cheeks. Wind pushed through my hair. Faraway mountains cast long shadows in the setting sun, swallowing the desert, and I floated somewhere in between the dark and the light. I wondered what came after the fear had gone.

I entered Nevada having gone too far west. Reaching a motel lit-up by the neon sign of a bar it shared a parking lot and wall with, I pulled in, got a room, showered and walked into the night. Two old men in front of the bar pushed each other, slurring something or other. One threw a useless punch at the other, knocking his hat off and him to the ground. The swinging geezer lost his balance and almost collapsed too, balancing himself against the side of a pickup. He helped the fallen man to his feet, supporting him with an arm over his shoulder. I picked the hat up and handed it to the puncher. He took it, placed it back on the other's head, made sure it was straight, and nodded to me. Then the men staggered off together, mumbling, and disappeared into the night.

I went inside and took a seat. It was a quiet town and the bar had the ambience of a place where wasted words weren't encouraged. I got a drink and a burger. The only other patron was a man sitting a few stools down from me. His upper lip was raised on the left side, always revealing a bit of tooth. I couldn't tell if it was a scar. Maybe he'd worn a snarl for so long his face had changed.

He looked at me but didn't say anything. We locked eyes for a moment, before I turned back to the baseball game on the television and ate my burger.

The sound of a bang exploded through the wall behind – the one shared with the motel. It shook the ground and the bottles behind the bar rattled and clinked together. The bartender checked his watch, continued chewing nuts and turned the game up. Another bang, bigger than the first, and then a man's scream. Neither of the men in the bar reacted. It didn't seem like the kind of place to ask questions; even less like one to get answers. Muffled yells and something heavy hit the floor. I tried to filter the racket out but couldn't. Was someone being murdered ten feet from me? After a few more thumps, I turned back to the wall. The man with the raised lip took note.

'Don't ask,' he said.

'Wasn't going to.'

The bartender shrugged at me and kept chewing.

'He lives in the motel,' the raised lip added. 'This happens every night.'

'What happens every night?'

'I don't know. He's in there alone. That much I know.'

'Right.'

'I live here too. I used to try to get him to answer the door at first. I thought he was killing someone or being killed. I used to bang on that old thing, but he never answered. It's a mystery. Starts at nine o'clock every night just like clockwork. Can go for fifteen minutes or an hour.'

There was a large thud on the wall, shaking my beer, then another scream. I thought I could make out words but they were incomprehensible. I looked up to the hands on the wall. It was 9.03 p.m.

'Have you ever seen him?' I asked.

'Yeah, all the time. Nice fellow – keeps to himself. I've never questioned him about … whatever it is he's doing in there though.'

'Do you think he's okay?'

'Seems it.'

'How strange.'

'Yeah, very. Hey, cheers,' the man grinned, lifting his bottle. His bent lip lifted so high I could see gum. Not a pretty smile, but an honest one. I brought my bottle to his, finished eating and went to my room. I lay in bed listening to the faint, drowned-out screams. That room could've been the closest thing to hell on earth or it could've been someone's nirvana. Was I a few doors down from the most sorrowful man in existence or the happiest? I tried to imagine what he looked like, what he did and how he'd ended up here, beating his fists or his forehead into the walls of the motel room he lived in. Was he a monster or an angel? How crazy a man could become before implosion fascinated me, and then I remembered what I was doing in that same motel. I laughed at myself then fell asleep to the sound of the nameless, faceless man marching to the thump of his own drum through the walls.

3.

The secret to the driving, much like the living, was to get enough air. If a car overtook me and pulled back in front, my radiator would starve and the temperature gauge rise. I'd have to slow down or move across lanes to catch air left uninterrupted. Most of the time only one option presented itself in traffic, but occasionally I was given neither. If two trucks sat side by side ahead of me on a two-lane highway, there was no choice but to drop way back. A good speed couldn't be averaged like that and the engine didn't have the gusto to accelerate around them before it became an issue.

I soon took to slotting the Miata's front bumper in the space between the trucks' rear wheels to scavenge any air pulled through. It was terrifying at first, having those metallic behemoths swaying left and right in gusts of desert wind, so close they almost took the dirt off my panels, but I quickly adapted to the way they moved and even to the confused, angry looks from other motorists. It was nice to drive east again. The sun would pass like some stranger travelling the opposite direction down some indifferent highway, neither of us taking much notice of the other.

I passed Flagstaff and Winslow, covering a section of Route 66 to reach Holbrook. The first motel I pulled into had a balcony; maybe the one from the letter, maybe not. I wandered the sidewalks, dust of the desert blown onto them crunching under my boots. Shrubs freckled the dry, empty land. There wasn't much happening. A motel's sign asked if I'd slept in a Wigwam lately and I couldn't say I had.

Almost all of the storefronts paid homage to Route 66 like some deity. A clerk sold me cigarettes and told me the town had been busier before the bypass went in.

Americans celebrated everything they could, even a road. In my mind, Australians didn't take as much pride in anything they had. I guessed it was because, to Americans, Route 66 wasn't just a road. It was an idea; some notion of greener pastures, better lives, the traversing of some great frontier. Constructed of dreams incarnate, not tarmac, stretched out across the land. But the American Dream was a farce, and just as imagination cannot be tamed into reality, a dream no longer exists once it has been attained. So then, it seemed to me, you either let your dreams run free like wild horses, watching their beauty from afar and accepting you'll never stroke them with your palm, or you catch them, break them in, own them, and know that in doing so you have dulled their fire in an irreparable way. The American Dream was just pornography for the soul, and anybody convinced it could be held in their hands was a fool.

I pushed the door of a bar on Navajo Boulevard in and stepped through. I ordered a drink, lit a cigarette, and felt alright. People really do go to remarkable lengths to feel a little better, ingesting ideals or diet pills or god, when all it really takes can be found inside any bar on any street in any town.

I drank into the night. Few letters remained – the thought of being without them, and what might come after, almost too much to bear. So many of my days had been spent living with the unanswered and the unknown that I'd become accustomed to them. In many ways, they were easy company, able to become whatever I imagined them to be, and nothing and nobody could tell me I was wrong. I ordered another drink, getting the feeling it was later than it seemed. The bartender shook his head, miming the slitting of his throat with straightened fingers.

'Well, shit, what does that mean?' I asked.

'Oowie! I've been drinking here twenty years and I've never seen someone get cut off before,' said a woman on the next stool.

'Yeah? What's the prize?'

'There ain't one. Your wallet's a little heavier tomorrow, I suppose.'

I stepped out onto the sidewalk and hobbled in the direction of my motel, making it halfway before I had to rest. I sat on a bench, then fell from it. Placing a cigarette between my lips, I shuffled backwards on my ass towards a shopfront instead.

There was an immense weight to the sky that night. It placed its hands against my shoulders and pushed down. I sat slouched against the wall, sucking breath in through my lips and pushing smoke out through my nose, looking up to it with an overwhelming sense of anticipation, as if it were a tidal wave or an explosion frozen above, readying itself to consume everything below.

I wondered what had stopped that from happening for so long. How this world contained all the happiness and the sadness; the good and the evil; the love and the hate. How each day there was more of it than the one before, and where it all went. It had to go somewhere, surely. It couldn't just dissipate into nothing, or there'd be no point to it at all.

Did it push back? Was that what held the sky up? Stars appeared like pinholes; maybe there to vent the pressure of this world's collective soul to some great, bright beyond. They throbbed as if barely able to control it. I wondered if the space taken up by just one more new mother's joy or widow's sorrow would become too much. That some cosmic seesaw might tip – rips spreading across the sky from star to star. That it might pop and expose that great beyond, flooding in and sweeping us away to salvation or crushing us under the weight of it all. That breaking point had never felt closer to me.

There was a tap against my boot. A man holding two large paper bags full of groceries stood beside me. He looked down his long nose.

'What are you doing?'

'Just sitting.'

'Why don't you get up?'

'Can't. Sky's too heavy. Don't you feel it?'

'Everything alright, son?'

I frowned and shook my head and blew smoke out through my nose.

'No, what a ridiculous thing to say.'

'How do you figure?'

'Some things are awful and some things are brilliant, and that's the way it is. I would never say everything is just okay.'

'I think you should go home. Do you need a ride?'

'No, I need another drink, but I was cut off,' I said, mimicking the gesture of the slit throat. 'Hey, did you hear? I'm the first person to be cut off here in twenty years. That means this town ain't seen a drinker like me in a long time.'

'You must be very proud.'

'Yes, sir, I am.'

'Get yourself home safe.'

I made a sloppy army salute. The man rolled his upper lip, pushing his white moustache into his nostrils, then disappeared down the street. A few more people passed, but no one else stopped. I sat for a while longer then walked back to my room.

4.

When I was sure the last of my vomit had washed down the sink, I turned on the radio, stretched out on my back on the motel bed, and began drinking again. I refused to go east or west, north or south. I had lost much more than any enlightenment, bliss or closure I'd gained from retracing these letters.

Each had seemed to steer me further from where and who I wanted to be. My father's travels had been his; attempting some poor man's recreation of them in search of answers was my own naive idiocy, and now I found myself with no compelling reason to carry on or to return home. I waited in self-imposed purgatory for answers to questions I hadn't asked yet – some clue I wouldn't recognise.

Slivers of light found their way between blinds and shadows began to move. A cobweb had formed in a corner of the room. It caught air rising from the back of a bar fridge beneath, making soft turns as it rose and fell. Its shape was like a child's drawing of a fish; an infinity symbol with an end left open. At certain angles, it caught in the light and shimmered. I watched it bend and twist as it swam through an endless ocean.

In the afternoon, I woke from a nap I hadn't planned to take. The view from my room wasn't spectacular, but over the tops of other buildings and through the gaps between, I could see the desert disappearing into the distance. The funny thing about the horizon is everybody has their own and it moves with them. I had spent my time in America convinced I could catch mine, but had made myself the butt of my own joke. For every step forward I took, my horizon took one back, taunting me. Trying to run it down was a fool's errand.

The great frontier isn't somewhere you go, I decided. It isn't something you reach by plane or car, bus or boat. It exists inside each man, when he takes that first big stride or timid step over the city limits of his own self. If my father was waiting for me at the end of all of this, I would shake his hand, buy him a drink and then break his nose. I would drag him from the bar, bloodied, and pin him on the sidewalk by his throat for everyone to see. I'd ask him if it was all worth it; if the two lives he ruined were worth it to forge the one he had for himself. If he were proud of himself – proud that the son he'd abandoned felt a flicker of hatred whenever he was told he looked just like his father. That his leather was too worn for his age and that he had become rotten inside like a piece of fruit.

The desert changed, white speckles appearing in the purple sky. It's strange how it happens out there; the darkness sneaks up on you. The cold is brutal and sudden, like warmth and life is looted from the land the moment the sun's vigilant eye wanes. I swayed down Navajo Boulevard. There were a few bars to choose from, so I decided to try an alternative to the one I'd been asked to leave the night before. I caught a few glances as I entered. Maybe I was already a celebrity in this town.

I drank and drank. Even when I didn't think I could stomach another, I tapped on the bar. I clicked my lighter shut and dropped it onto the bar in front of me. A man beside me, chatting up a woman another seat down the bar, picked it up. In a swift, finessed movement he clicked the lid open, turned the tip of the two smokes between his lips bright red and clicked it shut again. He handed one of the cigarettes to her. She smiled like they were following a script. A real fuckin' John Wayne.

'This is a nice lighter,' he either said to her or to me as he studied it between his fingers.

'Well, you can find one like it in just about any gas station,' I said, snatching it from his grip. 'This one's not for sale.'

'Hey now, I wasn't asking to buy it.'

'Yeah? What, planning on taking it? Go for it. Good luck.'

The bartender curved a brow and the woman seemed uncomfortable.

'Son, I was merely admiring your lighter. Used to have one a bit like it. Didn't mean any harm.'

'Marvellous. Thank you for sharing.'

I managed to get another drink before being asked to leave. A few patrons looked like they wanted to follow and bruise me up, but the man who'd used my lighter just watched with curious eyes. I stumbled up the street past the same bus stop. Even drunker than the night before, I skipped the first part, went straight to the shopfront and sat down on the ground.

Ash grew long on my cigarette before being taken in the breeze. I closed my eyes and listened to faraway trucks. The sky pushed down on my shoulder again, its pressure so extreme it roused me from sleep. The man with the long nose and the white moustache knelt beside me, holding a brown paper bag under his arm.

'Damn, how many groceries do you go through?'

'Not nearly as many as you do drinks, I'm guessing.'

'Did you hear I'm two for two?'

'Two for two what?'

'Getting cut off from bars in this shitty town.'

'What are you doing, son?'

'I'm sitting.'

'No, what are you doing with yourself and this life?'

'That's a hostile question.'

'Only for some.'

'I'm going to California.'

'Really? Because it looks to me like you're not doing a whole bunch of anything. Looks to me like you haven't moved an inch since I last saw you.'

'Why don't you fuck off?'

'Why don't you let me give you a ride back to wherever it is you're staying?'

I pondered his offer.

'Okay.'

Working myself up the brickwork, I stood and swayed, looking up at the man. He was a giant. 'Come on,' he said as we walked to his truck. I leant my head against his passenger window, looking up as we drove. The stars were bright. I watched as they faded to black through my tired, drooping eyes.

5.

A distant echo of hammering paused. An electric whir followed, then more banging. I opened my eyes. Only faint outlines of furniture and strips of light at the edges of the doorway and window could be seen. Dropping my legs off the side of the bed, I felt better than I'd expected to – the carpet lush against my bare feet. I rubbed them back and forth then stood, walked towards the outline of the window and ran a hand along the wall around. Finding a small knob hanging from a string, I pulled down and the blinds shot up, stacking against each other like dominos in reverse.

When my vision adjusted to the brightness, I leant my forehead against the glass and looked left to right. I was on the second floor of a property, but it wasn't the motel. A wooden fence traced a perimeter, rolling hills with scattered shrubbery disappearing in all directions beyond. Not another building in sight. I was in my underpants, with the clothes I'd been wearing neatly folded over a chair in the corner, my bags and boots underneath.

I searched my duffel. My passport remained, but the whiskey was gone. Feeling through my jacket's pockets, so too were my car keys, cigarettes and lighter. I got dressed and collected my bags. A flight of stairs descended to a large room with floors of black stone. Opposite the kitchen at one end was a large fireplace reaching up a triangular ceiling that must've been twenty feet high at its peak.

'Hello?' I yelled through the house.

No response. Pushing open what I assumed to be the front door, I stepped out onto a porch wrapping around the building. I walked down a few steps to a gravel path alongside a wall, opening to a large expanse, its far end forming a driveway meandering downhill to a gate in the wooden fence. A dog ran to me, jumping up with outstretched paws and a wagging tail. I pushed it away and kept walking. The man appeared from around a corner at the end of the wall and stepped towards me, smudges of dirt on his face.

'Ah, Mark, you're finally awake.'

I stopped and felt blood boiling in my veins.

'Where the fuck am I?'

'This is my home. A few minutes out of Taylor, another half hour from Holbrook.'

'Did I ask you to bring me here?'

'Not with those exact words.'

'Then why am I here?'

'Because you looked like you needed help, and you looked like you weren't going to get it for yourself.'

'You went through my bags.'

'I needed to know what kind of person I was bringing into my home.'

'Where are my keys? Give them to me.'

'Right here,' he said, pulling them from his pocket with a dirty hand.

He threw them. Gliding through the air, lambent in the sunshine, they found my palm.

'Take me to my car.'

'Don't have to, it's right here,' he said, tilting his head around the corner he'd emerged from.

THE ROADMAP OF LOSS

'Good. I'm out of here.'

'There might be a slight issue with that plan, son,' he said as I passed him and rounded the corner.

My duffel bag dropped with my jaw. Behind an open garage door sat the Miata, skeleton showing, front wheels suspended in the air, stands propped underneath. Its front bumper and bonnet were nowhere to be seen; the radiator and half of the engine were missing, cogs and gears and pulleys exposed like organs.

'Yep. Had my wife drive me to Holbrook this morning so I could bring it back here for you, and she started overheating straight away,' the man said, stepping up beside me with a crunch of gravel underfoot and hands on hips. The dog came and sat down too, making it three.

'What have you done ...?'

'Not much yet, really. The water pump's trashed, that's the problem. Already called the spares place in town. Unsurprisingly, they don't carry much for a little thing like this, so while I was at it, I also ordered a timing kit, gaskets, filters and whatnot. You know, just the basics.' He sucked in air and pushed it out between slack lips. 'I figured, hell, while we're doing the pump we might as well give her a proper once-over.'

'We?'

'Yeah, we.'

'We're not doing anything. You're going to put my car back together right now and I'm going to leave.'

'Sure, if you want, I could do that. Or you could wait a few days for the parts to arrive, we put her back together, your ungrateful smartass maybe even learns a thing or two along the way, and you end up with a car that might actually make it to California. Something tells me you're not in much of a rush to get anywhere.'

I stood there breathing through my nostrils. Stepping towards the Miata, I supposed that I should want to scream, tackle the man to the ground and beat him. Yet all I felt was an overwhelming calm all the way down to my bones.

'I can't afford all the things you just said.'

'It's on me, they weren't expensive.'

'I can't pay you to stay here either.'

'That's fine too. Let's get started on lunch.'

'Now?'

'It's two in the afternoon. You were out cold for almost sixteen hours,' he said, draping rags over uncovered parts of the engine.

'What's your name?'

'It's Jack. I'm gonna wash up now.'

Jack walked past me with the dog in pursuit, closing the front door behind him. I looked over the Miata then at the hills around me. It was quiet there like I'd never heard before. I picked up my bag and went back inside.

We had lunch but I couldn't have a drink. The house was dry. I was given my cigarettes and lighter back after an argument, but the whiskey went into Jack's safe.

'I've told you, there is no drinking on this property.'

'Fine, I'll drink at the end of the driveway past the property line.'

'Okay, have it your way if you're so desperately in need.'

He pressed a code into the safe, took the bottle out and handed it over. I walked down the winding driveway with the dog trotting alongside, its tail pointed proudly to the sky. Inching open the gate's hitch, I swung it open a few feet and stepped off the property, feeling uneasy right away. The cork came clear of the bottle's neck with a pop and whiskey stench filled the air.

Jack stood in the front doorway, leaning against its frame with crossed arms, watching me from a distance. I flicked a limp wrist to shoo him off. He shook his head and continued leaning and watching. I felt like a child needing supervision in the bathroom, but too embarrassed to piss in front of someone. The whiskey smelled sweet as I brought the bottle to my face, but I couldn't bridge the last inches of space between its rim and my lips. I pushed the cork in, closed the gate, and walked up the path past a silent, smug Jack back into the house.

Jack's wife returned that evening, introducing herself as Diane. They both seemed confused by my doubts at the dinner table. We talked, but there were very few questions about me. They were in bed by 10 p.m. Lighting a cigarette with shaky hands, I realised I couldn't remember the last time I'd gone a day without a drink. I sat on a bench on the porch, the dog asleep next to me. It was pleasant, but the land was bleeding warmth and would soon be cold. The moon seemed to take up half the sky, touching everything beneath with a gentle hum of blue.

The desert was so raw. There was an honesty and realness to it like nothing I'd ever encountered. It stood before you like a lover stripped for the first time, exposing themselves, letting you study every crease and bump and imperfection. Every place probably looked the same underneath; the oceans, the forests, the mountains, the fields; all deserts or something close, but covered with pretty things, like a woman insistent on makeup and pearls. If the earth had a pulse, then it could surely be felt most in the desert, where there was so little to obscure or dampen it.

I got into bed and stared at the ceiling for three hours, tossing and turning with exhausted frustration. What had I let myself become? I couldn't fall asleep without a few drinks swimming in my veins anymore. I'd only made it through my days bolstered by things that made them feel easier, not knowing how weak they'd made me in the process. I relaxed my clenched fists and let out a sigh into the pitch black of the room. There was a lot a man could learn from a desert.

6.

Reading filled my days. I'd close my eyes, reach towards the bookshelf and pull down whatever met my hand. Finishing or revisiting one rarely happened, but that wasn't the point; it was a welcome distraction from the drink and I couldn't watch television anymore. The people on there made me anxious with their white teeth and laugh tracks, and it made me want to drink. They all seemed like idiots to me, but they were idiots who managed to resolve their issues in neat, twenty-two-minute blocks. Mine had lived with me much longer than that. Their ease suggested I'd spent my life having the wrong conversations with the wrong people, or worse, that I was what was wrong.

If not reading or walking the slopes around the property with the dog, I scribbled drawings onto sheets of paper in my room or the kitchen. One of my works featured a stick figure in a little car with pop-up headlights – a horned stick figure in a bigger car engulfed in flames in pursuit.

'What the heck is this supposed to be?' Jack queried after uncovering the sketch one afternoon.

'Just a nightmare I had,' I answered.

By the fourth day, my withdrawals had peaked and begun

tapering off. The shakiness in my hands improved, as did my sleep. Parts started trickling into the auto store. Jack would thank some 'Marty', hang up the phone and yell out that something-or-other had arrived for me. 'Excellent,' I would reply, turning another page or scribbling another line, having no idea what he'd just said.

We made the trip into Holbrook each day to run his errands, and my evenings wound down on the porch. The dog and I got into a routine on its bench: I would read and try to have only one or two cigarettes; the dog would shuffle an inch closer each time the mercury fell. Jack never told me the thing's name and I never asked. The dog never mentioned it either. It was just a dog, but it would raise its ears and tail when it saw me and I liked that.

Diane forced me into a somewhat regular sleeping pattern, which I suspected was at Jack's suggestion. He revelled in giving me a hard time, though I felt he didn't want it to be all he gave. The three of us drank coffee on their porch in the early mornings. The dog took a diplomatic position on the floorboards between and nobody uttered a word, steam curling from our mugs and the rise and fall of our chests the only movement. Diane would leave for work at the same school Jack retired from years earlier. He was waiting for her retirement, but on the same day of each year following his own, she'd return home with tales of her new class of students.

'This life's no good spent waiting. It should be filled with nows, not soons,' I said one morning after she'd departed. Jack stared into his mug then over the land. He always had some quip, but had nothing then.

Returning with the final haul of new car parts, Jack lent me an old shirt of his that looked like a girl's sundress on me. He was a meticulous man, taking more pride in the cleaning and arranging of his tools at the end of a day's work than I perhaps had about anything in life. We tore the Miata down even further – every piece removed

THE ROADMAP OF LOSS

accompanied by some long-winded explanation of its purpose. This slowed the process considerably and annoyed me at first. But as we went on and I listened to Jack speak with passion only so I might know more than I did, it grew on me.

I learnt the garage, tools and engine. Lying in bed at night, I'd become excited about the next day's work, envisaging turning nuts and bolts. We'd finish at 3 p.m. sharp so Jack could be ready for Diane's return. She was maybe the only thing he held dearer than his pride. They'd spend the afternoons and evenings together and I'd feel like merely a substitute for when there was nobody else around. Walking the hills, I looked to the dog and wondered if he ever thought the same of himself.

At the dinner table that night, Jack began speaking in code to Diane.

'I'm gonna take him to see her,' he said.

'I really don't think he'd be interested,' she replied. I sat there with narrowed eyes, watching them speak about me like I wasn't there. Jack shovelled another piece of steak into his mouth and worked words out around it.

'It'll be good for him.'

'He doesn't want to see her. He just wants to get his car fixed and go to California.'

'There's no rush. California will always be there; it can wait another day.'

'If you say so, Jack.'

'What'll be good for whom?' I interjected.

He smirked and cleared his plate from the table.

'Jack wants to take you to –'

'Hey now,' he interrupted from the kitchen bench. 'He doesn't need to know yet.'

Jack had a strange air about him in general. Carefree but focused, like at all times he knew something you didn't and might lose interest at the very moment you figured it out. Despite this, he'd also done no evil to me or to the world as far as I could see, and giving him the benefit of the doubt had only resulted in good things for me. The two of them went back and forth. An argument between people as in love as them was an unusual thing to watch. It was the longest I'd ever seen them remain in a state of disagreement, and it piqued my interest enough to want to know what they both deemed worth it.

'I'll go,' I said, jumping between their parleying.

Diane seemed surprised by my response. Jack didn't.

'Good. Tomorrow morning then. Set an alarm for five and get a good night's rest. We'll be heading off before dawn,' he said, walking from the kitchen. He stopped and turned back. 'Wear those Converse shoes of yours and those shorts with the deep pockets,' he added, and then was gone.

'I really wish he hadn't gone through my things,' I said to Diane.

'I didn't agree with it, but I wouldn't have agreed with him not doing it either.'

'Is he always such a smug prick?'

'Smug mightn't be the right word.'

'No issue with prick though?'

She smiled and winked as she stood and cleared our plates.

'You have a more suitable word?' I asked.

'I'm not sure. Heck, I don't know if they've even come up with one for Jack. He just doesn't care much for any way other than his own.'

'You don't say ...'

'It doesn't bother me none though. You're going to find people like that all over the place. I'm just thankful he's got a good heart to go along with the attitude.'

Diane finished tidying up then was gone too. I leant under the table to the dog resting at my feet. 'I don't suppose you're coming tomorrow?' I asked. He huffed and lowered his head back to the floor.

7.

Jack was banging on my door by 5.04 a.m. The blinds were open but the bedroom was dark. I got dressed, putting on my Converse and shorts just like I was told. Diane was at the kitchen bench preparing lunches. 'Can you tell me where we're going?' I yawned. She sighed as she spread butter over bread.

'I'm just his wife. Now you get to meet his one true love.'

Jack and I drove west through the darkness, passing Holbrook and Winslow then turning north at Flagstaff. We passed a sign for the Grand Canyon. 'No ...' I said. Jack smirked and kept driving.

We parked on the canyon's South Rim. The sun was coming up, piercing the icy air and changing the sky. Jack pulled a pack from his truck and two sticks that looked like a skier's poles.

'Ha, really?' I asked.

'I'm not as young as I used to be.'

'Might as well skip the bullshit and go straight to an all-terrain walking frame, no?'

'Alright, we'll see how you feel about it later on.'

'Whatever you say, old man.'

Boarding a shuttle bus full of hikers who seemed a lot more excited to be there than I was, we pottered along the rim. A young couple rotated in their seat ahead and asked what trail we were doing.

'Maybe only to the river and back today,' Jack replied.

'Oh jeez, that's ballsy!' the girl exclaimed.

'Well, I'm just an old man, after all.'

The shuttle drove for fifteen minutes and we arrived at another site full of people.

'We're just walking back to where we got on the bus, right?' I asked Jack as we disembarked and he tied his boot against a rock.

'That's where we end up, yes. Let's get moving.'

'So a few miles?'

'Yeah, a few.'

'Doesn't seem too far.'

'It isn't,' he said, walking away without looking back. 'In a straight line.'

We set out, soon leaving the paved parking lot and entering a rough trail. We descended into the shadows one peak of rock drew onto the next and reached a cliff. It seemed impossible that a walkway might negotiate the gradient, but it managed to by switching back on itself with tight turns over and over, taking a nibble out of the precipice with each.

We would traverse hundreds of yards of path to descend what the near-vertical canyon wall did in twenty straight feet. I looked down, concentrating on aiming each step, trying not to slip as the worn soles of my Chuck Taylors skated on loose sand. Each step sent a jolt through my foot, up my knee and through the rest of my body.

'I don't think my shoes are cut out for this,' I said.

'Seriously? Excuses already? I don't think it's the shoes that aren't cut out for this,' he grunted. After a mile of thuds and slips, as we dropped further into the canyon, there was still no sign of the trail smoothing out or any climb back towards the altitude we'd started from. Jack powered on ahead, stabbing the earth with his poles.

'Where the hell are we going?' I yelled.

'Didn't you hear me before? Rim to river and back.'

'You know that doesn't mean anything to me. Where is this river?'

'You can't see it from here.'

I looked out over the canyon. Rock rose and fell without sympathy, stretching into the distance for miles and miles, but no hint of a river anywhere.

'Jack, how far is the river?'

'I'd say about another seven miles and, hmm, maybe four thousand feet of descent.'

'What ...'

'A little less than ten miles on the way back up though, which makes the incline a breeze.'

Dread washed over me. I stopped, almost slipping as I did.

'Fuck this, I'm going back.'

'Hey, wait a second now,' Jack ordered, turning and striding towards me. 'I don't bring just anybody here. I thought this might be good for you.'

'Well, thank you for the privilege, but I'm not interested.'

I turned and lifted myself up a step. He grabbed my arm, a lot stronger than he looked.

'Get off me.'

He didn't. I wanted to push him, but could've counted aloud how long something would take to find earth resting beyond the edge of the trail's steep edge. A couple passed by. I took notice of them and they of us, but Jack didn't seem to care.

'Let yourself be fixed. Let this place fix you.'

'What the fuck are you talking about?'

'You need to let go of all this anger you've built up. Walk the trail with me.'

'I'm not angry; I just don't want to hike through your goddamn canyon.'

'You don't want to, or you don't think you can?'

'It doesn't matter. Get off me, you senile son of a bitch.'

'If you don't, then it's because you refused to. If you can't, then it's because you never gave yourself the chance. The canyon doesn't say no, only we do.'

I looked along the trail. The couple had stopped within earshot, pretending to take a photo. They saw me watching. 'You looking to take the real fast way down?' I barked. They continued walking. Jack shook his head.

'You're an angry kid, Mark.'

'Get off me, Jack,' I said calmly.

He released my arm and waited.

'Have you done this trail before?'

'Yes, a few times a year for the last thirty.'

'Why?'

'Because once upon a time it saved me. It fixed me when I thought I was beyond fixing. And maybe it doesn't do a damn thing for you, but you'd be a fool not to give it a chance.'

A cool breeze blew. The day was still young and suddenly I felt the same. It, and maybe I, could still be made into something worthwhile.

'You're a cheesy prick, you know that?' I asked.

'It's possible.'

We stood facing each other. There was peace in Jack's eyes, his white hair tossed about in the moving air. He was the desert. I let out a sigh.

'How long does it take?'

'Most manage it in a little under ten hours.'

'Fuck me ... What have *you* done it in?'

'Eight, once, but I was a younger man.'

'Alright then,' I said, looking out over the expanse of indifferent rock. 'Let's do it in eight.'

'I can make it there and back up, but not that fast.'

'Seriously? You're gonna give me a pep talk then excuses with the same breath?'

Jack extended his upper lip, pushing moustache into his nostrils. I placed hands on his shoulders, which were the same height as mine with him standing down a step, and turned him around. 'Come on, old man. Let's go find enlightenment in the dirt. Shouldn't have forgotten your skis.'

I nudged him and we carried on.

'Cocky little bastard.'

Jack's strides were huge compared to mine. It seemed like I needed almost two for every one of his. Sections with stairs levelled the playing field as we each took them one at a time, but with his hiking boots and poles, Jack traversed them as if they were paved concrete, while I teetered left and right on each with a thump. I took to flexing my feet, curling my toes like a cat's claws, and stomping directly down instead of leaning forward. It helped for grip, but my feet and knees soon burned as they bore the brunt of my weight compressing them over and over.

We passed mile marker after mile marker, even catching and overtaking the occasional hiker. For a while, we managed to outrun the sun, staying inside the shadows as they receded down the canyon with us, but were soon consumed as the valley filled with heat. Rocks changed colour at various points, indicating how far we'd plunged. Jack listed the names of each layer and their order, trying to have me recite them. He still saw himself as a teacher and, I supposed to some extent, a guide. Every time I forgot a term, he'd get a little more frustrated, though I was only concerned with the balancing act of absorbing as little wear on my knees as possible while matching his pace.

I'd never concentrated so hard on walking while sober, but I'd have rather fallen from the edge than asked him to slow down. The canyon transformed in ways I wasn't expecting. The coarseness of the dirt, the shape of the land, even the air seemed different. We moved aside as a convoy of mules carrying tourists plodded up the trail in the opposite direction. The animals' eyelids sat low, draped over tired, black eyes – dust of the land coating their long lashes. They'd been born into a world that should've gifted them freedom, but were instead having their backs broken by fat sightseers. Each seemed to acknowledge me as they passed. We'd all been deceived that day.

Again and again, we reached a section's end, rounding a bend or arriving at a place where the land fell away, only to be greeted by the next, the path ahead navigating down a gully or snaking along a plateau to vanish at what seemed like some unreachable point. The canyon was made of them. Callous sections, one after the other, taking turns to break you, the only prize at the finish line of each being the realisation there was another one waiting. Your body and mind accumulated wear from the miles before, begging you to stop, and telling you that if you were going to fall, this would be the one. But, after that, elation from remembering you'd felt the exact same each time before. Laughing at yourself, you'd get moving, knowing you'd made it further than you thought possible and were about to again. Even though my body ached, I began taking pleasure in the chance to take a first step over and over. A person who looked at each day making up their life in the same way might just be damn near unstoppable.

Arriving at one of the points where the land fell away, I looked back up the steepness to the spot from which I'd gazed at it earlier. It too seemed impossibly far. I took a deep breath and pushed on.

THE ROADMAP OF LOSS

Soon, green dotted the otherwise barren land.

'Does that mean we're getting close?' I asked.

'Mhmm,' Jack replied. He'd become less chatty.

Scaling a short stretch of incline, I saw the river at last. It was way down, a bridge passing over it. From where we stood, the trail made a swift cutback away from the ravine, drawing a massive, tilted horseshoe around a gully. It led to an opening in rock on the other side – a whole lot of nothing and a huge fall the only things inside its wide arc. The tiny speck of a hiker moved towards the black dot of the opening on the other side like an ant. It must have been three or four hundred yards across, and a hundred down. I didn't want to know how long the walk around was. We kept going.

My feet were giving up; tendons and soles burning, my toes throbbing as they slammed into the ends of my shoes with every jarring step. With each step, they swelled a little more, making the next one perpetually worse. We reached the opening in the rock face and Jack stepped through. I stopped and looked back. Hikers stood at the beginning of the horseshoe-shaped section I'd just navigated. I wondered if they could see me, and if they were doubting whether they could make it, just like I had.

Stepping into the tunnel, I waited for my eyes to adjust to the darkness. They did, but just enough to make out faint licks of light accenting rock at my feet, the path worn smooth by so many tired steps before mine.

Jack hadn't waited; I was the only one in there. Sounds of rushing water could be heard like the whispers of a hundred faraway voices. Their chatter grew as I made my way through; it felt like they were speaking about me. Murmurs turned to talking, yelling and then screaming, deafening by the tunnel's end.

I stepped out into the sun and onto the bridge, the Colorado River wide and furious below, a huge fall between. Jack was there. His mouth moved but I couldn't hear him over the torrent. We crossed and began following the bank. My feet were giving out now, and Jack could tell. Passing a campsite, we headed up a narrow path into what looked like a garden. An offshoot of the river weaved through as a thin, gentle stream, a small clearing leading right to it. A large rock sat with half its mass in the dry and half in the wet, stained at the waterline.

'Soak your feet,' Jack said.

'That an order?'

'It's whatever gets you to do it,' he said as he left to refill our drinking bottles.

I stood up straight until he was gone, then slumped on the ground at the creek's edge, draping my tired body over the rock's hardness like linen. My throbbing legs melted into the ground as I pulled my shoes and socks off, running a finger along the distinct shift from desert brown to white skin where my sock had been. Maybe Mother Nature had decided I'd done enough damage to my body and was reclaiming it. I straightened my legs out and dunked them into the freezing water.

Pebbles of the creek's bank felt like coarse ice as I brushed my soles against them, its current so cold I felt my heartbeat in the bones of my feet. They tingled and the skin pulled tight like it was about to tear. Within minutes, they went numb, and I rested my head against the rock. I wouldn't have believed someone who said there existed a lush garden in the belly of the Grand Canyon, but here I was, recovering in its waters. I closed my eyes and listened to the trickling creek.

Jack returned and retrieved four sandwiches from his pack, handing two to me. Three Spanish-speaking women walked by our small clearing as we ate. My gaze met one of theirs and she smiled, pushing hair behind an ear.

'There's a lot of beauty here,' Jack remarked, a reflection of the canyon in his eyes. 'It's almost overwhelming. Bit like medicine for the soul.'

Her ass pushed against spandex, moulding and folding with her hips as they swayed into the distance.

'You're damn right, Jack,' I responded, chewing with a dry mouth.

The trail wound along the riverside. Having already reached the height of its arc, the sun was beginning to fall. We were on track for eight hours and to make it out before dark. Further down, another bridge thrust us back over the river and we were on the South Rim again.

'Ooh, boy's wearing Chuck Taylors,' a woman whispered to her friend, pointing to my feet as we passed.

'Out of his damn mind,' the friend replied, wiping sweat from her brow and returning to her water bottle.

The trail leading back up the canyon was different to the one that lowered us to its guts. It was wider, made of greyish rocks, not the dusty rust of the earth from earlier. More forested, too, with greens and browns filling the gorge, a narrow creek nearby. The incline began and the reduced strain on my knees felt like heaven in relative terms compared to the downhill.

I noticed Jack's tempo slow. He suggested I set the pace for a while, as he had for the entire hike. He was fading. It was a strength and endurance game from here, and I had him on both. The climb's grit gave good friction compared to the fine sand of the descent and my shoes seemed not to hinder me. My strides became longer and more confident; all I had to do was keep an eye out for stones big enough to trip over camouflaged among the smaller ones. We powered past three men who walked at the pace of people with nothing to prove. Whenever Jack picked up his pace to match mine, I shifted it another gear. Each time I sped up, Jack's breath became more laboured as he drove spikes into the gravel behind me with desperation. With each clink of their metal tips, I imagined myself as some master sculptor chiselling away at his stony will.

'Hey, grandpa, I'm kind of fading. Got any more words of inspiration back there?' I yelled.

'No, I just ... let me concentrate,' he worked out between stabbing breaths.

It wasn't graceful, but everyone has to eat and choke on their own words at some point. Jack had underestimated me, and now his moustache and his big nostrils and his goddamn ski poles were paying the price. The only way I was going to get his respect was by wrestling it from his grip; it wasn't going to be had any other way. And surely, I thought, he was smart enough to ask me to slow down before his heart gave out.

'Come on, old man. That all you got?' I asked as we stomped up the path. Even I was beginning to breathe heavily.

'Pace yourself, son, there's plenty more miles.'

'Tell you what,' I said, turning and walking backwards up the incline to face him. 'You just say the word and we'll take a break. I promise I won't tell anybody, not even Diane.'

'Cocky ... little bastard ...'

'You know, this canyon may be the love of your life, but I think she wants to take me behind the bleachers and make me her boyfriend,' I said, curling fingers of a hand and jerking it up and down in the air a few times.

Jack looked like a red-faced bull trying to charge me. My cackling echoed through the ravine like a hyena. He was about to break; I could feel it. Maybe I'd pour him a drink after I'd carried him home.

I took another few steps backwards, licking the teeth of my wicked smile, then turned to face up the trail. As I did, my left foot came down to find the top of a large stone, skating a few inches to the side.

THE ROADMAP OF LOSS

There was a throb in my knee unlike all the others. I'd been in pain for six hours; after six hours of rain, one droplet might be hard to tell apart from the others, but this one wasn't. Less of a pinch, more of a bang, like hitting a pothole in a car with blown shocks. A sting shot up my leg and hip like a twisting corkscrew, causing them to go weak.

I tried to keep the pace, placing my right foot underneath and thrusting up the canyon, but that same pain was waiting as I tipped back onto the left. My knee buckled as if I'd lost all connection to it other than via pain receptors, the leg about as useful as a crutch made of string. I toppled, slamming my kneecaps, then palms, into the coarse hardness below. Jack strolled up beside and stopped.

'Don't say a word.'

'Would I even need to?'

'I just slipped, is all.'

'Mhmm, I've found it helpful to face the direction you're going, especially when hiking. Maybe I should set the pace.'

'I'll set the pace.'

'Okay. Overtake me again and you can set the pace.'

I clambered to my feet, following Jack with grinding footsteps. The pain in my left knee amplified with each. Inside fifty yards, my eyes watered and the pain became overwhelming. The knee gave out and I collapsed again.

The three men we'd overtaken passed us. I looked up from the ground and waited for Jack's wisecrack; the sealed stamp of his victory.

He just looked at me like he had the first time we'd met. Bringing one hand to the other, he looped a pole's wristband over his thumb, lifted it off, then did the same with the other. He unfurled both hands towards me – one holding the poles, the other empty and upturned.

'You can take one or both,' he said, 'but you can't take neither.'

I deliberated, then forced myself back to my feet without help, unable to mask a groan as I did. It felt like someone was hanging off my back as another forced a nail through the space behind my kneecap. I rubbed my palms together, dislodging fragments of gravel embedded in them. Pricks of blood followed, mixing with the dirt.

'Wise choice,' he said, handing me the poles. 'There are a lot of miles left.'

Digging into his backpack, he withdrew two head torches, ensured they worked, and handed one to me.

'Why?' I asked.

'Something tells me we're not getting out of here before sundown anymore.'

We trekked up the canyon, every section becoming steeper than the one before. I transferred my weight onto the poles as I brought my left leg forward. They really did take a load off the knees. The old man wasn't a complete fool. Our trail became more populated as other paths merged onto it heading to the top. Group after group of hikers passed us as we moved with the most haste I could muster. After another mile, an ache began to build in my right knee. I had been carelessly shifting more and more weight onto it to save the left, but now its debt was due.

My pace dropped to a crawl as I clambered over even the slightest obstruction. Jack found a way to appease the situation, and his ego, by speeding off until just out of sight and waiting there until I caught up. 'Hey, look on the bright side, we'll both be old men by the time we're done,' he said at one point as I reached him, before powering away. 'Earlier, when you said eight hours, did you mean per mile?' he asked at the next before disappearing again.

The pain in my legs went beyond what I thought possible; my arms and back fatiguing as I propped myself up on the poles, now

THE ROADMAP OF LOSS

having to reset them for every step. When I reached Jack again, he didn't vanish, but instead walked ahead at my pace.

'You know, Mark, when I used to teach, there were a lot of Navajo children, and each new class liked to give me a Navajo name for the year.'

'Uhuh,' I mumbled, focusing on placing the pole tips between rocks.

'Well, I decided a while ago that I liked that, so I started giving them to people I took through the canyon. I mean, I dumbed them down, but I tried to base them on qualities they showed during the hike. The way they handled adversity.'

'Right.'

'For instance, I named one buddy "Wise Hawk" because he just seemed to intuit where the trail was going next, as if he were seeing it from above. I even named another "Selfless Bear", because he had the strength to carry his wife's pack and his own for their entire hike.'

'Is this going somewhere, Jack?'

'Yes. I've finally come to a decision for yours,' he said, stopping and turning back to me.

'Really?'

'Indeed, seeing you standing there like this, the way you're struggling to balance as you lean on those poles, huffing through your nose as you push yourself up this canyon. There's really only one name that makes sense.'

'Yeah?'

'Yeah. "Lame Horse."'

'Lame Horse? Lame Horse!? Are you fucking kidding me?'

'Ha!' he scoffed as he turned and began walking. 'I don't know why I would be. It's perfect!'

I swung a pole at him in anger, missed, and almost fell. He didn't notice and for that I was thankful, but still defeated. The whole place seemed to be laughing at me: the gurgling creek, the stones, the trees and the sky. The canyon's lesson, if there was one, was out of my reach.

Agony sent me into a sort of autopilot. I negotiated each step as a new, separate challenge, soon unable to discern whether I'd taken three minutes or three hours to reach Jack where he waited at the next turn. It was the canyon's own form of Chinese water torture. The only thing confirming I wasn't stuck in some infinite loop, taking the same steps over and over without moving, was when the shadows had climbed as far as me. My feet waded in them like the tide coming in. I tried to up the pace, but it was no use; soon my legs were submerged, then my sore, tired ass. Darkness crept up my neck and past my mouth. I lifted my nostrils but it got past them too, and then I was drowning. Still, though, I kept going. It astounded me I was still going.

When the grinding of sand and stone came up behind me, I'd move over on the narrow path to make room for faster-moving hikers. Some said thank you, some nodded, some did nothing at all. I hiked with my head down, staring at the ground in front. It helped place the poles, but also let me maintain the perpetual fantasy I was only a few steps from the top.

More footsteps. I shuffled to the side. They came up beside but did not overtake me.

'Are you okay?' a soft voice asked. She spoke with an accent; white teeth, blue eyes and blonde hair illuminated in the dusk light.

'Yeah, I'm fine,' I replied, feigning ease.

'What happened?'

'I hurt my knee. I'm alright.'

'Oh, I'm sorry. Do you mind if I walk with you?'

'Up to you; I'm taking it pretty slow.'

'That is okay. I have lost my group and it is boring to walk alone.'

'You're telling me … French?'

'Swedish.'

'Lovely.'

She smiled and slid thumbs down her backpack's straps from shoulders to hips. A skin-tight top glowed with the outline of her chest. Suddenly I felt better about the whole situation, relaxing my looking-forward-and-down policy. 'You can walk with me as long as you like.'

We reached Jack waiting at a switchback.

'Who's this? Your new hiking partner?' he asked.

'Yeah,' I said, passing without looking at him, the girl following.

'I'm offended,' he responded, strolling after us.

'Well, she's a lot nicer to be around than you. A lot nicer to look at too.'

'I can see that. Are you going to introduce me?'

'He did not even introduce himself,' she chuckled.

'A real charmer … Let me have the honour then. I'm Jack.'

'Hello, Jack. I am Alicia.'

'Well, nice to meet you, Alicia. Like I said, I'm Jack, and this is –'

'Shut up, Jack,' I barked, looking forward as I negotiated steps.

'This is Mark.'

I looked back with thin eyes. The old fucker was unreadable. Alicia looked at me.

'Hello, Mark.'

'Hi,' I said, turning back to the path.

'Well, I mean, he was called Mark, but I decided that name doesn't really suit him.'

'Oh? It does not?' she replied, intrigued.

'Shut the fuck up, Jack.'

'No, it doesn't, but I came up with a much better one. Would you like to hear it?

'Yes, of course.'

I sighed. I didn't want another minute in that canyon, but I couldn't pick up the pace. Jack's voice was inescapable, like one in my own head. I gritted my teeth and kept aiming the poles – it was all I could do.

'You see how he's walking now? Or, well, not quite walking.'

'Mhmm.'

'Well, I decided if he were here a century back, the Navajo would've named him Lame Horse.'

'Lame Horse …' Alicia repeated, pondering for a moment then giggling. 'Lame Horse – that is funny!'

'Isn't it?' Jack laughed along. 'Wouldn't you agree, Lame Horse?' he yelled ahead to me.

'Yeah, you're a riot.'

The three of us moved as the last light in the canyon drained away, soon so dark the only way to discern cliffs from the sky above was where the stars began. Torches clicked on all around – a string of lights plotting the now unseeable path ahead like fireflies. They zigzagged in wide arcs towards the sky, never letting me forget the massive trek still remaining. I looked back to see the same lights extending down towards the floor of the canyon. 'At least I'm closer than they are,' I murmured to myself.

Alicia didn't have a head torch, so she shared our light by following Jack while I followed her. She squeezed my shoulder as she passed, letting her fingers drag a bit. It was the first nice sensation I'd felt in hours and sent a little shot down my spine. Her ass swayed ahead like a hypnotist's watch. I found myself in a trance, dumbly mimicking the rhythm. Ascending each step, her shorts pulled tight and outlined her body ever so slightly.

Before I knew it, we were moving at a regular walking pace again. 'Those knees feeling better, Lame Horse?' Jack asked from the lead, jolting me from my fantasy and the only thing bringing any respite from the discomfort.

'Just keep moving!' I yelled back. I tried to ignore the pain in my body. She swayed to and fro. We were nearly at the top.

Light fixtures appeared, dust turned to paved stone and we'd made it. I was taken aback by how underwhelming it was. No parade or cheer squad waited, just the quiet, indifferent night. Alicia's party was waiting in the cold air, breathing steam. The three of us said our goodbyes as I pretended not to prop as much of my weight on the poles as I was. Jack went to retrieve his truck while I sat on a bench.

Fatigue may have been the only thing ascending the canyon slower than me, arriving a few minutes later. A toot accompanied the outline of familiar headlights and I dragged myself towards them. Collapsing into the passenger seat, we began the drive back. Jack pulled into the parking lot of a dive and we went inside, collecting strange looks as I struggled onto a stool at the bar. He ordered two burgers and asked what type of beer I liked. I shook my slumped head and sipped water.

The glass of the passenger door was icy against my temple as we headed east. I looked up at tired stars in a tired sky. People say they twinkle, when all they really do is inhale and exhale just like we do. I let air push its way up my nose and back out, as if doing my breathing for me. Jack was speaking about something but I couldn't hear him. The sky had that weight to it again. The stars began to fade and I didn't know if it was my eyes closing or if they were all finally being blown out like candles. I seemed to know less and less with each passing day, though I was beginning to realise nobody gets any better at seeing in the dark by spending all their time in it.

8.

I stripped the pillowcases, imprints of my face drawn in dirt folding over themselves as they landed on the chair in the corner. I stood naked at the window frame, bracing myself and looking out over the sun-drenched property. The shower drain gulped browned water, removing the canyon as it ran down my chest and back and balls. I sat in the corner letting it rain over me. With closed eyes I pulled in sips of the stuff as it ran past my mouth in little streams.

The wooden handrail bowed under my weight as I worked myself downstairs. Almost any bend in my left knee caused it to lock up and pain to shoot out in all directions. Either gravel or cartilage in my knee crunched with each hobbling step down the path. The dog emerged from around the corner, ran to me and jumped up. A paw dug into my knee and I yelped with the little energy I had. It was hard to get mad; he was excited to see me, crafting pleasure in the pain. I trudged around the side of the garage. Jack stood near the Miata with tools in hand, something between coy remorse and a smirk on his face. We locked eyes.

'What's with the cunty look?' I coughed.

He frowned, then laughed. I smiled.

'Cunty? You just making up words now?'

'Don't have to, really. Saw your face and it just kinda ... materialised before me.'

'Shame that mouth of yours ain't all worn out like that knee is. Might need to toss you back into the canyon,' he said, handing me a ten-millimetre spanner like a tiny baton.

'No, no more,' I said, raising hands in surrender and wincing a bit as I leant forward to take the spanner. 'I have been thoroughly deep-fried, flipped and fucked.'

'You've what now?'

'Doesn't matter,' I said, gazing at the still-disassembled Miata. 'And here I was worried you might've finished without me ...'

'That's some wishful thinking.'

'No, I mean, I'm glad you didn't. I want to be here to turn the key.'

He looked at me with screwed-up eyes, pushed moustache into nostrils with his lips, and waited for some inevitable, smartass remark from me. I was as sceptical as he when one didn't arrive. I thought I saw a flicker of real warmth, though it vanished as he took a breath in.

'No, we've still got a ways to go,' he said, walking to the back of the garage. 'Besides, bleeding brakes is a two-man job. And unfortunately we've only got you, so we'll have to make do.'

I hobbled over, lowering myself to the ground beside Jack with a thump and a groan. 'Stop being dramatic, he said. 'You're doing the dirty part of this job whether you like it or not. Now, a car's a bit like your body.'

'Yeah?'

'Hmm, well, this particular car's probably more than a little bit like your particular body,' he said, peeling a flake of rust from inside the wheel arch and holding it up to me as if comparing colour swatches.

'Uh-huh.'

THE ROADMAP OF LOSS

'Heh, sorry. It's like your body in that you can get a pretty good idea how the system's doing by the condition of its fluids. Think of brake fluid as urine. This here is clean, healthy, hydrated urine,' Jack lectured, tapping a bottle about one-third full of amber liquid on the floor. A length of clear rubber hose pushed over a nut on the brake assembly extended to it, submerging an end in liquid within. Jack stood, moved into the Miata's driver's seat, and pumped the brakes a few times. Wedging a length of wooden plank between the seat and compressed pedal, he then returned to the floor beside me.

'And this... this is what I imagine yours looks like.'

Taking the spanner from me and placing it over the nut, he cracked it open. Brown sludge shot through the hose and landed in the waiting bottle, frozen like a fossil before spreading and diluting the amber.

'Hey, how'd you know?' I asked.

'Nasty,' Jack replied.

The process from there involved me sitting at the brakes with Jack in the driver's seat. We couldn't see each other from the two positions, so I'd indicate the nut was closed by yelling, 'Pump!' Jack would then pump the brakes five times, maintaining pressure on the fifth. When this was done, he'd reply: 'Ready!' I would turn the nut, watching the mess of god-knows-how-many miles' worth of muck pass through the hose, accompanied by a thud each time as the system lost pressure and the brake pedal fell to the floor. I would tighten it again, yell, 'Okay, lift!' and Jack would lift the pedal to the top of its stroke.

We repeated the process until the fresh stuff came through the hose without bubbles. About halfway through each corner's brakes, a fluid reservoir in the engine bay had to be topped up again, requiring me to climb to my feet, hobble to the front of the car, hobble back and lower myself to the ground. Each trip hurt my knee more than the one before and soon I was in audible pain. Jack's initial amusement turned to concern.

'We should take a break,' he said.

'No,' I replied with a sharp breath, slumping down at the rear driver's side brakes. 'Ready.'

'No.'

'What?' I asked – a slight echo of my voice resonating in the dirty wheel arch I sat half-inside.

'You need a rest.'

'Like hell I do! Just pump the damn pedal.'

'That leg's too beat up. You're gonna do real damage if you keep going.'

'What the hell, Jack?' I yelled. 'You take me on that goddamn hike and destroy my knee, then say I have to work the bleed screws, and now you're telling me I'm not allowed to. The fuck do you want from me?'

There was silence. I leant back, craning my head from the wheel arch, looking along the car and up at the side mirror. Trying to catch Jack's reflection in it, I saw only the soft top's fabric. The door popped open and he stepped out, eyebrows almost meeting in the middle as they pulled towards the bridge of his nose. His fists were clenched and he stood at a slight angle to me. I was certain he was going to hit me and certain I wasn't going to stop him.

'You are worth something, you dumb shit,' he snarled, his mouth barely opening.

'Huh?'

'You heard me. You know, most people come to that realisation on their own. Hell, some even come to the conclusion they're worth a whole lot more than they are.'

'Are you having a stroke?'

'But then,' he yelled over the top of me, 'there are the people like you, Mark. Those who resist everything just for the sake of resisting. I'd say you need a little push, though it's proving to be more of an almighty shunt. Getting you to let go of this bitterness you've built up has been like trying to put a cat in the tub.'

'Ease up on the cryptic bullshit, will ya?'

The hairs of his moustache rustled as he sucked in a breath past them and calmed himself.

'This life is so much more than the things that have been done to you. You need to realise that, but you're either too stubborn or too stupid. You said yes to the canyon, you underestimated it, you showboated and you ended up hurt. Nobody else did that to you.'

'You think I don't know that?'

'Oh, I know you do. It's what you refuse to acknowledge that enrages me. That it was also you who reached out for those poles; you who shuddered with each of those ten thousand steps; you who dragged your sorry ass out of that mighty hole. Nobody else did that for you. It doesn't matter what you or anybody gets you into, it only matters how you get yourself back out.'

'Thank you for the optimism, Jack, but it's wasted on me. I know what I am and I'm nobody's idol. Self-realisation doesn't have to be some fuckin' euphoric epiphany.'

'Only a fool thinks they can't take with them a little piece of anyone and everyone they meet in this life. Sure, only some people do all of it right, but all do some of it right. You're worth something. You have something to offer. I look at you and see someone worth bothering with. Nothing's made you press on except your will to. I think you brought yourself here for something, and it's up to you to get what you came for.'

'What's that supposed to mean?'

'It doesn't matter,' he said, extending a hand towards me. 'You're almost there; let me help you finish.'

I studied his hand, the dirt under his nails, the fissures in his weathered skin, the stories they held but would not tell. I reached out for them. There was something so belittling about a hand so aged being the one to offer help. Mine looked so much suppler and stronger next to it, but his hands were aged because they'd seen time, and that same time had made them the kind of strong which can't be seen. I plunked myself into the driver's seat. I hadn't been there for almost two weeks. Gripping the wheel felt like greeting an old friend. Jack moved to the final set of brakes at the front-passenger-side.

'Alright, pump!' he said, his white hair just visible, bobbing over the edge of the fender across the hood from where I sat.

I pressed on the pedal. Even though my left leg had sustained the most damage, it was still an arduous thing to do with the right. I pumped once, twice, all the way to five. The travel in the pedal reduced with each, becoming immovable by the fifth.

'Ready!'

A faint tick of the nut opening accompanied the pedal losing resistance, falling to the floor with a hollowed clunk.

'Okay, lift!' Jack replied a second later.

I lifted the pedal and waited, starting to consider the situation. How each conversation I'd had with the man felt like a jigsaw piece that didn't quite fit with the one on either side. How Jack's motivations seemed not to match any stream of logic I could fathom. Then it occurred to me.

'Pump!'

I pressed down, then let the pedal wheeze back to its starting position.

'Hey, Jack?'

'Yes?'

'... Did you read all of them?'

'All of what?'

I pumped the pedal a second time.

'The letters in my bag. The ones written by my father.'

I watched the white hairs over the mudguard become still.

'Yes –,' he hesitated, then quickly added words, 'and I'm sorry for that, but understand, you were a stranger I'd taken into my home.'

'It's okay,' I said, pumping a third time, surprising myself with how calm I was. 'I'm not sure why you've been so nice to me, but thank you.'

'It seemed to me you were overdue some luck.'

I compressed and released the pedal a fourth time, staring at the rolling hills beyond the property as they became fuzzy in my misty eyes.

'I nearly ended it, Jack.'

'You mean you almost went home?'

I pressed the pedal in a fifth time, holding it there.

'No, I mean, I sat alone, about to end it all in some shitty motel room. It wasn't even that long ago, yet it already feels like some other life I used to live. I'd watched the sunset the day before and decided it was good enough to be the last one I ever saw. Jesus, I almost fucking clocked out for good. How fickle is that ...'

He didn't reply. I'd been speaking to myself and he'd just been there to hear it. The best and worst conversations of all time had probably happened the same way.

'Anyway, sorry. Ready.'

'You know ... they build bridges from each end to meet in the middle, but that's not the way anyone travels them. Something about that reminds me of you: too damn focused on how the pieces will come together to realise you're only halfway across,' he said with slow, considered words. 'Are you glad you didn't go out like that?'

'Maybe more than I've ever been about anything before.'

'Good. Then you still live with hope. That's a lot more than some people.'

'Just tell me it gets better, Jack. I can't have come all this way for nothing.'

'I can't tell you any of that, but I can tell you the fight is worth it.'

The pedal fell under my quivering foot, sending an echoed thump through the silent garage.

'Okay. Lift.'

September 6th, 1977

My everything,

My ride to California is due to leave in the coming days. I sense our departure will be sudden; the man's business in Holbrook hasn't quite gone to plan. What began as a raised thumb and a ride for me has turned into paid errands for him and they spring up without warning. I am writing this letter in haste from my table in a diner, so please excuse its bluntness.

    I've had a recurring dream. You and I are standing on the Santa Monica pier. Mark is there too. You are looking at me and there is forgiveness in your eyes. Not because what I have done is excusable, but because you see I have become the man you always wanted and needed me to be because of it. You see in me that waywardness is sometimes a necessary evil in the search for sensibility and our swelling ocean calms. We stroll the boardwalk of Venice Beach and I have my arm draped around you like a scarf while Mark runs a few steps ahead. We are laughing and he is smiling, and in my reverie, we are a family again. I wake from this in another bed in another place but always without the two of you. It has gone on too long, and it has gone on by my own doing.

    I want you to meet me in Los Angeles. I need you to meet me in Los Angeles. I can't find my way home without you, and to return to you an unfinished man would surely spell the end. All it takes is a chance. I think everybody gets at least one, though not everybody realises it. A second from you would be from on high. Not something I deserve, but something I hope you have still left in your heart for me. I am petrified to hear the sound of your voice again, but I will call when I reach the coast. I will scrape together all I have and all I am owed and I will find a way to get you here and get us both back. We must mend what is broken, my love, before it's too late. Before all of the pieces become *unsalvageable and before we become the very ghosts haunting our own memories. I think my time is up; the man has started screaming into a payphone outside the diner and a small crowd is gathering. Another errand is impending.*

1.

The Miata was pieced back together. I did what my body allowed, but mostly watched Jack work. He took few swipes at me. I guessed all he wanted or needed to hear me say was that I needed help.

Struggling into the driver's seat, I turned the key and the engine fired up first time – its pitch different and revs smoother. Still unable to compress the clutch myself, I switched spots with Jack and watched him take it through the gears. A sense of pride I hadn't expected washed over me as the rear wheels span in the air.

I made it downstairs on a Saturday morning later that week without the aid of the handrail for the first time since the canyon. It was an accomplishment of sorts, but left a sudden and sharp sadness in me. Jack and Diane seemed to feel it too as I moved into the kitchen with newfound pace. There was an unspoken acknowledgement that I'd stay only until healed enough to go. I didn't ask Jack how much, if any, of my story Diane had been told. We sat on the porch as steam was raised and robbed in the slow breeze.

Diane asked if I was excited to see California and what I had planned. Maybe he hadn't passed anything onto her after all. I said I would play it by ear. Jack furled a sad kind of smile, then sunk it behind his mug.

I unhitched the gate and stepped through. The dog rushed ahead on the path we'd walked many times before, circling back and ushering me to pick up the pace, becoming frustrated when I couldn't. I moved as fast as I could across the hills, using one of the hiking poles as a cane, but it was still a crawl. Soon he accepted the futility of his efforts and strode beside me in silence. We made it about two hundred yards before my knee began pinching and I had to stop. 'Sorry, buddy, this is about all I've got,' I said, our disappointment manifest in an unwagging tail.

I looked around. Everything seemed so hard and brutal, and me so soft and weak among it. But then, on top of that second hill, where the land could be seen for miles in all directions, came a realisation.

During one of these days in Arizona, I had become older than my father was when he wrote from Holbrook. The man I'd grown up envisioning as perpetually older, wiser and more weathered than I had suddenly become my junior. If there was some secret to living in this world, I'd now had more time to figure it out than he did. For the first time in my life, I saw my father as a boy, in all the same ways I still felt myself to be. I was alone on the other side of the world chasing some invisible monster in my mind, while he was here running from the one in his.

The resentment that shaped my image of him, and the world I blamed him for, began to fall away like dead leaves. Soon, only undecorated branches remained, unsure of which way to grow. How much time I'd lost; all the days wasted on sadness, only to stubbornly affirm the others that had come before and been wasted the same way. I began moving towards the house. My horizon shifted with each hobbling step, and I realised my father's had done the same for him.

THE ROADMAP OF LOSS

Jack carried my bags down the front steps as Diane and I followed. He'd moved the Miata to the gravel clearing outside the garage, its top down to make my entry easier. I pressed on the trunk, threw my backpack onto the passenger seat and worked arms through my leather jacket. 'Oh, just a second,' Jack said, hurrying back into the house. After a moment, he returned with my bottle of bourbon and handed it over like a dog that'd retrieved a ball. Diane curled a brow. I studied the corked neck and chewed-up label.

'You keep it,' I said, handing it back. 'Put it on your shelf or something. That way it'll be like I'm still here.'

'This could never replace you; it couldn't possibly be as annoying.'

'Yeah, but it'll be just about as much use to you.'

He took it from me with stormy eyes. I lowered myself into the driver's seat and fired up the engine. Bringing the clutch up, my knee shuddered in pain and the rear wheels spewed gravel. The engine stalled. I turned the key and tried again. More spat gravel, then silence.

'Oh, Mark, dear, that knee is too weak. You're not ready,' Diane said.

I looked down at the steering wheel and wondered if she was right.

'No,' Jack interjected. 'He'll be fine.'

'Jesus, Jack, he can't even get out of the driveway. How's he going to make it to California?'

'He can, he just hasn't yet. Maybe he's a little tougher than you give him credit for.'

I turned the key again, flexed the muscles in my leg to support the knee and brought the clutch up. The Miata coughed gravel, bucking forward without stalling, and coasted down the driveway. Jack, Diane and the dog followed on foot. I pulled the shifter back to neutral and waited at the gate. Diane hugged me as I climbed from the car, saying I was welcome anytime; Jack shook my hand, agreeing in as few words as possible. I held the dog's head in my hands, bringing our foreheads together for a moment, then sat back into the Miata and pushed the shifter into first. There was a hand on my shoulder.

'Go on. It isn't far now,' Jack said, leaning in, and not speaking loud enough for Diane to hear. He stepped back and I waved. It was hard to see the world as a bad place with such goodness waving back. I moved away from the property, turning onto asphalt curving around a hill. The Miata went into third gear with a jolt as I jerked the clutch up. The hill came between me and their waving arms as I watched yet another direction I could've taken shrink to nothing in the outline of a rear-vision mirror. What a petty and magnificent thing this life is.

I swerved into a gas station, filled up and bought a fresh packet of cigarettes. Humming along the section of Route 66 running through Holbrook, I slid my sunglasses on, yanked the wheel and floored it. The Miata surged up the on-ramp, its revs climbing with glee as it sang proudly into the desert. Orbison was on the radio. I moved the shifter and flew onto Interstate 40 towards the final letter.

2.

The highway descended towards Los Angeles as California tumbled into the sea. The more I pushed towards the city, the more I felt it pushing back. We were two magnets repelling each other when brought together. I rolled between hills, along packed freeways flooded with brake lights and horns, through endless, indifferent blocks and ended up in Pasadena. It was as close to the coast as I could bring myself to go.

I'd gone corner to corner across America, past packed strip clubs and empty bookstores, houses of god and all his children without homes. Seen beauty and ugly in extremes I never knew existed and locked eyes with both. I'd spread my pain like ashes over this land and hoped something would grow. Ten thousand hard, lonely miles, and I couldn't bring myself to traverse the final few.

I wasn't sure what incapacitated me that evening; whether fear of all that might be waiting, or fear of how little might remain after. Whatever it was, it paralysed me, just like it had a lifetime ago when I couldn't bring myself to read past the first letter in a Melbourne living room.

I got a room on East Colorado Boulevard as light pink sun disappeared behind the enormity of Los Angeles. Pushing in the door of a bar a few blocks down, I limped inside. The place was a shithole, but there were smiles and a jukebox and I didn't need much more than that anymore. I took a seat by two haggard men croaking to each other and convulsing in little fits of laughter; some peach concoction with a coaster atop in front of the next empty stool. I ordered a beer and sipped it without haste, slowly enough that even Jack might've approved.

'Mother of Mary ...' one of the men muttered to his friend through a cough. I turned to see them looking past me, then there was the tapping of heels and a whiff of something wonderful to my other side. She lowered herself into the seat, her face half-hidden behind waves of black hair which reflected the shimmering colours of neon behind the bar. A blue dress collapsed over her crossed legs, as though it was faint at the thought of caressing them. She removed the coaster from the glass with brown fingers and indigo nails. I tried to look away but couldn't, soon realising most in the bar were suffering a similar ailment.

She turned her head, dark eyes staring through me. I'd played this game before, but I'd never won. Perfection was her burden. She was a vinyl record holding an unheard masterpiece, and anybody willing to lay a needle against her, knowing they would have to carve a piece out of her to hear it, would not be worthy of her song. What she was doing in the place was beyond me.

We studied each other for a moment, her blank expression unchanging. I nodded, turned back to my beer and laughed at myself. The hour hand chased the minute hand around the clock above the bar, only to have it sneak up behind, slap it and run off into the distance again, giggling like a child. She ordered drinks with a soft voice wrapped in a Hispanic accent. Men approached with dreams cradled in cupped hands, hoping she would be gentle with them. None of the fools got anywhere with it except back to their own seat. I smoked and took in the music, trying to pretend she wasn't there, but couldn't ignore the very air around her tightening with each glance she took at her watch. I smiled and snickered into my glass.

'What? What is funny?' she shot towards me after a few repetitions.

She wore every facial expression imaginable at once.

'Pardon?'

'You keep looking at me and laughing.'

'No, sorry, nothing's funny.'

She turned away. Scratching my beard, my jaw fell open. I couldn't help myself.

'I'm just trying to figure out if you're early or he's late.'

'Excuse me?'

'Well, you keep looking at that watch ...'

'So I have to be waiting for somebody?'

'You don't have to be doing anything, but nobody comes to a place like this, looking like that, unless they want to be taken somewhere much better.'

'And it is a man I am waiting for? This somebody must be a man?'

'Yes.'

With a scoff, she looked towards the bar but not completely away from me.

'Listen. It has to be a man, because somebody risked your heart tonight and I think they've done it before, and I refuse to believe there's a woman alive that careless.'

I recoiled a bit, shocking myself I'd uttered those words without the aid of drunkenness. She glared at me, locked onto my cigarettes and swiped them. Even her anger was perfect. 'Sure, knock yourself out. I'm gonna use the little boys' room,' I said. She threw my lighter down, and blew out smoke. I gestured that I wanted to close out to the bartender.

Empty seats and the delicate waft of smoke rising from a half-smoked cigarette resting on the ashtray awaited my return. The haggard men turned from me back to each other with little convulsions. I'd joined the ranks of fools. I threw down a ten, tasted her lips and breath on the cigarette, ground it out and forgot about it. I limped outside to find her standing by the street.

'It's alright; I'm not following you,' I said with raised hands.

'That's a strange thing to say.'

'Is it?'

'I would not mind if you were.'

She pinched a clutch bag in front of exposed thighs; her little shoulders shivered.

'Okay, well, I'm not. Goodnight.'

I turned and hobbled a few steps towards the motel.

'You seem kind, but you pretend you are not. It is sad,' she said, her voice carrying in the night.

I stopped, turned and took a few painful steps towards her, not sure what she thought I was. Her heels tapped closer, a princess in the presence of some lame beggar.

'I don't have anywhere better to take you.'

'It's okay. The bar is not very high after tonight.'

'Keep lowering that thing and you're gonna trip over it.'

She smiled. I was fucked. I took her hand in mine and we began walking.

3.

Lauren. Her name was Lauren. It sounded a lot better coming from her lips than mine, but then so did everything. I hadn't expected her to be there in the morning, but when she opened the blinds I found myself angry at the darkness for having ever hidden her. We sipped coffee for breakfast and feasted on each other for lunch. That night, she directed me to a nearby house. I parked up the street while she went inside and filled a backpack. The house's porch light flicked on as we departed, and she sank into her seat. We stayed in Pasadena four more days, finding ourselves in that same bar each night. Lauren worked the jukebox as if pulling a playlist from my own mind. I swam in her eyes, unconcerned with drowning. We hid from the world inside each other.

At an ATM the following evening, I waited longer than usual for the all-too-familiar DECLINED and monotone buzz. I looked at Lauren standing down the busy street, pushing out smoke. She smiled to me. 'This won't do,' I mumbled. Pushing coins into a payphone, I called my Australian bank for the first time in months, daunted by the prospect of how tiny the balance I expected a teller to recite could be. It didn't matter though. I would move it all over, every cent, just to spend more time with her. I quoted account details from a weathered card in my wallet and almost choked when the teller responded. I made him repeat himself a few times before accepting it.

'Yes, all of it. Same account as before, thank you,' I said into the phone. Lauren noticed my seriousness and came over.

'Is everything okay?' she asked as I hung up the handle and stared at nothing.

'It would appear I just sold a house.'

'Is this one of your jokes I don't understand?'

'Not quite. Hey, you ever been to San Francisco?'

'No.'

'Ever wanted to?'

'Yes.'

'Let's go to San Francisco in the morning.'

'Okay.'

The Miata hummed a happy tune as we cruised up the coast with the top down the next morning. I ignored signs for Santa Monica and Venice on the way like they were company not welcome at the party. Lauren placed a hand over mine as it rested on the shifter, almost causing us to sail from the cliffs of the Pacific Coast Highway when she dragged it to her lap and slid my fingers into her.

I watched her move inside a gas station as I squeezed one of pump's triggers outside, wondering what life could be made with her. We got back in the Miata and carried on. I asked her how to say, 'I love you.'

She replied, *'Te amo,'* curious why I wanted to know. I told her I might need it soon. She pushed on my shoulder and hid a smile behind her wrist.

A haze sat over the harbour, radiating blood orange from the setting sun. The peaks of the Golden Gate Bridge poked through like it was being consumed by a brilliant, gentle inferno. I watched the

THE ROADMAP OF LOSS

colours reflect in Lauren's eyes and felt the same way. We drove to a hotel on Mason. The valet seemed offended by the Miata.

'Be careful, she is a very special lady,' I said as I closed the door for him. He scowled and I listened to the rotted exhaust drone all the way into the far corners of the car park below.

Waking from sleep beside Lauren made me need less of it somehow. I'd rise with my soul on fire, my heart pulling me around like some unruly dog on a leash. Love until that point had been a radio wave for me, undulating and ambivalent, but with her I was a tiny rowboat being heaved over a never-ending wave.

I returned from an early morning walk to find her still asleep. I looked her over: at the sheet ending where her lower back rose; how the light climbed and fell over her features like brush strokes. I refused to believe we'd grown from the same soil. Plotting kisses from her ribs to neck, I watched lips curl into a smile as she woke. My heart was full to the point of bursting, but then I felt undeserving of her company. A woman like that needed wonder and awe and magic to match what she gave to the world. Anyone could give her a beat-up car and a hotel room.

We walked to the wharf arm in arm, sharing heat and safety.

'Why do you keep this jacket?' she asked.

'What do you mean? I like it.'

'The leather, it is hard and rough,' she said, rubbing her nails against the tattered sleeve like a file.

'Yes, it is, but it still keeps me warm.'

'Do you not think it is ruined?'

'No, it's not ruined. It's just seen time, my love.'

'Oh ... then I like it too.'

We reached the wharf. There was somehow clear skies and fog at the same time. I kissed her forehead.

'Would you like to go to New York City?' I asked. 'We could fly.'

'To do what?'

'The same as we've done here. Walk and talk.'

'Hmm, no, I don't think so.'

'Fair enough, how about Chicago? Maybe Philadelphia? We can go wherever you want.'

'I think I want to go home.'

'We can do that. Let's stay in Beverly Hills.'

'No, baby, I mean I want to go back to my home and my family and my life.'

'What? Why? You're not enjoying this?'

'It has been nice and I like you very much, but this feels... it feels like running. These hotel rooms and bars, they are not life. It has been fun, but it is time to go home.'

I looked over the bay, cloudy and sunny all at once. She buried a head into my shoulder and I put an arm around her.

We reached Pasadena that night. I left the engine idling in case she changed her mind. 'Smile, Mark, this life is a happy thing,' she said. I nodded because she was right, not because I wanted to. 'Goodbye, maybe we will meet again someday,' she added, kissing me. I felt her lips tear something from me as they pulled away.

Heels clicked across the street to the house I'd been directed to before. She pressed a buzzer and waited. Its front door opened, illuminating the path and front lawn. She looked up at someone, sunk her head then walked through. A man stepped out to where she'd stood. A husband or boyfriend, maybe a brother or a friend. He looked at me with low, uncertain brows as I leant on the Miata under a street lamp across the street. I nodded. He took a moment, reciprocated, then went inside and closed the door, the light spilling onto the front lawn thinning until it was gone. I let out a breath, lit a cigarette and got in the Miata. Love was just something I'd read on a

Hallmark card. Pop-up headlights lifted and showed the way. I let the clutch out and drove west.

A room on Lincoln Boulevard near Santa Monica welcomed me. I washed my face and stared into the bathroom mirror. Retrieving my razor, I ran it back and forth until my beard was gone. A younger, kinder face I thought I'd lost stared back in the mirror. I crawled under the covers and stared at the ceiling through darkness, unable to feel upset. I'd run fingertips along perfection and not been burnt.

4.

I traced California's winding roads the next day, visiting Griffith Observatory and ending up in Malibu, unsure if the drive was for leisure or merely postponement. The sun began to sink as I parked outside a bar near my hotel. I'd gone no closer to Venice than Lincoln – the coast looming, felt but not seen. I stared at nothing through the Miata's windshield, fidgeting with the letters inside my jacket pocket.

'The fight is worth it,' I said to myself as I pulled them out. Skimming through their top left-hand corners, the final date appeared. I took a deep breath and began.

Shuffling towards a stool at the empty bar, I dropped into it, ordered a drink and sipped slowly. I stared at the wall, the neighbourhood and entire continent behind it, around the globe and back at myself. The bartender asked if I was alright. I tilted the bottle and swished around what remained.

'Yeah, sure, another. Why not?'

'I meant ... are you feeling alright, sir?'

He couldn't have been much younger than I, but seemed like a child as we looked at each other over the bar. His eyes were bright and they waited on my reply with an abundance of hope. Mine hadn't looked like that in a long time. I hesitated to give an answer because I didn't know if I had one. He reached down, retrieved a bottle and fumbled with a bottle opener.

'On the house,' he grinned, as if he'd wanted to say that for a long time.

'What do you do?'

'I, uh, I go to school.'

'Which school?'

'UCLA, sir.'

'And what do you do there?'

'Economics, but I think I want to do something creative.'

'Then why not do it?'

'I don't know. Most people want numbers and dollar signs, not bars and notes.'

I let out a laugh and he smiled. He may have been a kid but was already the wiser of us.

'How do you get to this school?'

'The bus, mostly. Sometimes I ride my bike.'

'You like that car out there?' I asked, gesturing to the Miata with my head.

'Oh yeah. The Miatas are cool!'

I got up and walked out. 'Sir! I just meant the one beer on the house …'

His voice trailed off as the door closed behind me. I reached into the Miata, came back to my stool and sat.

'Oh, I thought you were a walkout,' he said, his cheeks pink.

'Got a pen?'

'Yeah, sure.'

Rummaging around the till, he retrieved one and handed it to me. I bit off and spat its lid onto the bar, and hunched over behind my bunched-up jacket.

'What's your name?'

'My name? Why?'

'Your name. Your full name.' I dead-eyed him.

'It's Mike Burns.'

'Mike or Michael?'

'Michael.'

The pen whispered against the paper as I scribbled. Mike tried to peer over but I looked up and he leant back like he was looking at something else.

'How much do I owe you?'

'It's, ah, three-fifty.'

I threw down notes then the folded sheet of paper.

'What's this?' he asked, nervous.

'Your tip. The title to that Miata out there.'

'Sorry?'

'It's yours now. She's been good to me. She'll be good to you too.'

I dropped the key onto the pile and threw my jacket on. Mike unfolded the sheet, his eyes widening when he realised it was no ruse. He grasped the key and studied its cut with a slack jaw.

'Have a good life, Michael.'

'You too ...' he paused, studying the title, 'Mark Ward.'

I stepped outside. The footprint I'd left on the Miata's bumper in the desert came off with a rub of my sleeve. I ran my hand across its hood, feeling the coarseness of the paint. We'd both come a long way from a driveway in Staten Island.

'Goodbye, old friend,' I said. 'Thank you for everything. Be well.'

The sunlight descended through yellows. I strolled up Lincoln and headed west.

October 12th, 1977

My dear Celeste,

I will not write or send another letter after this one, I promise you. You could not begin to imagine the happiness you brought me in these past weeks. I really did not believe you would come, but watching you walk through those gates at LAX that morning was like seeing you again for the very first time. Do you remember how we met? What a state I was in. To think I took offence to your gaze. Though I realise now that was probably what separated me from all of the others trying to capture it in that moment. I'm sorry, this is no time for nostalgia – I have the rest of my life for that.

I had a feeling our time together was to be a goodbye. I think we both knew you would be leaving this country alone and leaving me alone in this country long before you arrived. To watch your lips and listen to your voice say you were going home without me and not to follow you cut me to the bone. But it would be ridiculous for me to expect anything less than your honesty. That same strength and conviction is what made me fall in love with you in the first place. It's the same that lets me know Mark will always be safe under your wing too. You are right, though; the loss will be mine, not his. I do not deserve anything from you and even less from him, but I need him to understand he has not been forgotten. I need him to understand that I carry him with me wherever I go, and if he ever needs to find me, I'll be there in every smile and every tear, every sunrise and sunset, in the very fire and the rain. Just as he is for me. Just as he is for you. And just as you will surely be for him.

Holding you two so closely was my greatest accomplishment. How a mutt like me could have anything to do with something as incredible and beautiful as Mark coming to be still makes my hands shake and my heart soar. I will not be around because I have been rough with *fragile things.* Anything less than absolute commitment to you two is an insult, and perhaps it is not in my nature, or perhaps I am just still too young to be capable of it, but I knew you could tell the second you stepped off the plane and stared into me that way you do. Time is a rolling boulder, my love, and Lord knows I've placed myself in front of it, dug my heels into the earth and pushed back harder than I thought possible, only to be crushed by it again and again.

I am writing this from the same bench on the Venice promenade where we sat and watched the sunset. I've had the photo taken of us developed and attached a copy. I had one printed for myself as well. It sits in my wallet next to one of the three of us taken at Mark's fifth birthday. To walk from the pier to the boardwalk with you on our final day was a special kind of bliss. It was just how I'd dreamt it. I only wish Mark could have been there too, though I understand your reasons for not bringing him. If it is in your heart to, please speak kind words of me, but don't lie because it sounds pretty. Make him understand all the things I was not strong enough to. That the world is abundant with beauty and joy, but only if we have our eyes open to it. He will surely learn of its hardness and ugliness in his own time, though he must learn true strength is being able to meet with and wrap your arms around happiness even after having bumped shoulders with pain along the way.

And you, my sweet Celeste. I do not believe men are born fathers, but I do believe women are born mothers. Your lives begin and then you have the ability to begin life. A constantly expanding ball of energy capable of bringing more capacity for joy and sorrow and everything in between into the world. What a marvellous thing each and every one of you are, but none so much as you. In you, I discovered all the things I pray Mark will become. If you find another, please marry. If you do not, I'll know it was because your heart was already filled by Mark and by the world. Please take care of yourself. Do not let your soul gather dust. Keep your fire fed and it will keep you warm.

The sun is sitting low and I have heard the patter of my tears against this page. Now seems as good a time as any to say goodbye. I love you and will always love you. You have given me nothing more and nothing less than everything I could have ever hoped for, and that is all.

Forever yours and Mark's,

Dylan Ward

I finished Route 66 on foot, the air full of sound as I slowly lapped the Santa Monica Pier. Waves came to a stop somewhere below as children chased each other over its creaking boards, screams rising and falling with the tracks of a rollercoaster. I descended stairs and began walking towards Venice Beach, sinking hands into my pockets as the path wound between the city and sand. Bicycle bells rang and joggers overtook me, beautiful women with unforgettable smiles passing by. Chaos resumed as I reached the Venice promenade and moved through a jungle of umbrellas and stalls, freaks and models, bodybuilders and junkies, hobos and artists. All extremes of the world collided there and my parents had stood in the middle of it, arm in arm.

I sat by myself on a bench as the sun and ocean collided, but did not feel alone. My mother had done all she could to protect me from this world and I had done all I could to protect her. My father left us to become a man, and in his absence, I'd become one. For all he'd taken from my mother, he'd given something back that she had never tried to replace or say wasn't enough. He didn't have to worry; they were always together because she had me and I had her. It didn't matter to me if he was out there anymore.

LIAM MURPHY

The beach groaned underneath my boots, the noise of the boardwalk fading as I moved away. I reached the water, and with it, the end of some invisible path I'd been walking for so long. Home hadn't been this close since I'd run from it. I sat, feeling the cold sand through my jeans.

Removing the letters from my pocket, I read them again from beginning to end, running my fingers against depressions in the paper carved out long ago. Those curves and lines marking the timeline of my father's doubt and pain as he'd tried desperately to make sense of the world and have it make sense to him. The lies my mother told to protect a boy who would never have understood. The secret and burden they became, which she carried for so many years. I wondered why she'd kept these pages, perhaps always intending for me to someday find and make sense of their pleas for reconciliation. Well, I had, and now no one else could lay them to rest.

I tugged my boots off, stuffed my socks inside, and placed them on the sand. The last sigh of a wave filled the spaces between my toes like tiny lagoons as it crept up the beach to meet me. Frosty water seeped into my jeans, pulling my skin tight as I waded out far enough for the ocean to lick the waist of my jacket. I clasped the letters between shivering fingers, the tired pages slumping at their folds. They too had borne the weight of what they carried for too long and were finally ready to rest.

One by one, in the order written, I let them go. The ink ran and the paper became transparent as they took in salty water. I held the last page to my nose, breathed in the scent of my mother and father for the last time, then relaxed my grip.

All around me, the words and pages and story were taken by the sea, fading to blue until they were gone. I drew breath like it was the first of my life. The sun sat low – fiery orange skating along the Pacific. Light and warmth were about to leave this place, but were only arriving somewhere beyond that horizon. It burnt my eyes, but I couldn't bring myself to blink or look away. I'd never watched a sunset behind the ocean before. It was nicer than I'd ever imagined.

Acknowledgements

To my agent, Michael Cybulski, whose expertise and coolheadedness when I had none was crucial in steering this work down that long, bumpy path from desk drawer to bookshelf.

To the amazing assortment of women – Susan Cutsforth, Sue Andersen, Jessica Friedmann and Diana Hill – who not only edited and improved my little story, but were also able to deal with me while they did so. Your insights, suggestions and challenges proved invaluable, and I'm a better writer for having worked with each of you.

To Debra Adelaide, my teacher and mentor, who saw potential in this project and in me perhaps long before I did.

To the Echo Publishing team. Thank you for letting me run free like a daft farm animal when I felt I needed to, and reeling me in when you felt you needed to.

To everyone who made it to this page, I hope you got as much out of reading this as I did from writing it.

Thank you.